"WE'VE GOT HIM ON SONAR. MAKING FIVE-TWO KNOTS, BEARING ONE-SEVEN-SEVEN. COMING DIRECTLY AT US, FIVE THOUSAND YARDS."

"TAKE HIM OUT, MEMPHIS."

In the rearview screen, Badr saw two of the patrol boats lined up directly behind the *Sea Spectre.* Machine gun muzzles on the foredecks winked whitely.

"Aim first for the pursuit boats," Badr said.

Heusseini worked his controls, pressed the launch key once, then a second time. The darkness ahead was erased twice as first one missile, then the second, launched toward the rear.

"In-coming!" screamed the radio.

In the rearview screen, he saw both boats veer off as they took evasive action.

The two detonations came within two seconds of each other.

Both boats disappeared in the middle of white, then yellow-red fireballs.

Other Thrillers by
William Lovejoy
Coming Soon from Avon Books

RIPCORD

WILLIAM LOVEJOY

AVON BOOKS  NEW YORK

SEAGHOST is an original publication of Avon Books. This work has never before appeared in book form. This work is a novel. Any similarity to actual persons or events is purely coincidental.

AVON BOOKS
A division of
The Hearst Corporation
1350 Avenue of the Americas
New York, New York 10019

Copyright © 1991 by William H. Lovejoy
Published by arrangement with the author
Library of Congress Catalog Card Number: 91-92057
ISBN: 0-380-76577-2

First Avon Books Printing: November 1991

AVON TRADEMARK REG. U.S. PAT. OFF. AND IN OTHER COUNTRIES, MARCA REGISTRADA, HECHO EN U.S.A.

Printed in the U.S.A.

RA 10 9 8 7 6 5 4 3 2 1

As always, for Jane, Jodi, and David,
and for Clete,
who once shared twenty-eight days at sea with me

1

The light from a three-quarter moon left a blue-white trail on the black water to starboard. A mile ahead on the right, sodium vapor lights floated on the shoreline like yellow polka dots. A foggy haze obscured similar lamps on the coast to the left. Low-lying clouds hid the stars from the western horizon to almost directly overhead. Black on black.

The *Scarab* gurgled along, piercing the bay and the blackness at less than ten knots, but McCory could feel the subdued vibration of the 350-cubic-inch V-8 engines in the steering wheel. A light breeze plucked at his shirt sleeves.

White light of a marker buoy a quarter mile to starboard.

"Jesus, Mac. Turn on the running lights."

"And have somebody spot us?"

"And get out of here," Daimler told him. "We get caught, it's my ass."

"And mine."

"My boat. They'll confiscate it, and I paid sixty grand, damn it!"

1

"Not so loud, Ted. Sound carries."

"Shit! Look . . ."

The night filled suddenly with halogen light off the port side, starkly bright. McCory was on stage again, high school production of *The Man Who Came to Dinner*.

A bullhorn blared. "This is the U.S. Navy gunboat *Antelope*. You are in restricted waters. Heave to, and prepare to be boar . . ."

McCory slammed his palm at the twin throttles, and the *Scarab* surged forward, leaped to the plane, and shot out of the floodlight.

"Mac! Goddamn it, Mac! Shut her down!"

He spun the wheel slightly and rolled into a broad turn to the right as the searchlight chased him, missing, going far to the left.

The instrument panel was unlit, but McCory figured he had forty knots by the time he swung back to the left. The engines screamed, rising close to maximum revolutions. The coast on the starboard was much closer.

The man controlling the searchlight would be looking for a wake.

Whipping his head around, he saw the running lights of the gunboat illuminate as it rose to the chase. Sneaky bastard had come up on him unlit in the darkness of the fog. Probably had him on radar.

Searchlight sweeping back, probing.

Forty-five knots? The windstream tore at his shirt sleeves.

"Goddamn it, Mac!"

"We can outrun him!" McCory had to shout over the scream of the wind.

"Not in here!"

The gunboat was behind them to port and had the mile-wide mouth of Carr Bay covered. The bay would narrow rapidly on him from here on in. Already, the dim lights in the mist on the left coastline were becoming sharper.

Daimler was right.

A siren started to scream from the *Antelope*.

"They'll sink my boat!" Daimler yelled. He was getting panicky.

Fifty knots? The *Scarab* could do it.

The gunboat could only make a bit over forty knots, but it had time and space and angle for advantages. Probably calling his friends on the radio, too.

McCory reached below the helmsman's seat, found his blue plastic bag, and pulled it up onto his lap. Probing with his left hand, he located a fragmentation grenade, removed it, and rezipped the bag.

He pulled the pin and tossed it overboard.

The searchlight swung close, passing just off the port side. The coast was about a quarter mile off the starboard bow. Shallow waters ahead.

McCory turned the helm left as soon as the light went behind him.

Tapping Daimler on the right shoulder with his left hand, he held the grenade close enough for him to see.

Daimler's face was not visible, but McCory heard the man groan.

"Hey, Ted!" McCory called. "What say we get out right here?"

"You son of a bitch! Sixty thousand bucks!"

The searchlight found the boat's wake and raced toward them.

McCory dropped the grenade.

It bounced once, then rolled aft down the incline of the deck.

He scrambled out of his seat listening to Daimler's screams as the boat's owner did his own scrambling. Hanging on tight to his plastic tote, McCory pulled himself up to the gunwale, rolled over it, and hit the bay on his back.

At sixty miles per hour, he skipped like a flat stone six times before the water caught his leg, flipped him over, and dragged him down.

When it came, the concussion hurt his ears.

2

"Allah Akbar!" yelled the young man in the bow.

Ibrahim Badr kept his own exclamation to himself. He had more self-discipline than the young Muhammed Hakkar.

Still, the detonations were impressive. He gauged them to be almost two kilometers away, near the western coast. A boat or ship, of course. In the dark, the first explosion had been a flare, a blue-white visual crash that stunned eyes accustomed to the night, followed momentarily by deep thunder. The second explosion—fuel tanks, no doubt—was yellow-red. Flaming debris arced out of the center of the fiery maelstrom.

Badr turned the handle throttle of the outboard motor to full idle. The rubber Zodiak boat slowed, skewed about, and bobbed in the light chop of the Chesapeake Bay. Far away to his left, he could see the lights of Annapolis struggling through the fog.

The explosion receded and became simply fire on the water. The ship with the searchlight and siren—the one that had first caused him to retard his throttle—was slowing, moving in on the wreckage.

5

"We must leave," Hakkar said from his seat in the bow of the rubber boat.

"It appears to be the best course," Badr agreed.

Already, the lights of another ship had appeared in the north, coming toward the scene of the fire—and toward them—at a fast pace.

A night that had been so shining with promise had become a disaster.

"And we must hurry," Hakkar urged.

"No," the leader said. "We must think."

Too many of his subordinates were disadvantaged in the matter of thinking. They promoted action without thought, reacting on impulse to outside stimuli. They thought little of consequences and almost never developed credible or practical alternatives.

"There is nothing to think about, Ibrahim Badr. We must try another time."

"But time grows short, young Muhammed, and opportunity slips away. Instead, we must remember that at the eye of the hurricane there is calm."

He could not see Hakkar's face but knew there would be a grimace of disgust on it.

"I do not know what you speak of."

Which is why it is I who am in command, Badr thought.

"The hurricane is over there, and we are in the eye. We will take advantage of this diversion," Badr said.

He twisted the throttle grip and turned the bow of the Zodiak toward the west.

0121 hours

Commander Martin Holloway stood to the left of his helmsman in the wheelhouse and looked down on the bows of his gunboat. The decks were crowded with crewmen, but few were gawking. His crew was well trained.

Beyond, the flames were dying away as the flammable liquids were consumed. Tongues of fire reached a few feet off the surface. Several searchlights were in play now, their beams slicing the night, seeking whatever was left. The forward half of the civilian boat was still floating, but barely. As he watched, a deck hatch popped open from internal pressure, let the air escape, and the bow started sinking.

"Mr. D'Angelo, let's come to five knots."

"Aye sir, five knots."

"And, Jones, we'll circle counter clockwise."

"Aye aye sir," the helmsman said.

"Mr. D'Angelo, contact Lieutenant Dyer on deck. He's to put two boats out. We want survivors, and we want anything that will identify the intruder."

"Aye aye sir." Chief Petty Officer Dennis D'Angelo turned to his intercom station.

The phone on the bulkhead in front of him buzzed, and Holloway picked up.

"Commander, Captain Norman of the *Prebble* wants to speak with you. He's on Tac-Two."

The *Prebble* was a destroyer, probably the ship converging from the north. She had been around the bay for months, and Holloway supposed she was being outfitted with some kind of experimental gear.

"Patch him through, then notify CINCLANT that we are investigating debris from an unknown civilian boat that exploded within restricted waters of the Research and Development Center. Explosion of undetermined origin. We did not, repeat, not, open fire."

"Aye aye sir."

Holloway waited for the two clicks, then said, "Captain Norman, Commander Holloway here."

"We're bearing on you, Commander," a gravel-filled voice told him. "What have you got?"

"I'm not certain, Captain." Holloway repeated the gist

of the message that he had sent to the Commander in Chief of the Atlantic Fleet.

"Pleasure boat?"

"Yes sir. Forty feet, at least, and fast. My radar man said she was doing fifty-two knots when she exploded."

"Survivors?"

"We're just starting to circle the area. There are none as yet."

"All right, Commander. We'll be joining you in about . . . four minutes."

Holloway hit the intercom button for the communications room. "Comm, Bridge."

"Comm. Milliken, sir."

"Milliken, send a copy of the CINCLANT message to the commander, Naval Ship Research and Development Center."

The center was the site of innumerable classified projects. Holloway had no idea what they were. His job was simply to patrol the area.

By the time Lieutenant Dyer had his boats in the water, the destroyer *Prebble* had arrived, and the flames were almost extinguished. The two naval ships flooded the scene with their lights, but there were no bodies, or parts of bodies, to be found.

0127 hours

McCory had abandoned his shoes, then unbuckled his belt, slipped it through the handle of the plastic bag, and rebuckled it. Swimming with the bundle dragging at his midsection was hard work, but he was a good swimmer. He had grown up in and on the waters around Fort Walton Beach, Florida, where the elder McCory, Devlin, had operated his marina. Kevin McCory was built for swimming, lean and long, with elongated and sinewy musculature. He was firm and hard, but he wouldn't be mistaken for Mr. Atlas by anyone.

The U.S. Navy was four hundred yards behind him, now two ships strong as they patrolled the spot where the *Scarab* had gone down. When he stopped to rest, dog-paddling in the oily water, he saw by their running lights that two launches were now cruising the waters closer to the western shore of the bay. The people commanding the small boats would naturally think that anyone who had lived through the explosion would head for the closest available land.

Which was why he had struck out for the eastern shore.

The bay waters were relatively calm, mediocre swells passing under him, bobbing him up and down a foot in either direction. To the east, the ships were clearly out-lined against their own searchlights. To the west, the view was more forbidding. Dank. Mist hanging low. At the apex of a wave, he could see the diffused lights around the naval complex. It looked to be a long way off.

Voices from the ships floated across the water, but he couldn't decipher any meanings. The sounds and the words overlapped.

He heard water slapping to his left.

"Ted?"

"Asshole." Daimler's voice was a stage whisper.

"Glad you made it, buddy." McCory started swimming toward the whisper.

He found Daimler floating on his back twenty feet away and moved in close enough to see his friend's face, a pale blob against the dark water.

"You all right?"

"Twisted my knee, I think. I'll live, thank you. But I'm not sure I want to."

"Sure you do."

"Not in prison."

"We're not going to prison."

"You son of a bitch. What're you doing with grenades?"

"Souvenirs. Happened to have them along." In reality, he had chased down an arms dealer in Miami. Arms dealers in Miami were easy to find.

Daimler mulled that over for a bit, then said, "You broke my boat."

McCory grinned, but it probably went unseen. "Insured, wasn't it?"

"You actually think I'd make a claim?"

"I'll buy you a new one."

"You don't have any money."

"I'll figure out something."

"Figure out how we're getting out of here."

"What we want," McCory said, "is Pier Nine."

"Pier Nine, what?"

"Pier Nine of the Ship R&D center."

"You're out of your everlovin' mind, you know that?" Daimler continued to float on his back, taking deep breaths.

"That's where I was going to have you drop me off."

"Midnight boat ride, that's what you told me. Just like college days, ol' buddy, buddy."

McCory and Daimler had attended the University of Florida together, then spent four years in the Navy SEALS together, mostly in San Diego. A long time ago, it seemed now.

"I could apologize, I guess," McCory said.

"Good goddamned start, but far short of need."

"Can you swim?"

"How far?"

"Less than a mile, looks like."

Daimler swung his head to look to the northwest. "You're lying to me again."

"Maybe a little more than that."

"Shit. How come I owe you so much?"

"You don't owe me."

"The sheet's going to be even after this, for damned sure. Let's get going."

Daimler rolled over onto his stomach and launched himself toward an objective that could barely be seen in the dark and the fog.

McCory watched the remembered easy, slow, and strong stroke until Daimler disappeared into the darkness, then he swam after him. There had been uncounted night operations, albeit training operations, when the two of them had parachuted into a similar situation, then swum side by side for miles.

It took them nearly an hour, making four rest stops before they made landfall. And then it was the wrong place, Pier Seventeen. McCory figured out the right direction, and they swam parallel to the maze of docks and warehouses, a hundred yards offshore. The security lights spaced along the quay lit a skeletal array of cranes and booms, transfer platforms, and other equipment. They were eerie forms, almost alive in the writhing movement of the thin fog. Trucks and tractors were parked in haphazard fashion. Moored at the docks were a wide variety of vessels—a frigate, a missile cruiser, several destroyers, and smaller boats. Two hydrofoils. Something that looked like a miniature helicopter carrier, big enough to handle five or six choppers. He saw the glow of a cigarette near the bow of the cruiser, on board her.

Behind them, over a mile away, a third ship had joined the search for ex-passengers aboard Daimler's ex-boat.

Through a gap between buildings, McCory saw a navy blue sedan pass by. Night patrol, maybe.

He kept looking for SPs on foot, working the docks, but didn't see any. Except for a possible personnel contingent aboard the cruiser, the place was as deserted as he had hoped it would be on a Friday night. He could hear the wave motion against the nearby concrete docks. There was a high level of fuel oil in the water. It burned his nostrils and made his hands feel slippery.

Pier Nine was long and wide, about five hundred feet by a hundred feet, and enclosed. There were windows in the corrugated steel sides, but they were high above the surface of the bay. A faint glow from inside suggested someone had left a night-light on for them.

"This is it?" Daimler whispered.

"Yup."

"What is it?"

"Follow me."

McCory breaststroked his way to the corner of the dock, studying the wall facing the bay. There was a large roll-up door in the center of it, indicating that the pier was actually two fingered, with open water between the fingers, inside the building.

It was.

He had to dive six feet down to find the bottom edge of the door, pull himself under, then rise slowly until his head broke the surface inside.

McCory used his left hand to wipe the polluted water from his eyes. His eyes were stinging badly. The inside of the building was partially lit from half a dozen ceiling-mounted bulbs.

And there it was.

Daimler's head emerged soundlessly from the water beside him—the SEAL training had stayed with both of them.

"Jesus Christ!" he whispered. "What in the hell is that, Mac?"

"That's mine."

"You've got to be shitting me."

"Come on."

McCory swam quietly toward a ladder mounted on the right side of the pier. The ladder rungs were of steel bar, bent into U-shapes, and sunk into the concrete of the pier.

When he reached the ladder, he worked his way slowly out of the water, aware of the greasy water sluicing off of him. He moved slowly, diminishing the noise, alert to the movement of any guard. But there was no guard. This was a classified project, but not a high priority one.

When he reached the top, five feet above water level, he rolled out onto the pier. His muscles yelled damnations at him, complaining about over-utilization. As Daimler climbed up beside him, dripping loudly, McCory unbuckled his belt and freed the plastic bag.

"How's the knee?"

"Hurts like hell. You're going to get a stack of medical bills, too."

They stood up, and Daimler tested his weight on his knee. He could hobble along, but he, too, had lost his shoes. Unlike McCory's feet, Daimler's were no longer accustomed to barefooting it on alien surfaces. Ted Daimler's feet were normally encased in lovingly hand-fitted leather appropriate to a Washington, D.C. attorney, who acquired large fees for introducing one set of influential people to another set of influential people.

Daimler looked daggers at him.

"Okay, I'll spring for a pair of Reeboks, too."

"Those maybe you can afford."

With Daimler leaning on him, the two of them worked their way along the dock toward the boats. As outside the building, there was a lot of equipment parked on or bolted to the pier. Winches, bollards, welders, lathes, drill presses. Set against the walls were large, metal-clad cabinets that McCory guessed were ovens and casting machines. Everything inside the building was clean and appeared to be well maintained.

There were two boats backed into the slip, moored one behind the other on the right finger of the pier.

They appeared identical from the exterior view.

McCory's practiced eye measured each of them at forty-four feet in length and about fourteen feet in width. Exactly as on the preliminary drawings. The bow was blunt, curving in abruptly from the sides, sharply angled toward the back and downward on the lower side. Along the gunwale edges, the deck also curved downward to meet the sides of the hull, the stern, and the bow. There wasn't a sharp angle visible. No railings, no safety lines. Chocks and bitts were countersunk into the deck, hidden when sliding doors were closed over them.

There was no cockpit and no apparent cabin.

Instead, from the stern forward, the deck angled upward, curving to level at midships, flowing forward, then rolling into the compound-curved, black Plexiglas windshield eight feet back from the bow. Along the sides, more curved, black Plexiglas had been molded into the plastic sides. The sun would not reflect off of those windows, and nothing of the interior could be seen through them.

Nothing protruded from the sleek surface. No radio or radar antennaes, no stanchions, no masts. The top of the craft was almost level with the dock, making its above-surface profile about five feet above waterline.

The night-lights sixty feet up didn't provide much illumination, but there was enough to tell that the boats were finished in a flat medium blue that seemed to absorb light. On a sunny day at sea, they would be all but invisible. On a cloudy day, they would also blend into the ocean.

And that was the idea.

"It is a fucking boat, isn't it, Mac? I mean, I'm just taking a wild guess."

"Sure enough."

"Not a sub?"

"Wasn't planned that way."

"How'd you know it was here?"

"Article in *The Washington Post*. There's nothing like a hungry reporter delving into the Pentagon's secrets, Ted. They're better at revealing classified data than the KGB.

They even had a fuzzy picture of it, taken during sea trials.''

"And you liked it, huh?''

"Hell, the minute I saw it, I knew it was mine.''

Daimler gave him a look that McCory knew was searching for his sanity.

"Not mine, really. It belonged to Devlin.''

"Your dad?'' Daimler was beginning to get the picture. The attorney had met Devlin first in 1972.

"That's right. He called it the *SeaGhost*.''

"What does the Navy call it?''

"I'm dammed if I know. X-twenty-two, I think.''

"So now you've seen it,'' Daimler said. "What do we do about it?''

"I'm going to take it home.''

"Bullshit.''

McCory shook his head. "Nope. And I'm going to get myself a few spare parts, too.''

He pointed to the far corner of the building where three oddly shaped gray blobs rested on wheeled dollies.

Daimler sighed. "I'm not going to be surprised anymore. What are those?''

"Engines. They're made from ceramic castings.''

"No shit? No radar echo?''

"You got it, my friend.''

McCory left Daimler standing on the dock, walked past the bow of the first boat until he found the hatchway, then sat down and dangled his feet just above the curved outer gunwale. Leaning way out, he was able to reach a recessed latch and pop it open. The hatch rose with hydraulic silence, like the doors on a classic Gull-wing Mercedes. Reaching out with his left foot, he wrapped his toes around the surgical rubber weather stripping at the bottom of the doorway, then pushed off the dock.

The interior wasn't laid out quite like he had expected. A short, steep flight of three steps took him down to the inside deck level. He was in a narrow cross passage with another hatch on the starboard side. Several coiled lines hung on the bulkheads on either side, secured by Velcro loops. A couple of flashlights and two fire extinguishers were also mounted on the bulkhead. He noticed they were made of plastic. Midway across the corridor, there was a door leading aft and a corridor leading forward. The overhead was low, barely two inches above McCory's six-two stance.

Dropping his vinyl bag on the deck, McCory tried the door. It opened easily, and he felt around until he found a light switch.

Flipped it. Bright light from several recessed overhead and bulkhead bulbs.

Cargo bay.

Or weapons bay. It depended upon the mission for which the boat was outfitted. Somebody was testing this boat as a weapons platform. Part of the cargo bay was taken up with a collapsed missile launch platform of some kind. Locked into racks along both sides were about forty slim, short missiles. They didn't look like any missile he had ever seen before.

Oh well. Something new to play with.

There was a control panel next to the light switch, protected by a clear plastic door. Opening the door, he located a toggle identified as "CRGO DRS" and flipped it upward. He heard the repetitive clicks of bolts being drawn, then the decking above him began to lift. The whine of electric hydraulic pumps could be heard. The molded plastic doors each served as half of the outer deck and opened initially like the clamshell doors of the space shuttle, then slid downward into recesses between the hull and the cargo bay's inner lining.

He went back through the corridor and scrambled up onto the dock.

"You're actually going to do this?"

"Damned right."

"I'm an unwitting accessory," the lawyer told him. "Jesus! Grand theft, boat. Boats. Let's count mine. Classified DOD secrets. Probably traitorous activities. Conspiracy. When the rookie lawyers at Justice get done with me, I won't have anything left. Won't need it in maximum security, though."

"You worry too much," McCory said.

"I'd worry less if I'd never met you."

"Go on aboard, and see if you can figure out how we start her."

While Daimler grimaced and shuffled his way aboard, McCory went to the far corner and moved two dollies out to the edge of the dock. The strange engines were big, about twice the size of a Caterpillar diesel, but flattened, the major component standing about sixteen inches high. They appeared to be complete, with compressor, starter, pumps, tubing, and other accessories already attached. A wiring harness led to a black box resting on top of each engine. That would be the controlling computer. The design was similar to that of the Wankel rotary engine, which McCory expected. They were rotary engines, though they were fueled by diesel. They were also heavy as hell, requiring a great deal of effort to get each dolly underway, then just about as much effort to stop it before it went over the edge of the dock.

Fortunately, he had powered assistance available. An electrically driven block and tackle, suspended from an overhead track, was parked near the wall. McCory grabbed the cable, moved it out from the wall, snapped its hook into a lifting yoke attached to the first engine, then pressed the lift button on the suspended control box. The electric winch whined, the engine lifted clear of the dolly and of the foot-high exposed edge of the cargo door, and he pushed it gently out over the cargo bay.

Daimler emerged into the hold and guided the descent

clear of the missile launcher to the far, starboard side of the bay, then disengaged the hook. The boat settled in the water a little, canted to starboard. Six minutes later, they had the second engine loaded and the boat back on an even keel. McCory walked back to the tall metal shelves in the corner, picked up a couple of empty cardboard boxes, and began filling them with odds and ends from the shelves. He didn't know what he was grabbing, since they were in clear plastic bags identified only with part numbers, but he wanted at least two of each—gaskets, seals, bearings, valves, solenoids, filters, and the like. He had to get another box when he ran into sets of large turbine blades that appeared to have been cast in carbon-impregnated plastic. Then he reboarded to stow the boxes and help Daimler rope the engines in place, tying them down to nylon loops sunken into the deck.

As McCory was closing the cargo hatches, Daimler asked, "You realize, of course, that this son of a bitch is armed? With missiles?"

"Yeah, I saw that."

Daimler shook his head sadly. "Now we can leave?"

"Now we can leave."

McCory went back to the pier to release three of the four mooring lines, then walked out to the end of the dock, looking for the switches controlling the roll-up door.

He found them easily enough and was about to try a momentary test, checking on the noise level, when he heard an outboard motor.

He froze in place, listening, but the sound died away, replaced by the whir of an electric motor and the whistle of moving air as Daimler blew the bilges.

Pressing the UP button, McCory raised the door six feet, just enough for clearance, then stopped it. He walked back to the *SeaGhost,* released the last line, then stepped aboard and closed the hatch.

In the corridor leading forward, he found a small storage compartment, opposite a narrow head that included a shower. Forward of those spaces were two tiny cabins, each with two bunks stacked against the outside bulkhead. Storage drawers were built-in under the lower bunks. A pair of narrow hanging lockers were the only other amenities in each of the cabins.

The main cabin was dimly lit with red light. It contained a small galley and a banquette-type booth on the port side, aft, and a complicated radio console and a desk on the starboard side. Daimler was in the helmsman's seat, a heavily cushioned, gray Naugahyde, bucket-type seat bolted to the deck. It was located on the starboard side behind an ultra-tech instrument panel with an amazing array of red and blue digital readouts. Opposite the helm side were two more of the bucket seats, situated behind electronic consoles mounted in the forward bulkhead. Vision through the tinted windows was good forward and to the sides but blind toward the stern.

The boat rocked a little, and McCory could see that they were drifting away from the pier. He looked around again at all of the electronics and estimated that there was a couple hundred thousand dollars tied up in the *SeaGhost*. Hell, he thought, given that it was the Department of Defense, double the dollar estimate.

He began to have doubts about what he was doing but quickly brushed them aside.

"I'm going to try 'em," Daimler said.

"Go."

The lawyer hit an ignition switch, but McCory didn't hear anything.

"That one's alive," Daimler said.

"You're shitting me." McCory leaned over his shoulder, found a blue readout labeled "PORT RPM," and saw that it was registering 825.

Daimler started the starboard engine, and the RPM indicator quickly came to life on that one, too. McCory became aware of a minute vibration in the deck, just a shiver under his bare feet.

"They're jets, Mac."

"I thought they would be." The propulsion system sucked water from vents in the lower hull, channeled it through the rotary engine-driven turbines, and streamed it out the transom through steerable nozzles.

Daimler crawled out of the seat and moved to the port side. "I don't know from jets, Mac. You run it. Besides, you have to remember that I'm a hostage."

McCory grinned at him and dropped into the seat. He found that the throttles were the two longest of four short levers mounted in the front of the right armrest. The two outboard, short levers were marked for "Forward" and "Neutral." Beyond those controls were two even shorter levers marked "Reverse." He suspected that they would drop cuplike devices over the jet nozzles, channeling the thrust forward.

He tried the throttles and ran the RPM's up to 4000. The result was a baritone whine rising from the stern quarters. The power-rumble of a typical V-8 was absent.

Pulling the throttles back, McCory slapped the shift levers into forward, then eased the throttles back in.

The *SeaGhost* responded immediately and headed for the gap under the overhead door. They slid under the door, into the thin light from shore-based lamps, and McCory felt free.

As soon as he was clear of the pier, he pushed the throttles forward some more. The boat reacted, leaped forward.

"Jesus Christ!" Daimler shouted.

McCory squinted his eyes and saw the rubber boat in the darkness.

Just as he hit it.

3

It was a few minutes after six in the morning in Norfolk, Virginia, and the dawn mist had already burned off. The sun was up, casting its rays through the partially opened slats of the venetian blinds in Admiral Bingham Clay's office. The gray carpet was striped in sun, as were Commander James Monahan's khaki-clad legs.

Monahan sat in one of two low chairs on either side of a matching couch, self-consciously rubbing his cheeks with the fingers of his right hand. He had not shaved very well in the sleepy moments after he got the call to report. There was a minor forest of stubble below his left ear. The day was shaping up badly. He was supposed to have a three-day weekend, he and Mona and the boys going over to Fredericksburg.

A rear admiral, a captain, and a lieutenant commander took up the rest of the conversational seating. The diminutive Admiral Clay, commander of the Atlantic Fleet, sat in his tall swivel chair behind a teak desk the size of an aircraft carrier. A large model of an F-18 Hornet was parked in one corner of the desk.

Clay was talking to Admiral Aaron Stein, who headed the U.S. Navy Ship Research and Development Center.

21

The conversation was amplified over the telephone's speaker and shared with the visitors.

"Hit me with it again, Aaron; my people are all here, now. Some civilian boat has been sunk?"

"It's worse than that. Both of the *Sea Spectre*s are gone, Bing. Vanished."

"They can't be."

"They are."

"Shit. What did the *Antelope* recover?"

"No bodies yet, if that's what you mean. But we've got lots of fiberglass and cushions, and we've got a registration number. We're tracing the owner now."

"As if that's going to lead us anywhere. Any media people show up yet?"

"No, and I'm not holding any press conferences, Bing. Hell, if it hadn't been for that *Post* story, nobody would have known about the *Sea Spectres*. The damned Air Force kept the F-117 Stealth fighter buried for seven years."

"Yes, well, that's history, Aaron. We've got to . . ."

"Hold on, Bing. My exec just came in."

Clay wiped his hand across his eyes. They were reddened and droopy. The admiral had been called away from his bed early, too. Clay was only five feet, six inches tall, but he had the presence of a six-footer. His build was blocky, with a strong torso always clad in an immaculate uniform. Monahan could picture him at sea, in the middle of a Force 10 typhoon, every crease in place. He had hard, dark eyes under thick gray eyebrows that matched the iron in his hair. Rusty iron, as the original red hung on for as long as it could. There were a lot of lines in his face, brought on by weather, worry, and the weight of command.

Stein came back. "Now we've got a body, Bing."

"Damn! That's just great. It's going to be difficult to keep it quiet now. Civilian?"

"Yeah, but get this. My people recovered the body off Pier Nine, not at the site of the sunken boat."

"What?"

"That's right. And we've also got a sunken Zodiak."

"What's going on, Aaron?"

"Damned if I know. I've got Navy Intelligence on the way over here from suitland."

Monahan was not so sure that would help matters. He knew some people who belonged to the NIS, and he had yet to be impressed.

"Any ID on the body?"

"None. It's been mangled pretty good. And Captain Melchor tells me it appears to be of Latin heritage, or possibly Middle Eastern."

"Anything else?"

"Not now. I'll keep you posted."

Clay leaned forward and cut off the phone. Resting his elbows on the arms of his chair, he pursed his lips and swiveled his chair toward the couch. "Gentlemen?"

Rear Admiral Matthew Andrews, who headed the Second Fleet's intelligence arm, said, "Seems to me, Bing, the bigger boat brought the Zodiak in from somewhere. They may have intended to scuttle the larger craft but blew it up as a diversion when the *Antelope* spotted them. After they transferred to the Zodiak."

"Perhaps, Matt. Check it out. What abut the body?"

Andrews shrugged. "Accident? Discord within the group? Who knows."

"Okay," Clay said. "I want you to get in touch with Defense Intelligence, the CIA, and the FBI. Let's see what they know about any group who would be interested in having their own *Sea Spectre*s. What's the mission for them, Jim?"

Monahan sat up straighter. "Night assault and reconnaissance, Admiral. The prototypes use stealth technology. The RCS—radar cross section—is so thin, the boat has to be within a couple miles of a heavy duty radar to be picked up. And then on the screen, it looks like a sea gull at rest. Sonar can ping it, but by the time it does, it's probably too late. During daylight hours, they can be spotted visually, but at night, they're all but invisible.''

"All but?''

"They do leave a wake.''

"Yes, okay. How many do we have?''

"That was it,'' Monahan said.

"Damn.'' Clay flicked his eyes toward Captain Aubrey Nelson, the man in charge of the morning watch in the Operations Center. "What's the range of those boats, Captain?''

"As I recall, Admiral, those rotaries are very fuel efficient, even with their turbochargers. With a full fuel load, it seems to me they have a range of nearly four thousand miles.''

"They can cross the Atlantic?''

"Easily, sir, at a cruise speed of forty-five knots.''

"What's the top end?''

"Sixty-five knots with a full crew of four and a medium load.''

Clay shook his head dishearteningly. "Okay, Captain, I want you to set up a search. The area is going to have to be as large as the range at maximum speed at,'' he checked his watch, "possibly five hours. Cover the entire Eastern Seaboard and the Atlantic. Be prepared to extend into the Caribbean. Bring in the Coast Guard and start canvassing marinas and ships at sea. We're going to have to have some visual sightings from witnesses to go on.''

"Aye aye, sir.''

"Jim, I want you to coordinate all of this and report to me on the hour.''

"Yes, sir.'' Monahan had known that, as Clay's aide, he would end up with the duty. It would go round-the-clock until the end, and there would be short tempers and jealousies involved. Mona's would be one of the short tempers. Monahan got along well enough with Aubrey Nelson, but Rear Admiral Matt Andrews got highly irritated anytime he sensed that his channels to Clay were required to go through a lowly commander.

The phone rang, and Clay flipped the toggle.

"Bing? Aaron again."

"Something new?"

"And bad," Stein said.

"How bad?"

"Both of those boats were armed. We were conducting trials."

"Armed with what?"

"M61 Vulcan cannon and the new Mini Harpoon surface-to-surface-missiles. There were forty-four on each boat."

"Son of a bitch! How difficult are they to operate, Aaron?"

"You ever watch an eight-year-old at a video arcade? These are easier."

Admiral Clay looked over at his subordinates. "Get cracking, gentlemen."

0630 hours, 35° 12' North, 74° 17' West

Ibrahim Badr had begun to worry that he had made the wrong decision. There were so many blips on the radar screen, and he was totally unfamiliar with the particular radar set. Yet, when he finally spotted the tanker hull-down on the horizon, he was elated.

He pushed the throttle forward and felt the boat pick up speed. The readout indicated sixty-two knots, but the noise level was surprisingly low. Or perhaps the insulation was very good. The engines seemed to only produce a heavy, low whine at high speed.

Very high speed.

It was amazing.

He had traversed the 190 kilometers of the Chesapeake Bay to its mouth in slightly more than two hours, staying close to the western edge of the shipping channel. If any of the commercial ships plying the passage had seen him racing south at over ninety kilometers per hour, none of them had sounded an alert. Lookouts stationed aboard freighters, tankers, and cargo ships would probably have only seen the white flash of his bow wave or his wake, anyway.

Badr had been so intent on his piloting and on avoiding other traffic that he had not learned to use the radios or the radar until long after he had passed under the Chesapeake Bay Bridge and headed east into the Atlantic.

And when he finally activated the radar, he had found the screen cluttered with dozens of targets in the coastal shipping lanes. He had had to rely on the tanker captain having his ship located at the coordinates where he was supposed to be at six-thirty, 160 kilometers off the coast of North Carolina.

Badr hated relying on anyone except himself. That was because so many of his compatriots were unreliable, while he had absolute faith in himself.

Hakkar, for instance, had been a man requiring careful watching.

He was now a martyr to the cause and mercifully joined with Allah. Badr would tell others as much.

During the torturously slow trek to the west, then up the eastern shore of Carr Bay, he had cut the speed of the rubber boat to less than five knots, to keep the outboard motor quiet. It seemed that infinity passed before he located the right pier, the one mentioned in the newspaper story. Badr had shut off the motor as soon as he saw the watchman stationed aboard a large ship, and he and Hakkar took up paddles for the last several hundred meters into the dock.

He had been shocked when he saw the door rise, spilling interior light on the the surface of the water.

Hakkar went flat into the bottom of the boat, dragging his pistol from his pocket.

And then the silhouette of the boat moving toward them. Suddenly accelerating.

Badr grabbed the motor housing and pulled himself over it, launching into a dive that took him out of the path of the oncoming boat. Just before he went under the surface, he heard the sickly crunch as the bow of the boat hit something, very likely Muhammed Hakkar's head.

He dove deep, and when he came up, the big boat was gone. He could hear a miniature moan off to the south, quickly abating. Beside him, the Zodiak was hissing, nearly deflated, and already slipping below the surface. One of Hakkar's arms hung over the gunwale.

Badr paddled close to check on the man. His face was coated in blood, and his right temple looked mushy. He was breathing, but raggedly. Badr reach up, grabbed the man's neck, and pulled his head underwater, finding only feeble resistance.

Casualties were a hindrance to any mission.

He scanned the shoreline, taking time to stare into the crevices and between buildings. The collision had not raised an alarm, apparently.

But time was running perilously short. He must get away from there before some patrol came by.

The Zodiak gurgled and went under, taking Hakkar with it. A stream of bubbles broke the surface, sounding unnaturally loud as they popped.

Badr looked toward the pier numbered nine, under the partially opened door.

And there was another of the boats, just as pictured by the newspaper photographer.

His blood sang in his veins.

Badr had been certain that he was too late. Someone else had stolen his boat.

He swam into the building, found the ladder rungs on the right side, and climbed to the dock. His heart was beating fast, and the sense of fear elevated his awareness. Everything inside the structure appeared sharp and clear.

Badr ran along the concrete dock, the leather soles of his shoes slapping loudly, spattering water.

It was such a sleek boat, and it took him several seconds to locate the hatchway and open it. Another two minutes were devoted to releasing the mooring lines, then he went aboard and found his way to the controls.

The instrument panel dismayed him. He had never seen anything like it. The face was flat black plastic, completely smooth except for a few touch-sensitive pads. In the vague light coming through the windshield, he searched it and tried various switches until the panel lights came on, a wild array of red, blue, yellow, and orange lines and letters. Fortunately, each control and readout was neatly labeled in blue. Americans insisted on labels—on their cigarettes, their cereal, their highways. Waiting for the bilge blower to ventilate the engine compartment felt like forever. The engines started so silently that, on the first one, he tried the starter again while the engine was already running. A horrible screeching from the back of the boat caused his heart to leap.

And then he was moving.

And four hours later, he was closing on the Kuwaiti-flagged *Hormuz,* steaming easily and very slowly in the calm blue ocean.

The tanker was moving at less than seven knots as Badr brought the *Sea Spectre*—the name was imbossed in blue at the top of the instrument panel—alongside it. He adjusted the speed to match the tanker's, held the wheel over to keep the boat in place against the rusted steel plates of the oiler's hull, and tightened the steering lock.

Pulling himself out of the seat, he ran to the back and opened the narrow door into the cargo compartment. His legs and back were stiff after so many hours at the helm, and he realized that he badly needed to relieve himself.

He found the switch and flicked the lights on. Studying the hatch controls, he moved the identified toggle switch and looked up to see the doors first rise, then slide downward. Sunlight flooded in.

And struck all those missiles.

Badr felt the grin widening his face.

Allah was so good to him.

The cargo hatch doors settled into place, and Badr watched as the crewmen scampered down the netting suspended from the tanker's railings. Quickly, they moved over the *Sea Spectre*'s decks, slipping and falling on the smooth, sloped surfaces, trying to locate the lifting rings.

Within five minutes, cables from the ship's crane had been attached, and the *Sea Spectre* rose from the sea.

Badr hurried back inside the cabin to the helm and shut off the engines.

He returned to the cargo bay, smiled at the missiles, and watched the activity on the tanker's cluttered decks as the *Sea Spectre* was brought aboard.

The hatch cover of the false tank had already been removed and the stealth boat was slowly lowered into the tank. Leaning out, Badr looked down and saw a half-dozen crew members scurrying to adjust the cradle secured in the bottom of the tank to the contours of the boat's hull. To fit within the tank, the assault boat had to be lowered diagonally into it.

He watched them carefully, because he did not want the hull damaged after all of his work.

When the boat finally settled into place, Badr felt a great sense of achievement.

The boat was now his.

As were all of those lovely missiles.

1530 hours, 21Sep86, the Pentagon

Devlin McCory was a quick man with a temper. He had the scars to prove it—little dashes of hard tissue on his jaw, forehead, cheekbone, shoulder, arms. In earlier days, there weren't too many saloons he hadn't loved. And cleaned out.

He was six feet tall, with a chest like a barrel of Ireland's own, and he had big gnarled hands and the hard muscles of a man not afraid to do his own work. His hair was the color of weathered orange brick, and his blue eyes could pierce egos. His face always gave him away, though. It went through fifty shades of suffusion in direct proportion to his temper.

It was medium red as he sat on the other side of the desk from Lieutenant Commander Roosevelt Rosse, who was somewhere in the chain of command of the Navy's Weapons Procurement Division. Rosse was, by Devlin's reckoning, far too young and far too low in the chain to be making this decision.

He handed McCory's drawings back to him, leaning out across his gray metal desk. "I'm afraid, Mr. McCory, that you're a bit too late with this. Our specialists looked it over, but the Navy has already undertaken a similar program."

"The hell it has! You've already got this boat?"

"Well, no sir. But negotiations with the contractor have been concluded."

"What the hell happened to open bidding, Commander? I want to be part of the process."

Rosse didn't respond to that. Instead, he asked, "What are your qualifications, Mr. McCory?"

"Qualifications! Qualifications! I spent twelve years in your damned Navy. CPO. I've got my own marina. I build boats. I'm a master mechanic. I know boats."

"But no degrees? As it happens, Mr. McCory, the contractor has a staff of marine architects and marine engineers. The Navy is impressed with their qualifications."

If the lieutenant commander's office had had a window, Devlin would have put the gray steel desk through it, followed shortly by the lieutenant commander. He managed admirably to hang on to his sanity, however, and found his way out of the Pentagon's C-ring and back to his Ford pickup in the parking lot.

He counted the money in his wallet and figured he had enough for gas back to Florida, if he didn't eat much. Pulling out of the parking lot, Devlin McCory finagled his way onto the Henry G. Shirley Memorial Highway and headed south.

Feeling fully defeated by his own Navy and his own country.

And planning the letters he would be writing to anyone holding some kind of power in the Navy.

0800 hours, 34° 2' North, 73° 46' West

Ted Daimler owned a cabin on the Chesapeake Bay, just below Rose Haven. It was a rustic thing of three rooms used for poker games and weekends away from the hurdy-gurdy of Washington political life and intrigue.

McCory had let Daimler off on the dock below the cabin at three in the morning. He lodged himself in the hatchway, holding onto the rotting wood of the wharf as Daimler stood on the planks and tested his knee.

"Tell me again, Ted."

"Hey, I've got it down, Mac. I tell the deputy I got down here after dark last night, beat from a long day, and went right into the sack. Get up this morning, and see my *Scarab*'s gone. That's when I report it.''

"Good."

"But, goddamnit it, Mac! We hit that boat."

McCory could still hear and feel the thump when the hull collided with the Zodiak. "Yeah, I know. It shouldn't have been there."

"Like ourselves?"

"Look, Ted, all we can do is watch the newspapers."

Daimler's face was haggard in the light from the corridor behind McCory. "I suppose so."

"If it gets too tense, Ted, you spill it all. Name me."

"Ah, shit."

"Just do it."

"I'm not going to give you up, Mac. We go back too far." He didn't mention the almost brotherly relationship that had developed over two decades, the things they had done for each other.

"This is me and Devlin, Ted. I don't want your ass in a sling because of us. They're not going to find me, anyway, not until I want them to."

"Ah . . ."

"Sorry about the knee and the boat. I really am. More about the knee, though."

"I'll bill you."

"Do that."

"Kevin."

"What?"

"Somewhere down the line, you're going to need an attorney. I want you to keep me up-to-date on what you're doing."

"Ted, I don't think I'll . . ."

"You are going to negotiate?"

"Maybe. I don't know yet."

"Do it through me," the lawyer said.

McCory looked up at his friend. 'I'll let you know."

"Go on. Get the hell out of here before my backyard fills up with submarines and battleships."

McCory backed inside, closed the hatch, and made his way to the helm. Three minutes later, the dock, with Daimler still standing on it, disappeared into the gloom.

He had taken the *SeaGhost* down the bay at full bore, which amounted to fifty-seven knots. He assumed the weight of the spare engines and the missile launcher were taking a toll on the maximum speed.

By eight o'clock, he was 225 miles off the coast, headed south at a leisurely forty knots, and the radar didn't show another vessel within forty miles of him.

McCory had figured out a few things. The navigation system was keyed into the NavStar Global Positioning Satellite System and precisely plotted his position for him. The automatic pilot was linked into the same system. After a few trials at different speeds, the computer had calculated his rates of fuel consumption. He didn't yet know how big the fuel bladders were but guessed they were large. A fill-up would wipe out his VISA card. The readout told him he had three-quarters of a fuel load left.

The radar was exceptional. At thirty miles of range, it picked up tiny things that he suspected were flotsam, but he could squelch them out. It looked to him as if the maximum range was about two hundred miles, which meant that an over-the-horizon set of electronics kicked in, bouncing their signals off the ionosphere. The radar was normally operated from the center seat, but one of two small screens behind the plastic face in the helmsman's panel repeated the signal. The cathode ray tubes in the pilot's panel could also be switched to show fore and aft views from video cameras mounted in the bow and the stern. The video had low-light and infrared capacity. Besides repeating the radar image, the CRT's also repeated the information found on the sonar set, which was operated from the left-hand seat.

Either of the CRT's could also serve as the display device for the on-board computer. The small numerical keypad was mounted to the right of the instrument panel, but so far, McCory had only learned how to tap into the fuel consumption program.

Below the instrument panel bulkhead, in front of the radarman's chair, was a hatch into the bow, accessed on hands and knees. McCory had taken a look, finding electronics bays on either side. The radar antenna was mounted on the port side, with clearance enough for a 180-degree sweep. Very likely, there was a similar antenna in the stern, covering the rearward 180-degrees. He figured that the radio antennaes, or most of them, were inlaid into the fiberglass of the deck. Directly in front, in separate insulated compartments, he found the video camera mounted behind a transparent panel in the hull, and to his amazement, a six-barreled Gatling-type gun. He thought it was probably twenty millimeter, an M-61, and when he pounded on the side of the fiberglass magazine, it sounded full. The magazine and the gun were apparently accessed for service from a hatch in the deck above. Except for a variable up-and-down arc, it was solidly mounted and, like a fighter aircraft, had to be aimed by steering the boat.

There wasn't any food in the galley, and he went back to the cross-passage and retrieved his vinyl bag. There were two grenades left, and he put them in the desk drawer on the starboard side. Somewhere in the middle of his rage had been the idea to blow up the boat if he couldn't appropriate it. Probably, he should have dropped the grenades in the second boat in Pier Nine, but he had forgotten about it.

The peanut butter sandwiches were slightly soggy and tasted of salt, but the coffee in the Thermos was almost hot. He sat in the U-shaped dinette booth to eat his breakfast.

Looking through the tinted windows on the other side

of the cabin, he could see stratocumulus clouds building up in the southwest. He might run into some weather—light squalls—in the late afternoon. Right now, the seas were calm, with one-foot swells running, and the *Sea-Ghost* took them smoothly.

McCory thought the boat would also take to heavy weather gleefully. With her smooth topsides, wind and water would sluice right off her. She might even cut right through the tops of tall waves, playing submarine. He would have to calculate her weight and displacement. As far as he had determined, all of the flat surfaces—well, curved surfaces—were comprised of a fiberglass impregnated with a carbon compound for strength. There was almost no flex in the major panels. If the engineers had followed Devlin's drawings, the keel, structural beams, and ribs would also be cast in carbon-filled plastic, with lots of angles and cutouts to foil radar returns.

He thought she would be light for a boat her size. There was no armor plating of any kind. A direct hit by hostile fire in the twenty millimeter or larger calibers would be all it would take. But then, hostile fire would have to find her first. Computer-controlled guns, using radar data, would be useless against her.

The interior fittings, in the cabin at least, were also of fiberglass and plastic, from cabinets to instrument panels. Two ceramic burners on the galley range. Even the sonar, radar, and CRT screens were plastic.

The interior was navy spartan. The deck was covered in a light gray industrial carpeting—sound-insulating against sonar-seeking footfalls, and the bulkheads were painted a slightly darker gray. The chair and dinette cushions were upholstered in a heavy gray Naugahyde.

It was comfortable though. Outside the tinted windows, a fierce sun was building up heat, reflecting hot off the water in the far distance, but inside, the air conditioning was doing its job.

McCory slid out of the booth and walked forward to lean against the instrument panel bulkhead. Through the windscreen, the sea appeared to be a bright blue this morning, but the coloring of the foredeck blended right into it. He scanned the ocean but saw nothing. He was completely alone, a condition that never bothered him. In fact, it was a situation that he often sought for himself.

The left CRT in the helmsman's panel, set to rearview, also showed emptiness.

If anything bothered him, it was being so fully enclosed. McCory had been on boats from the age of six months onward, but he was accustomed to sun and wind in his face. His face demonstrated the history—deep sea-tanned and weathered, with squint lines at his eyes and deepening crevices at the outside edges of his nose. His eyes were Devlin's, sharp and clear and a radiant blue, but his mother had played a part in his coloring. Her darkness was in his skin tone and his hair—it was a dark auburn and cut short. He didn't like maintaining elaborate styling.

He went back to the stations behind the helmsman's chair. Against the rear bulkhead on the starboard side was the communications console. It was complex and, as far as he could tell, state of the art. Running his finger down the stacks, he noted UHF, VHF, HF, FM, AM, low-power, marine, and ship-to-shore telephone sets. Scanners. A printer recessed in the left side of the desk surface suggested telex and cable capability. On the right side of the desktop, a panel slid back to reveal a computerlike keyboard. There were two scrambler interfaces and what looked to be an encryption device. If for nothing else, the Navy would be very excited about the loss of those top secret black boxes.

McCory turned on the AM component and searched for a shore-based radio station transmitting news. When he found one out of Atlanta, he turned the volume down and left it broadcasting on an overhead speaker. He could select from a variety of speakers sited within bulkheads of the cabin, and there were a bunch of cushioned headsets lying around.

Maybe he'd make the news.

Next to the communications console, facing outboard below the window, was the commander's station, primarily a chart table. There were drawers in a stack to the left, but they were locked. A shallow center drawer held some drawing instruments, pens, pencils, and now, two fragmentation grenades. On the right, under the table, were tubes for chart storage, and the only navigation chart aboard was for the Eastern Seaboard. There were also two shelves full of manuals. McCory pulled the manual for the radar and, as he did, found the boat's log.

He opened it, found a pen, and dutifully entered the beginning of this morning's voyage. He signed off as "K. McCory, Captain." He had only made lieutenant in the Navy, but he had captained a lot of boats.

Then he scanned the radar manual. It was an operator's manual, rather than a maintenance manual, and he was surprised by what he found. Carrying the book forward, he sat in the radar operator's chair and experimented with the set.

One of the drawbacks to radar in a battle or war setting was that, when it was actively seeking, it emitted radiation that could be detected by hostile forces. If a boat commander used his radar, he knew what was out there, but what was out there also knew where he was.

This radar set had its own computer, and after a few tries with the keyboard mounted to the right of the screen, McCory had it programmed as explained in Chapter Eight of the manual. The range was set for thirty miles and at randomly selected intervals of time to avoid setting up a routine. Between twelve and seventeen minutes, the set would go active, make one 360-degree sweep, utilizing fore and aft antennaes that were electronically synchronized, then return itself to an inactive state. If that single sweep picked up a blip, a low-toned alarm would buzz.

Pleased with his discovery and his new-found computer programming ability, McCory checked on the autopilot, then dialed in a new heading of 190 degrees. He would begin to slowly close with the coast. He was going to enter his safe harbor way after night had fallen once again.

He reset the air conditioning thermostat to a lower setting, entered the port-side bunk cabin, and sprawled out on the lower bunk. As always, he was asleep within a minute.

2303 hours, Glen Burnie, Maryland

The eleven o'clock news caught Justin Malgard by surprise. He and Trish were in bed, but Trish was already in a near-coma. She believed beds were for sleeping or making love, not watching the late news.

Malgard grabbed the remote control on the bedside stand and turned up the volume. When the piece was over, he turned the volume down and slipped out of bed.

He slept in the nude, so he grabbed his robe from the chair beside the dresser and donned it as he went out into the hall. Jason's bedroom was quiet as he went by it, but Patty, who was fifteen, had her stereo going, playing something that would have shattered eardrums if she had not been trying to sneak it past the ordained shut-off time. Malgard stopped, opened her door, and started to reinforce the house rule verbally. Patty, however, was already asleep, on her back with her mouth open and her blonde hair spread carefully over the pillow.

Malgard went in and shut off the stereo, then closed the door and took the stairs down to his den.

It was a nice den. Trish was not much of a decorator, and he had paid outrageous fees for a professional to design every room in the fifteen-room house. Patty and Jason did not understand the cost, of course, and it was a constant struggle to get them to maintain their rooms and the recreation room located in the basement.

The den was his refuge. The deep-pile, rust carpet absorbed sound. The furnishings were finished in dark oak and brown leather. There was a full wall of bookcases housing leather-bound books ranging from classical literature to hard science. It always felt very academic, very intellectual, and very professional to Malgard. When he retired, Malgard intended to read every one of those English, French, and American authors.

It was a while away, yet, because he was only forty-five years old.

Malgard went around behind the desk and settled into the soft leather of his chair. Picking up the handset of the telephone color-matched to the room, he punched the memory button for Rick Chambers's number.

Chambers was listed on the organization chart of Advanced Marine Development, Incorporated as an assistant vice president. Malgard himself was at the head of the chart, president and chief executive officer.

When the phone on the other end was picked up, the voice was alert, but irritated. "What?"

"Rick, this is Justin."

The voice softened. "Justin? Yeah, what do you need? I'm in the middle of somethin' here."

"Did you see the news?"

"Hell, no! I ain't got time for that."

"Well, listen up."

"Can't we do this in the morning?"

"No, damn it!" Malgard erupted. "Are you listening to me?"

A long sigh. "Okay. I'm sittin' up."

"My two *Sea Spectre* prototypes were stolen this morning."

"No shit? The Navy call you?"

"Not yet, and I'm pissed that they haven't. Damn it, I'm the prime contractor, and the media got it first. As soon as we're done, I'll call the Pentagon."

"What happened?" Chambers asked.

"It's difficult to tell from what the news had, but apparently they've identified a body they found as Middle Eastern. From the dental work or some damned thing."

"Arabs stole your boats?"

"That's what it sounds like. Or that's what it is supposed to sound like."

"You don't think so?"

"Let's say that I harbor a doubt," Malgard said.

"I don't know what the hell you're talkin' about."

"This body they found could have been just a hired hand. There's Middle Eastern people looking for work all over the country. No, I think the Navy's jumping to a conclusion they want to jump to."

"You know somethin' they don't?" Chambers asked.

"Of course, and you do, too. I think I know exactly where those boats are headed, and I want you to be there when they arrive."

Chambers's voice showed a little excitement now. "Bonus time?"

"Yes, Rick, it'll be a nice bonus."

4

Ponce de Leon Inlet's marker buoys were clearly visible in the moonless night. The moon had dipped below the horizon an hour earlier. A pale glimmer of dawn was cracking the eastern horizon, but McCory only saw it in the rearview screen on the instrument panel.

McCory saw no other marine traffic, either entering or leaving the Intracoastal Waterway. There were a few nightlights visible in Ponce Inlet, on the northern point.

He scanned the instrument panel, having become accustomed to the placement of its blue lettering, identifying the readouts—and its red, green, orange, and yellow numbers and lines—the indicators of activity. Then he retarded the throttles until the readout showed him thirty knots. Once he had cleared the marker, he turned the wheel and headed south along the eastern side of the waterway. Within minutes, the lights of New Smyrna Beach appeared on his right oblique, somewhat diminished by the tinting of the windscreen.

McCory felt invisible. The invisible man, as well as boat. The *SeaGhost* made the waterway seem a few miles wider than it actually was.

As he passed New Smyrna Beach, a large cruiser, run-

41

ning lights ablaze, left port and made a wide turn to the north. McCory instinctively gave it room, easing the helm a few points to the left. The cruiser passed him half a mile away, and there was no indication that he had been spotted.

Three miles further south, he saw the lighted public pier of Edgewater, then shortly after that, the dock lights of his own place, Marina Kathleen. McCory had never known his mother, but he thought Devlin would have approved of using her name again.

He continued on a southerly heading for another five miles, then spun the helm to starboard, crossed the waterway, and closed in on the mainland. Captain John Barley's Marine Refitters was dark except for a tall, hooded lamp in the graveled yard near the office. It was a chaotic place of five acres, with shanties, sheds, and cradled boats spotted where they had been needed at the time. There were eight dry docks lined up on the shore, three of them enclosed by gargantuan structures built of wood that had lost its paint years before. The wind and water and salt had eroded every board and every plank within the chain link boundaries of Barley's to a silver gray that gleamed in the night. John Barley didn't care how it looked. He was seventy-four years old. He worked when he felt like working, and if one of his sheds collapsed, he figured he would not be needing it again.

McCory had leased one of Barley's enclosed dry docks when he took on the hull-refinishing of Pamela Endicott's *Mimosa*. She was fifty-two feet in length, four feet more than he could comfortably get out of the water at Marina Kathleen. The rented dock was empty now, but McCory still had an active lease because John Barley would not lease for less than a year, a point of honor, and income, for him. He wanted the hundred bucks a month. At any other place on the East coast, McCory would have paid twelve hundred for a two-week rental.

With the *SeaGhost*'s engines barely whispering and still in gear, McCory nudged the bow up against the closed door of the dock, slipped out of his seat, and hurried back to open the hatchway. The original drawings of the *SeaGhost* had had a hatch from the cabin to the bow, but some engineering jerk had eliminated it.

With the hatch lifted, the predawn air on the water was cool. It refreshed him after the long trip and made him feel more positive about what he had done. Gripping the edge of the hatchway, McCory worked his way around the raised door and pulled himself onto the top of the cabin. The surface was slick under his bare feet, and he was cautious as he moved forward and slid down over the windshield onto the steeply inclined foredeck. He sat down, dangled his legs off the bow, and searched the wooden face of the door for its handle. When he found it, he tugged upward.

The door hardware had been stiff when he first rented the dock, but McCory had reconditioned it, and now the sectioned door panels rose easily and silently. As he raised the lower edge of it above his head, the *SeaGhost* obediently inched forward. Water dripped from the door, splattering McCory and the deck.

McCory rose to his feet and stayed with the door, hanging onto it, and walked backward up onto the cabin and back over the cargo hatch until he reached the stern, where he finally let go of the door, shoving it downward.

He slid his way back to the hatchway and inside but not before the *SeaGhost* traveled the full eighty-foot distance of the slip and banged into the dock head.

As he killed the engines, he thought about motorizing the boat house door and installing a remote control. It might preclude his killing himself or severely denting the boat, either event undesirable.

After securing all of the *SeaGhost*'s electronic systems, he found a coiled line in the cross-corridor and used it to rope a stanchion on the dock and pull the boat close enough to step ashore. It took several tries, since he was working in the dark.

Making his way around timbers and braces, McCory reached the front of the building and found the switchbox. He turned on several overhead lights.

It took a couple of minutes for his eyes to adjust to the radiance.

It was a utilitarian structure. A twenty-foot wide dock head crossed the front of the building, supporting workbenches, heavy tools and a latrine stuck in one corner. Overhead, a steel-legged rack contained the winches that lifted canvas slings that went under a hull. Once a boat was elevated above water level, the side docks could be cranked out under it. Everything was old. Most planks had splintered, and some had large chunks broken out of them. Any moving surface requiring grease was coated with both grease and dirt. The casings, rods, drive shafts, and bolts of ancient machinery were tinged with rust. The tops of wooden beams and steel I-bars had once been layered with dust, but McCory had washed it out before refinishing the *Mimosa*'s hull two months before.

There wasn't a pane of glass left intact in a window, and fortunately, McCory had simply boarded them over with plywood. It made the interior private.

He went back to the side dock and rigged several spring lines to secure the boat, then walked out to the end and made sure the door was locked in its down position.

Then he walked back to the front of the building and lifted the telephone from its wall mount. It was connected to the same number as the Marina Kathleen.

He dialed.

"Mmmpf?"

"Good morning, Ginger."

"Mmmpf! You mmmpf!"

"Me?"

"Bastard!"

"It's 5:10 in the morning. Beautiful day. You should be getting up, anyway."

"Your memory is fading, Kevin. I don't get up until noon," she said, and hung up.

He dialed again.

She let it ring three times before picking up.

"I need a ride, hon."

"Where are you?"

"You know John Barley's Refitters?"

"That's only five or six miles. Walk it."

"I don't have any shoes."

"Why?"

"It's a long story."

"If I get out of this bed, you have to tell it to me."

"You don't want to know."

"Good-bye."

"I'll tell you."

"Give me ten minutes. Oh, hell no! Give me twenty minutes."

0650 hours, Dulles International Airport

Rick Chambers smiled at the waitress, who was too tired to notice. She placed the coffee cup in front of him with a weary clatter and turned away, stifling a yawn.

Chambers didn't like being ignored, especially by women. He almost said something to her, then thought better of it.

He was on an operation, and attention was the last thing he needed, even in an airport restaurant.

There hadn't been many interesting operations in the last few years. Sometimes, it seemed like he'd become nothing more than an errand boy. He didn't like the feeling, though the salary and the free time were acceptable.

And he wasn't a boy. Richard Chambers was fifty-one years old. He'd done his twenty years as a Special Forces trooper, rising to master sergeant, after a couple of demotions, before his retirement. If he cared about proving his competency in the Green Berets, he could point to a stack of blue, flat, cardboard boxes somewhere in his mother's house that contained a Distinguished Service Medal, a couple of Silver Stars, three Bronze Stars, two Army Commendation Medals, four Purple Hearts, and a few other trinkets with his name engraved on the backs.

He didn't much care about the jewelry anymore. A Silver Star didn't buy zilch. Greenbacks were better. He had become a little complacent, enjoying the restaurants around D.C. a bit more than he should have, lolling around his Arlington Heights condominium, taking long weekends at AMDI's hospitality condo in Palm Springs.

There were maybe fifteen pounds around his waist that shouldn't be there. Otherwise, he was still fit enough. The shoulders and neck were as thick, hard, and strong as ever. His hair was a trifle longer than in his military days but still maintained in a brush cut. His cheeks and jaw were slightly padded with new flesh, but the hard angles of his cheekbones and the somewhat sunken sockets gave his hazel eyes a menacing appearance. His nose had been broken a couple of times and wasn't quite lined up with the rest of his face. On the left side of his neck was a thin, angry white scar, the result of a 7.62 round that had passed a little close.

Chambers wore thousand-dollar suits that were tailored to his six-four, 240-pound frame. This morning's suit was a silver-gray with thin, dark red stripes, and as customary, he didn't wear a tie. On the table beside his plate—wiped clean except for the sprig of parsley—was a thin leather portfolio. It contained all of the paperwork that Malgard had given him. There wasn't much there.

He had sent his carryon through Delta's baggage check,

because he didn't want the magnetometer sounding off when he entered the concourse.

Checking the time on the stainless steel Rolex strapped to his wrist, Chambers tossed a couple of bills on the table, stood up, and strolled back into the terminal. He never gave anyone the impression that he was in a hurry or late for an appointment. He sauntered his way down the concourse to his gate in the Delta Airlines section, leaned against a post, and studied the Boeing 737 parked on the ramp.

When the girl at the counter called the flight and the people clambered out of their chairs and scrambled for a place in line, Chambers remained where he was. He didn't like fighting mobs. Besides, he had reserved a first-class ticket. Window seat. He always got a window seat.

The line dwindled down, and Chambers joined the end of it, passed down the skyway, and entered the aircraft. He pulled his ticket and boarding pass from the inside jacket pocket and handed it to the girl.

"Good morning, sir. Off to Tallahassee?"

"Right." Connecting to Pensacola. He hadn't been down that way in years.

"Fine, sir." Glancing at the boarding pass, she said, "You're in row three, on the right, aisle seat."

"No."

"Sir?"

"I reserved a window seat."

She checked the ticket, then the boarding pass. "Oh, I believe there's been a mistake. The window seat's been taken."

"Then correct it."

"Sir?"

"Correct your mistake."

She studied his face for a moment, then said, "Just a moment, sir. I'll see what I can do."

Rick Chambers always got his way.

1120 hours, Carr Bay

The *Antelope* was holding position some two miles off the western coast of the bay. Nearby, a salvage barge had been anchored, and a hill of fiberglass chunks was slowly growing on its deck. The two V-8 engines and part of an outdrive from the once-proud *Scarab* were lashed down near the gunwale.

Several small boats and launches chugged about. Sailors in blue work uniforms scampered about the decks or leaned against railings, grabbing a smoke. Infrequently, a diver's head popped free of the water's surface.

The gunboat was not large enough to take a helicopter, and James Monahan was lowered to the aft deck by the helicopter's winch. He was met by a chief petty officer and led forward to the bridge.

He heard a triumphant shout and looked over the railing. A scuba diver was treading water, holding aloft a bottle of Chivas Regal. Treasure from the deep.

The sun had come up hot and gotten hotter. The armpits of Monahan's khakis were already stained after the long flight from Norfolk in the back of the *Sea Knight*.

The CPO rapped on the door of the captain's quarters aft of the bridge, then opened the door for him. He found Commander Martin Holloway and Admiral Aaron Stein inside. Holloway was bleary-eyed and a little bedraggled and, like Monahan, young for his rank. Stein was in whites, the space above his left breast pocket rainbowed with ribbons picked up in Vietnam and Grenada. He was of medium build but sported a beginning paunch.

"Come in, Commander," Stein said.

"Thank you, sir." He had met Stein several times before but shook hands with Holloway for the first time.

In the cramped cabin, the admiral had commandeered the sole chair at a built-in desk, and Holloway and Monahan sat on the bunk.

"Bing tells me you're coordinating the search effort," Stein said.

"Yes, sir. I thought I'd better take a look at the scene here, then run by your base and look around Pier Nine."

"Unfortunately, you're not going to see much at Pier Nine," the admiral told him. "The bastards even helped themselves to two of our three spare engines. Plus a full stock of replacement parts."

"Spare engines?"

Stein nodded. "Those rotaries aren't common, of course. We have, or had, the only ones in existence, as far as I know. Somebody thought this thing out."

"Somebody who is planning to use those boats, rather than just copy them," Holloway suggested.

"Anything out of Walter Reed?" Stein asked.

The body found in the water off Pier Nine had been transferred to Walter Reed Army Hospital for autopsy.

"Definitely Middle Eastern," Monahan said, "from the word I got around ten o'clock. His head was caved in, and the forensics people seem to think he was run over by a boat. He died by drowning."

"Shit. Well, those stealth boats would be useful in the Persian Gulf. With their capability against oil tankers and even small warships, damned nearly any nation could be held hostage."

"I haven't even seen them," Holloway said. "May I ask why we had them?"

"Sure, Commander," the admiral said. "When we got tied up in Vietnam, we found out we didn't have anything in inventory that was suitable for coastal and river fighting. We ended up using old LCM's until we could get *Antelope* class boats, like the one you've got here, built. After that nonwar, we gave away a few gunboats to friendly nations, because we knew we wouldn't need them again. Then, we ran into a bunch of zealots in the Gulf, attacking tankers with anything from rowboats to high-power ski boats. The

Sea Spectre was envisioned as a counter to those kinds of threats. They're small, maneuverable, and very fast.''

"As well as being useful for reconnaissance and infiltration," Monahan added.

"Extremely useful. We want them back." Stein looked very determined. Recovering the boats would go a long way toward easing the censure he was bound to get for losing them in the first place.

Monahan was not going to say anything about the security measures that had been utilized. Bingham Clay had already ordered that investigation.

He turned to Holloway. "Are you finding anything of value here, Commander?"

Holloway looked directly at him. "Puzzles, maybe. It was a *Scarab,* but it was blown up on purpose."

Monahan raised an eyebrow.

"The aft sections of the hull are peppered with shrapnel. We think they used a grenade to blow it."

"After boarding the Zodiak?"

"Must have been," Holloway said. "We thought we were chasing a guided boat, from the maneuvers it made. Hell, I still think it was manned. But from the other evidence, I guess they climbed out, set a timed grenade, shoved the throttles all the way in, and let her go."

Monahan felt a little uneasy at Holloway's indecision, but before he could pursue it, the commander continued. "The boat belonged to a man named Theodore Daimler. He's a Washington lawyer, the way I heard it, and he has a cabin on the bay somewhere south of here. He had reported the *Scarab* missing this morning."

Unbuttoning his shirt pocket, Monahan retrieved his small notebook and entered the information. "You know anything else about him?"

"No."

"I'll ask the FBI to check him out."

They talked for a few more minutes, then Monahan said, "I think I'll go on over to Ship R&D."

Admiral Stein stood up. "You have room for me in your chopper?"

"Yes, sir."

"Good, I'll ride along."

After they had been lifted aboard the *Sea Knight* and were enroute to the Research and Development Center, Stein pulled his headset aside and leaned over to almost shout in Monahan's ear.

Monahan pulled his own earpiece back. The racket of the turbines made nonintercom conversation difficult.

"You got your search grid set up?"

"Yes, sir."

"As if they're going to sneak those boats back to the Middle East."

"That's correct, Admiral."

"You'd better tell Bing to check his back door."

"Sir?"

"The *Sea Spectre* would be an effective guerilla weapon anywhere in the world, Commander. It doesn't have to be in the Persian Gulf."

1530 hours, Southern Chesapeake Bay

"Newport News coming up, Captain."

"Contact the *Mitscher,* Evans, and tell her we'll join her outside the bay." Captain Barry Norman's voice was particularly raspy this afternoon, after spending the night and the morning overseeing the search efforts in Carr Bay.

"Aye aye sir." The seaman crossed the *Prebble*'s bridge to an intercom station.

Norman could see the Chesapeake Bay Bridge coming up about five miles away. It was starkly outlined in black against a blue sky.

He turned to Commander Owen Edwards, his first mate. "Owen, you have the conn. I'm going down to my cabin to sack out for a couple hours."

"Aye sir. Do you want me to notify you when we rendezvous with the *Mitscher*?"

"No. Just put us on the course CINCLANT designated."

He scanned the instruments on the bridge's forward bulkhead once again, then went aft and descended to the officer's wardroom. He filled a mug with steaming coffee, added one cube of sugar, and carried it to his own quarters.

Inside, he sat on his bunk and unlaced his shoes, kicked them off. He was tired. Barry Norman was sixty-two years old, with over forty years in the Navy. His hair was short and gray, almost matching the color of his eyes. There was more sag to his jowls than he liked, more softness around his waist. He found that fatigue crowded him more easily.

Norman was a man of the sea. He had served on more classifications of ships than he bothered remembering. Only aircraft carriers and battleships had eluded him, but Bingham Clay had promised him at least a year on the *New Jersey* before he retired, now just three short years away.

Norman would never make flag rank, not that he cared. He did not have the ability to cow-tow to either Navy or civilian politicians. On each of his shore-based assignments, he had managed to offend as many admirals, senators, and congressmen as possible, insuring a return to sea duty.

He belonged on the bridge of a warship, especially since cancer took Elizabeth twelve years before. His instinct for unhesitating and appropriate command decisions was well known among his superiors. They could trust him with an expensive ship and a few hundred lives, though not with a congressional hearing room and thin-skinned legislative staffers. Norman's comfort with naval strategy and tactics was the sole reason he was still in the United States Navy after being passed over for promotion so many times.

He shrugged out of his uniform jacket, tossed it toward a chair, and swung his feet up onto the bunk. Leaning back against the bulkhead, he sipped his coffee.

Norman had been rethinking his desire to command the *New Jersey.* Sure as hell, some admiral would have his flag aboard her, and Norman would not really have full command.

Besides, in the two years he had been aboard the *Prebble,* he had come to appreciate the competency and loyalty of her crew. Even Susan Inge, his second mate. He had damn nearly rebelled when Inge had first been assigned, but after a couple of months, he had also rethought his position on women aboard warships and changed it.

Additionally, the last ten months working out of Ship R&D had been interesting. The Navy was not totally stupid. When they developed a weapons system, they also considered a counter system. For almost a year, the *Prebble* had been serving as a test platform for weapons systems that could cope with the *Sea Spectre.*

High-power, sea-level radar had been tried, but without success.

Enhanced infrared sensors mounted on the *Prebble's* two Seasprite helicopters had been able to detect the heat of the *Sea Spectres* at five miles.

The *Sea Spectre* engines and exhaust systems had been altered with coolant wraps to decrease the heat radiation.

The helicopters' infrared sensors had been boosted once again, and they were able to locate a stealth boat that was within a range of four miles, providing the boat was operating on both engines at over two thousand RPM's. They were great boats.

The five-inch guns—one forward and one right aft—

were computer controlled but were now linked, not only
with radar but with laser designator and night-sight targeting systems. In computer-controlled games in the past
three months, the *Prebble* had sunk four *Sea Spectres* in
simulation. Of course, the *Prebble* had lost five encoun-
ters. Still, Norman thought that, given more training, his
people would change those results.

If any ship in the U.S. Navy could locate and destroy
the *Sea Spectres*, it was the destroyer *Prebble*.

Which was why CINCLANT had pulled her out of the
northern Chesapeake and sent her on the search for the
missing assault boats.

Barry Norman had taken a few rides in the *Sea Spectre*
to acquaint himself with her weapons and capabilities. He
had liked the boat.

He did not want to blow it out of the water.

But he would.

2145 hours, Edgewater

Kevin McCory remembered that his father had often
taken late-night walks through the marina at Fort Walton
Beach, acting as his own security guard, stopping to talk
to the live-aboard residents, checking for safety violations,
yanking on the padlocks attached to storage cabinets placed
along the docks.

It was something he liked to do, too. Marina Kathleen
was not a large enterprise. It would not be described as
thriving. Still, in the eighteen months he had owned it, he
had made some transformations. The office, storage buildings, and docks had been repainted white. Slowly, as he
could afford it, he was replacing sections of the floating
docks that had rotted or canted due to corroded metal.
The original docks floated on empty fifty-five-gallon

drums. The replacement sections were attached to foam-filled fiberglass canisters.

There were a hundred slips available, and seventy of them were rented, mostly to people who weekended aboard small cruisers, sailing boats, and ski boats. Twenty-two people lived aboard houseboats, sloops, fishermen, and cruisers that would not be called yachts. Six charter fishing boats operated out of Marina Kathleen.

On the south side was a storage yard for boats on cradles or trailers, a maintenance building, and a small dry dock. McCory employed a super-mechanic and a lazy, but expert, hull and fitting man. Dan Crips and Ben Avery. He also employed two high school girls who tended the office-cum-general store after school hours on alternate days. Marge Hepburn, who was sixty-six years old and lived aboard an old Cape Hatteras, watched over the office—and everyone else—in the mornings and early afternoons in exchange for her slip rental, her groceries, and an occasional six-pack of Dos Equis.

Debbie Trewartha, a green-eyed senior at Edgewater High, was sitting on the counter talking to Hanna Wilcox when Ginger arrived.

Ginger Adams's parents had named her before she was born, expecting a redhead. What they got instead was a platinum blonde, hazel-eyed package of frenetic energy. Though she was now twenty-eight, five-ten, and proportioned along the lines Hugh Hefner demanded, she had not lost any of the energy. It did go dormant in the mornings, which was a problem, since McCory was a morning person.

She was sometimes irritatingly independent, maintaining her own apartment and working her twelve-to-eight shift at the Edgewater Bank and Trust, where she was a vice president and assistant manager. She had been almost married once, when she was eighteen. The union had faltered when she discovered the groom was not planning on letting her go to college. Ginger took on causes. Whales, seals, environment, politicians, bureaucracies, Kevin McCory. Nothing was sacred to her.

Ginger came through the front door like she owned the place, said hello to Debbie and Hanna, and leaned on the counter to stare at McCory. Her eyes were full of fire and ice.

McCory got up from behind his beat-up, ancient teacher's desk, crossed to the counter, and kissed her lightly on the lips.

"Hi, hon."

"I'm awake now."

"How was your day?"

"Fine."

"Nobody robbed the bank?"

"Not illegally, anyway."

"Want a beer?"

"Not now. You have a story to tell me."

"Story?"

"You promised, damn it!" She pouted.

"Come on," he said. "I've got to make my rounds. Deb, you can go ahead and lock up. Leave a note for Marla, will you? The back windows could use some Windex."

Debbie slipped off the counter. "Gotcha, Mac."

Hanna said, "I'll walk down with you youngsters."

Hanna Wilcox couldn't have been more than fifty years old, but she thought of anyone younger as an agile teenager.

The three of them went out the back door, took the ramp down to the floating docks, and strolled toward the end of it. The night was balmy, a nearly full moon on the rise, and the stars clear. A light breeze kept the insects offshore. At the second cross-dock, Hanna turned off for her *Indigo,* a new thirty-six-foot Trojan sedan.

McCory and Adams walked out to the end of the dock,

then turned and came back. He eyed the locks on storage lockers. They turned off on the fueling dock, and he checked the pumps for leaks and locks.

"You're not eager to tell me tales," Ginger said.

"I'm organizing my thoughts."

When they reached the *Kathleen,* moored in Slip 1, McCory took her hand and guided her up the three steps to deck level. They stepped aboard, and McCory hooked the safety cable between the railing gap back in place.

The *Kathleen* was the first boat Devlin McCory had designed, a tribute to his far-sighted vision. She was forty-six feet long, and though she had been built in 1954, her lines were as sleek as any motor yacht produced currently. A long, rakish bow, gunwales that swooped downward toward the stern. The foredeck was long, the cabin had large side windows and windshields, the stern deck was raised to accommodate the master's cabin below. From the stern deck, a short companionway on the left rose to the flying bridge and another, centered, companionway descended to the salon. The hull was wooden, but every piece was hand fitted. Her chrome fittings gleamed in the moonlight. The teak deck was polished to a high luster. Except for updated electronics and two new Cummins 320 diesels that McCory had installed, she was as his father had built her. As far as McCory was concerned, the craftsmanship could no longer be found. Similar, new boats could bring better than a quarter of a million dollars.

McCory followed Ginger down the companionway and reached around her to push open the door. She turned on the salon lights.

"Now, a beer?"

"Is it a long story?"

"I can make it that way."

"White wine."

McCory went to the galley and opened the overhead wine cabinet. Devlin McCory had built the racks from teak. He pulled a bottle of Chablis from its cradle.

"It's not cold," he told her.

"That's okay. I can live with it."

Ginger was wearing a white summer cotton dress, hemmed just a fraction above her smooth knees. The belt matched her shoes and was pale aqua. To maintain her banker's image—what there was of it—she also wore a pale blue scarf tucked into her collar.

She kicked her shoes under the helmsman's seat, then went around pulling the off-white drapes over the windows.

McCory got himself a bottle of Michelob from the refrigerator, then found two glasses, one stemmed, in another cabinet.

Ginger unknotted her scarf, slipped it from her neck with a whisper, and tossed it on the dinette table. She unbuckled her belt, zipped through a half-dozen buttons, and peeled off her dress.

Clad in panties and a half-cupped bra, she settled into the corner of the sofa under the windshield and watched him fumble with the glasses.

He nearly dropped the stemmed glass.

Unplugged the Chablis and filled her glass.

Unscrewed the top of the beer bottle and filled his own glass.

"I can see this is going to be a tough story to tell," he said.

"Want me to get dressed?"

"Unh-uh. I'll struggle."

Handing her the wine, he sat down beside her.

"Start at the beginning," she suggested.

"Let's see. At one o'clock yesterday morning, the U.S. Navy tried to board me."

Ginger almost spilled her wine. "What!"

"That was just before the boat blew up."

Eyes wide, she asked, "That was the damned begin-ning?"

"Well, not quite."

5

"Advanced Marine Development has had a long relationship with the United States Navy," Malgard said. "Since 1956. It would have been courteous to have notified me of the theft of my boats, rather than let me find out by way of television. I've had to wait two days for this meeting. And then come in on a Sunday morning."

Malgard thought his indignation sounded sincere. He stood in the small conference room and glared at the men sitting at the table. Commander Roosevelt Rosse, the black man from Procurement with whom he normally worked sat at one side of the long table. Next to him was another commander, named Monahan, who did something with the Second Fleet. At the head of the table was a rear admiral. A skinny, tall man with a horsey face and a protruding Adam's apple, Matthew Andrews, was in charge of fleet intelligence.

"Sit down, Mr. Malgard," Andrews said, rather firmly.

Malgard slowly sat down but kept the anger showing on his face.

Andrews tapped a thick file resting on the table in front of him. "The Navy's relationship with AMDI was primarily conducted with your father, I believe. A series of

60

contracts for marine fittings and accessories over the years, all of high quality and delivered on time. From what I read here, it was a satisfactory arrangement.''

Malgard nodded, not certain where the admiral was leading the discussion.

"In late 1985, your father passed away, and you assumed control of the company.''

Andrews paused.

Malgard nodded again.

"Since then, I note quite a few instances of late shipments and cost overruns.''

The son of a bitch was questioning his management. Malgard looked to Rosse for support, but the man's face was noncommittal. Commander Monahan sat with his elbow on the table, his chin resting in his hand, and his eyes showed intense interest in the accusations.

"In the fall of 1986, AMDI proposed its first major contract, that is, for a complete program, rather than as a subcontractor. It was awarded the XMC-22 stealth assault boat program.''

"Is this what you've been doing for two days, Admiral? Reviewing history, instead of looking for my boats?''

Andrews's eyes bored at him, and he continued as if he had not been interrupted. "The XMC-22 program is nineteen months behind schedule, and there have been cost overruns amounting to three hundred and sixteen thousand dollars.''

"Don't lay that on me, Admiral," Malgard said. "Your people have a big hand in there.''

Rosse cleared his throat and said, "That's true, Admiral. We have made some design changes, after testing, that have contributed to the delay. The sonar was changed out. Intake baffles were redesigned. There were some cooling system alterations, also, I believe.''

"Nineteen months' worth?" Andrews asked.

Monahan spoke for the first time. "Mr. Malgard, as I

understand it, once the test sequence is approved, AMDI is to begin production of twenty boats. The basic program has already been approved by the Department of Defense and Congress.''

"That is true, Commander, but with exceptions. Any additional costs due to design changes would have to be approved by Congress.''

"So you're almost two years behind the time you thought you would have contract income for your company?''

Malgard suddenly felt as if he was under interrogation. It was supposed to be the other way around. He looked to Andrews, but the admiral's face suggested he was in favor of Monahan's line of questions.

"Almost two years. That is correct,'' he said cautiously. "Research and development payments have been made on schedule, of course.''

"Of course. Along with additional payments for unexpected costs. You've been pressuring the procurement division to get the full program underway?''

"I've talked to some people, yes.''

"The reporter for *The Washington Post* told us that he received an anonymous tip that led to his story on the *Sea Spectre*. You wouldn't know anything about that, would you?'' Monahan's gaze was unwavering.

"I don't know a thing about it,'' Malgard said. "What the hell's going on here?''

"It seemed to me,'' Monahan said, "that that article in *The Post* was intended to generate interest in the boat, maybe put some pressure on people to get the production program started.''

"That's absurd.''

Monahan shrugged. "We've certainly got exposure now. Classified information on secret weapons system leaked to the press. The boats stolen. Television and newspaper reporters all over the building. Dead man, too.''

Malgard felt his face reddening. From anger. "Commander, are you suggesting that I stole my own boats?"

"The boats belong to the U.S. Government," Andrews said. "You're the contractor and designer."

"Listen, goddamn it!" Malgard said, "I'm here, because I want to know what you're doing about recovering them."

"We would like," the admiral told him, "a complete listing of your personnel."

"What!"

"We want to know the background of everyone working for you. There may be a possibility of insider information."

"Ridiculous!"

"The dead man," Monahan said, "has been identified as Muhammed Hakkar. According to the CIA and Interpol, he has connections with a terrorist group known as the Warriors of Allah. We want to make certain that he did not also have connections with someone working in either your plant or your office."

"That would be unbelievable. We have an enviable security record, and our procedures are approved by DOD. And it was the Navy who blew the security on the boats. You listen to me, Admiral. The loss of these boats is nothing but a setback for AMDI. Until the testing is completed, we are at a standstill. I want them back more than you do. Instead of harassing me, you should be chasing down the Warriors of Allah, or whatever the hell they are."

"Do you think the Warriors of Allah took the boats?" Monahan asked.

"I don't know who took them. You've got more information than I have."

Malgard did not like the way the commander looked at him. He also did not care for the son of a bitch's questions. As soon as he got home tonight, he would toss the telephone bill from last month.

He did not want anyone seeing the call made from Glen Burnie to *The Washington Post.*

1040 hours, 30° 51' North, 62° 5' West

Abdul Hakim, master of the *Hormuz,* was skeptical of Ibrahim Badr's claims about the *Sea Spectre,* but then the tanker captain was a cynic of high degree.

He was also as slovenly in appearance as was the *Hormuz,* Badr thought. The tanker, built in 1959 and capable of transporting only 16,000 tons of Arabian crude, was long past her useful lifespan. Her hull plates were streaked with rust that was thick as pita. The decks were littered with paper, chicken bones, and coagulated oil.

Hakim's skin was a streaky yellow, the result of an unsuccessful battle with jaundice. He wore a beard that was untrimmed and skimpy. The whites of his eyes were orange, and his fingernails were black. The skin of his hands was impregnated with stains of unknown origin.

Despite his appearance, he was lord of the tanker, and he ruled his realm with the steadfast ruthlessness of a nineteenth-century pasha.

He had been apoplectic over Badr's stationing of armed guards in the hatchways of the *Sea Spectre* while Badr slept for almost a full day, regaining the forty hours of sleep he had lost during the infiltration of the American mainland and the foray on the Naval Ship Research and Development Center.

Now, Hakim stood at the bottom of the tank, like an arrogant goat, looking up at Badr in the hatchway of the *Sea Spectre.* Despite the blowers and ducting intended to ventilate, the heat at the bottom of the tank was ferocious, and the sweat dripped from the man's face.

"I want to see for myself, Colonel Badr."

"I think your orders simply state that you are to assist

the Warriors of Allah in any manner possible, Captain Hakim.''

"Though not blindly," the captain retorted. "I am still in charge of my vessel, and I will not place it in jeopardy for reasons of minor importance."

Badr considered that Allah meant for him to make the journey through his lifetime suffering the idiocy of fools.

"Very well. You may come aboard, but you are not to reveal to anyone what you see." Badr nodded to Amin Kadar, and the man lowered the rope ladder to the bottom of the tank, which was about five meters below the hatchway.

The fat captain struggled valiantly with the swaying ladder and finally reached the hatch. He was panting loudly, and the massive stomach under his filthy khaki shirt heaved as he pulled himself inside. He wore a red-and-white-checked *kuffiyah* that hid his dirty black hair. His khaki pants were torn at the knees, and he wore rubber sandals.

Badr backed up and turned forward into the short corridor leading to the control center. At the hatchway on the other side, Ibn el-Ziam leaned against the open portal and grinned at Badr.

Badr nodded his head, agreeing with el-Ziam's silent appraisal of the good captain Hakim.

In the main cabin of the boat, Heusseini and Rahman looked up as Badr and Hakim entered. The Warriors of Allah claimed a membership of fifty-six, but only the five men—now four—Badr had brought with him were fluent in English. He was happy that he had recognized the necessity. The manuals that Omar Heusseini and Ahmed Rahman were poring over were filled with engineering and scientific terms that none of them had ever heard, much less seen in print, before. It would have been so much magical gibberish to the Arabic-only speakers in his band. As it was, there was more guesswork taking place in the interpretation of the manuals than Badr could have wished.

Badr stopped and leaned against the table in the eating area while Hakim looked around the cabin, some degree of wonderment growing in his face.

Badr felt himself the captain of his own kingdom. He was tall and lean in fresh khakis, though the extreme heat was already taking its toll. His black hair was cut short and combed back on the sides. The experience of combat was in his dark eyes, and the hard, abrupt planes of his face were finished in flat olive. He folded his muscular arms over his chest and let his eyes follow Hakim as the man peered at the radios, the sonar, the radar, the intricacies of the instrument panel.

"It is but a toy," Hakim said.

The man operated his tanker on a compass, a barometer, and an ancient radar set; everything else was broken.

"But it is a lethal toy."

Hakim spread his hands expansively, rapping Heusseini on the back of the head in the process. "I do not see it."

"Come."

Badr led the man back down the short corridor to the missile bay, opened the door, and turned on the lights.

The missiles gleamed dully in their racks along the side of the hull, each of them painted a midnight blue and identified with small white letters and numerals. Each was about a meter-and-a-half long and fifteen centimeters in diameter. Four short, movable fins were located at the rear, and two stubby wings were fixed at midlength. Badr had tried to lift one from its cradle, but the weight was too great. It explained the small cranes set into the forward corners of the cargo area.

The missile launcher itself was an engineering marvel, as far as Badr was concerned. The base was composed of interlocking beams made of some matte gray material he had not seen before. It collapsed into the hold by a scissoring action and, when fully extended, probably stood two to three meters above the boat's deck. The top of the launcher had rails for four missiles, with a blast deflector plate mounted to the rear. It appeared that the launcher head rotated in a full circle, as well as moved up and down in an arc of perhaps forty-five degrees.

"Is that lethal enough for you, Captain Hakim?"

The captain crossed to the side bulkhead and caressed a missile with his dirty hand. "They are impressive, Badr. How do they perform?"

Badr shrugged his shoulders. "Who knows? We will find out soon enough."

"As soon as we reach the Gulf." The captain smiled, revealing a broken tooth.

"There has been a change in plans," Badr said. "We will not immediately return to the Arabian Gulf."

The Westerners called it the Persian Gulf, but they were in error about that, as they were about almost everything in his homeland. In reality, Badr did not have a homeland. He was Palestinian, a guest in Iraq, Libya, Syria, and Lebanon for all of his life. He was determined to right that wrong, and the means to the end required the elimination of western influence in the Middle East.

In that quest, he had been tutored by the best of his brethren, studying under such as Abu Taan of the Palestinian Armed Struggle Command and Abu Nidal of the Black June Organization.

Originally, he had planned to use the boat to sink the supertankers that plied the Gulf, choking off the energy so vital to the Americans and Europeans.

That was the plan Hakim was following. "We are already underway for the Gulf, Badr."

"Your orders are to support my cause, Hakim. And my cause is to strike at the infidels where I can." He stuck a finger out, pointing at a missile. "That weapon allows me to bring the battle to the American shore. That is what we will do.''

Hakim frowned. ''I will put your boat over the side and leave you to it, then.''

''No. You will do as you are told, or the *Hormuz* will find itself with a new master.''

Hakim's arms and shoulders went rigid. Badr thought the man might have thrown the missile at him, if he could have lifted it. He tried to stare Badr down for a moment, but then his eyes sidled away.

''What must be done?''

''First,'' Badr said, ''you will reverse course. We are going back to where we came from.''

1350 hours, 27° 16' North, 80° 44' West

The eastern coast of Florida was hazy, muted, and variegated greens that muddied into one another. Seven miles offshore, the *Kathleen* cut the long swells easily, cruising at twenty knots. The stereo speakers on the flying bridge and the stern deck reverberated with Elton John's ''Bennie and the Jets.'' Unfortunately, the clients had brought along their own cassette tapes.

McCory was on the bridge, dressed in cutoffs and a red-and-white striped soccer shirt, his feet up on the instrument panel. He wore sunglasses and a baseball cap adorned with the Miami Dolphins' logo. From time to time, he checked the automatic pilot.

On the wrap-around bridge lounge seat, the two kids—boys, ten and twelve years old—were playing checkers. The view of the sea had bored them a half hour out of Edgewater.

The clients, two couples in their thirties, were on the aft deck, in the shade of the white canvas awning he had rigged. They were sitting in deck chairs around the table, drinking margaritas. Having a good time. Their laughter swelled and ebbed.

McCory didn't run many charters. He didn't want to infringe on the business of the charter captains who based themselves at Marina Kathleen. Occasionally, if they were fully booked, he would take a party out on the *Starshine,* his thirty-eight-foot sport fisherman. Today was different. The outing was an early-morning run down to Cape Canaveral to watch a Titan IV launch. It had been booked three weeks before by the two men, who were engineers with one of the aerospace companies.

The launch had been expectedly delayed three times before it got off successfully and spectacularly. White fire and heavy contrails arcing into the bright blue Atlantic skies. McCory had enjoyed it. Then, he had grilled sirloin steaks for lunch, hot dogs for the boys.

He kept resisting the impulse to nudge the throttles forward, hunting for the *Kathleen*'s top end of thirty knots. He felt restless. It was difficult to maintain his normal, easygoing demeanor. He wanted to get up and pace the deck.

Grab an airplane for Washington.

March into the Hoover Building and say, "I did it."

The fact that the Sunday papers down in the salon reported that the dead man, Muhammed Something-or-other, was some kind of terrorist didn't make it any easier.

McCory had killed another human being.

Didn't know the man but tried to paint a picture of him. Guessed he was a killer of innocents, assumed he had created carnage in Italy, Beirut, the Gaza strip, somewhere, but it still caused him to ache deep inside.

Like a drunk, driving a lethal weapon, swerving into a teenager on a dark road. *Didn't mean it, officer.*

Didn't make it right.

He was beginning to question his own motives in taking

the *SeaGhost,* too. When he first saw the newspaper pho-
tos, it had been anger that ruled heart and head. That had
evolved into a basically simple plan of grabbing the boat,
composing an elaborate analysis of the boat in comparison
with Devlin's drawings, then making some kind of big
splash. Press conference, maybe. Humiliate the damned
Navy.

That had changed in the millisecond of impact with the
Zodiak.

Everything was different. From the papers and newscasts, it was apparent that the Navy thought the . . . Warriors of Allah had taken both boats. There was a massive
search underway all over the western Atlantic. McCory
had seen the Navy and Coast Guard ships out in force. A
Coast Guard cutter had put into New Smyrna Beach and
Edgewater on Saturday afternoon, disgorging a bunch of
sailors who ran along the coast asking the citizens if they
had seen anything. Showing them *The Post* photo of the
SeaGhost.

A lieutenant (j.g.) had hit up Marge Hepburn, she told
him. Marge hadn't seen any strange boats.

Now, he wasn't certain what he would do. Admitting to
the Navy that he had taken the *SeaGhost* also meant sub-
mitting to a charge of manslaughter, or reckless endan-
germent, or something along that line. Daimler could tell
him. Would tell him, in fact.

McCory had been on the run before, but he had been
running from an insurance company, not the law or the
Navy. He was tired of running.

Still, he had to do something.

By the time he tied up in Slip 1, disembarked his clients, hosed the salt rime from the decks, and cleaned the
salon, he had not stumbled over any solutions. He changed
the sheets in the bow cabin. The sea had made one of his
couples romantic. It was three-fifteen.

McCory checked the office and found that Marla Fox

had replaced Marge. She already had the Windex and the paper towels out and was eyeing the back windows with some distaste. She was a cheery and chunky seventeen-year-old. She was also a trusting soul, somewhat daring, and not afraid of some of the things she should be afraid of.

"You really think those windows need cleaning?"

"Marla, you can't see the other side of the waterway."

"Isn't this supposed to be in my contract, or something?"

"You don't have a contract."

"Oh."

"Anything new?" he asked.

"Dan called in and told me to credit him with a couple hours on his time sheet. Somebody lost a water pump, and he replaced it."

"I can't believe Crips would work on Sunday."

"He was probably drunk," Marla said, and she had a point.

He spent a couple more minutes talking with her, then searched under the kneehole of his desk for the cardboard tube he wanted. He went out to the fueling dock where he kept the *Camrose* tied up. She was a nineteen-foot Chris Craft runabout that he had fully disassembled, rebuilt, and refinished. Born in the same year as McCory, she sported a Vee-drive and a Chrysler marine engine. Mahogany wood and blue leather. More elegance than get-up-and-go, but he liked her. The *Kathleen* and the *Camrose,* he owned outright. He owed over fifty thousand dollars on the *Starshine,* but her charters brought in just enough to meet the payments and the maintenance. No profit in her, just yet.

He also owed a quarter-million dollars on the marina. The cash flow was sufficient to meet his overhead and give him a couple thousand a month in salary. McCory had long since given up the notion that he would one day be a millionaire. More likely, he would die owing a million.

Then again, he had never aspired to millionaire status. One day at a time, with enough left over to buy a bottle of Dos Equis.

Releasing the spring lines, he clambered aboard and blew the bilges while she drifted from the dock. The engine caught on the first revolution, and McCory slipped it into gear and eased out of the marina while the engine warmed up. The exhaust gurgled in the water behind.

The flat planes of the windshield glass reflected the bright sun in little shatters of light that bounced back onto the highly polished mahogany of the foredeck. He guessed the afternoon temperature at above ninety. The sweat trickled down his sides.

The five-mile trip down to Barley's Marine Refitters took eleven minutes, and he tied up at the finger pier next to Dry Dock One. John Barley was up near his office and had the hood off of a big Merc outboard motor. The motor was mounted on a small ski boat sitting on a trailer behind a GMC Suburban. The boat's owner stood by anxiously as Barley probed for the solution to some fault in the motor.

McCory waved at him, and Barley waved back. Spit a wad of chewing tobacco in a twelve-foot curve.

McCory entered his rented building and locked the door behind him. He turned on the lights.

God, she's beautiful. Like you knew she'd be, Devlin.

He walked down the side dock, reached out, and opened the hatch.

Thought about the articles in the Sunday paper.

Thought about Ted Daimler.

He tossed the cardboard tube aboard the boat and went back to the telephone over the workbench. He had to check his wallet for the phone number of Daimler's home in Chevy Chase.

"Daimler residence. This is Ricky."

"Hi, Ricky. This is Uncle Kevin."

"Hey, Mac! How you doing?"

"I'm doing just fine. How are you?"

"Somebody stole Dad's boat. You know that?"

"I heard about it. You'll have to come down here and go fishing with me."

"Neat. When?"

"Maybe later this summer. We'll talk about it. Is your father around?"

"Yeah, hold on."

Daimler picked up the phone a couple of minutes later. "You trying to steal my boy, now?"

"Must have picked up a new habit."

"Jesus. That's all Reba and I will hear about for the next two months. When can I go, when can I go? By the way, get rid of the habit."

"You read the papers, Ted?"

"Read the papers! For Christ's sake, Mac! I've been calling you for two days."

"Yeah, I saw some notes Marge left. I've been busy."

"Get yourself an answering machine. Then answer it."

"I've got an answering service. She's a nice lady."

Daimler paused for a moment. Maybe composing himself. Then, he asked, "You get that thing hidden away?"

"Yep. In fact, I'm standing here looking at it right now."

"This is getting way out of hand, Mac."

"I know. Shit, I feel awful."

Surprisingly, Daimler didn't chastise him. "I don't know that you need to feel too badly. The guy was a real asshole. The CIA links him to the murders of some twenty people, Mac. We probably did the world a favor.''

"It may take me a while to come around to that point of view. What have you heard?"

"The Pentagon's in an uproar. The White House is alarmed. The FBI is investigating me.''

"What!"

"Probably checking my story. They talked to one of my partners and a couple clients, but it got back to me. Reba said a strange sedan was poking around the neighborhood, checking our house. She thinks they're burglars casing the joint. So far, I've kept her from calling the cops.''

"Damn. I'm sorry I got you involved, Ted.''

"Well, let's not worry about the history. Let's worry about you and me. What are the plans?"

McCory told him about his original scheme, including the press conference.

"Not a good idea, not now," Daimler said.

"Yeah, that's what I thought.''

"Time is our best bet. Let's let it blow over, drop back to page fifty in the papers. As long as the Navy thinks the Arabs have both boats, we've got some breathing room. Hell, maybe they'll catch them.''

"It'll be tough, Ted. That's one fine boat.''

"Keep in mind that I was the second civilian to ride in one, Mac.''

"Yeah. I want to find some solution that keeps you out of it.''

"Hey! You're my kind of man.''

"I mean it.''

"Well, you wouldn't be surprised if I told you the same thing has been on my mind? Keeping me out of it?"

"I'm not surprised," McCory told him.

"I'm still working on it. There's a conflict of interest, since I was part of the caper, unwilling participant though

I was. We don't want to be in court, where the wrong
questions could come up, the kind I'd have to answer. At
some point, we're going to have to negotiate a settlement,
but let's not rush into it until we're ready. Send me a check
for a hundred bucks.''

''What for?''

''Retainer. I want the attorney-client privilege locked
in.''

''Hell, you've always been my lawyer,'' McCory said.
''You settled the insurance deal.''

''Earned my fee, too.''

''Took you four years.''

''Did it right.''

''Debatable.''

''Fuck you.''

''You think I'm in deep shit?'' McCory asked.

''Of course. What else? But send me the check. I want
it formalized.''

''Then what?''

''Then we wait and watch. There'll be a place where
we can jump in.''

''Yeah, maybe.''

''What are you doing now?'' Daimler asked.

''I've got Devlin's drawings, and I'm going to start com-
paring them to the craft.''

''Okay. Take your time. Stay out of trouble.''

''I intend to. I'm maintaining my normal schedule.''

''You have a normal schedule? Look, Mac, not a word
of this to anyone. Got that?''

Involuntarily, McCory cleared his throat.

''Oh Christ! Who'd you tell?''

''Ginger.''

''Ginger? She's the dream girl we met last time we were
down?''

''Hey, you dreaming about my woman?''

''You planning on marriage?'' Daimler asked.

"It hasn't been discussed."

"Start discussing it."

"What the hell? You my social advisor now?"

"We don't want her testifying against you."

"You just said we weren't going to court."

"Just in case."

After he hung up, McCory spent an hour lifting the spare rotary engines out of the cargo bay with an overhead engine hoist. He parked them in one corner of the dockhead, stacked the cardboard boxes of parts with them, and covered everything with a paint-splattered tarpaulin. Then he inserted several clean sheets of paper in a clipboard, found a tape measure and a roll of black electrical tape, and climbed aboard the *SeaGhost*.

First things first. McCory went forward to the helm and used his pocket knife to cut a small piece of plastic tape. He carefully pressed it in place on the instrument panel, covering the title, *Sea Spectre*. She was the *SeaGhost*, and he was going to prove it.

He pulled Devlin's drawings from the cardboard tube and started at the stern. There was a small access door in the aft end of the cargo bay. He had to stoop to get through it.

He found a light switch and flipped it on. Four small bulbs lit up, and he looked around. Most of the space was taken up by four individual fuel bladders. There was an electronics compartment that contained another radar antenna, a camera, and a few black boxes. He skipped all of that, since Devlin hadn't included specifics about the electronics in his drawings.

In the decking was a large hatch. He pulled it up and found the jet housings below. The rotary engines were mounted forward of them, under the cargo bay. It was a nice installation. Everything was clean, painted gray. There was a sheen on the housings, and when he tested it with his finger, he discovered light oil. A leak somewhere, but then, there were always leaks.

Spreading the large drawings on the deck near the hatch, McCory extended the tape measure and started by measuring the width of the keel.

If he stayed busy enough, he wouldn't think about Coast Guard lieutenants questioning his employees or prison or dead Arabs.

6

1520 hours, CINCLANT

Monahan and Andrews got back from Washington at three o'clock on Sunday afternoon and went their separate ways, Andrews's driver dropping Monahan off on Mitcher Avenue, near the headquarters building. Monahan was halfway amazed that the day spent with the intelligence chief had gone so smoothly. So far, apparently, Monahan had not issued silly orders, stepped on the wrong toes, or otherwise gotten in the way of Rear Admiral Matthew Andrews and his concise view of naval life and command.

Monahan went directly to Operations.

The Operations Center of the Commander-in-Chief, Atlantic Fleet was a well-disciplined beehive. Behind the scene, a few thousand people all around the world and a large number of electronic surveillance mechanisms fed data to the computers at CINCLANTFLT. Routine reports from warships, task forces, and fleets were entered into the data base. CIA, Defense Intelligence, and Navy agents in foreign ports, satellites, reconnaissance aircraft, and hydrophones resting on the sea bottom provided their information about the movement of both hostile and friendly sea vessels.

Most of the activity—telex, data, and voice communi-

78

cations, data entry, analysis—took place in another room. In the Operations Center, the focal point was the massive electronic plotting screen mounted on one wall. Currently on the screen was a map of the normal operations area of the Second Fleet. All of the Atlantic Ocean area was displayed, as well as the Caribbean. Land masses—the eastern coasts of North America and South America and the western coasts of Europe and Africa were shaded in gray. A hodge-podge of symbols defined ship types at sea, each colored to represent its nationality. The predominating color was blue, for American ships. Dotted blue rectangles outlined the operating sectors of ballistic missile submarines. Nobody knew exactly where they were, which was the idea.

Soviet naval vessels were shown in red. The assumed location of Soviet submarines was projected by dotted lines from their last point of contact by a U.S. ship, an ASW helicopter strewing sonobouys, or with SOSUS—the Sound Surveillance system composed of listening devices sited at "choke points," narrow passages above the sea bed.

COMSUBLANT, the commander of the submarine fleet, had responsibility for all subsurface vessels. The rest belonged to Admiral Bingham Clay, and he took his responsibility seriously.

Captain Aubrey Nelson was the watch officer when Monahan entered the center. He waved Monahan to a chair beside him at the long table in the center of the room.

"Well, Jim?"

Monahan sagged into the chair. His sleep was coming in two-hour chunks lately. "Nothing, Aubrey. Personally, I think Malgard is behind the leak to *The Post*, though I don't think we'd ever prove it. I don't think he's involved in the theft."

"Intuition working for you?"

"Basically, yes. Plus, from what NI can find of Advanced Marine's financial records they look to be right on the edge of solvency. They're borrowed to the hilt, using the XMC-22 contract as collateral. My gut tells me he leaked the data, trying to pressure Ship R&D into completing the tests and approving the construction phase.''

"So we're back to the Warriors of Allah?"

"If Hakkar hadn't jumped ship to another group before he met Allah.'' Monahan retrieved a sheet of paper from the inside pocket of his uniform blouse. "This is the listing I got from CIA.''

Andrews took it and scanned it quickly.

"Jesus! Forty-three of them?"

"That's only the ones they know about, Jim. I doubt they all participated in the operation.''

"Ibrahim Badr. He's the leader?"

"Palestinian, and apparently a pretty fair commander. Langley thinks he's had training from the Libyans and maybe even the Soviets, in addition to on-the-job training with a couple of far-out groups. On actual and suspected terrorist operations, he's credited with almost four hundred deaths. The profile suggests he's a fanatic, but that he doesn't let it get in the way of his thinking.''

Nelson shook his head and looked up at the plotting board. "And we've got him out there, somewhere.''

"What all have you got involved in Safari?" Monahan asked. The search for the *Sea Spectre*s had been given the code name Operation Safari.

"Mr. Dean,'' Nelson called to an ensign sitting at a console at the side of the room, "give me Safari.''

All of the odd-colored symbols blinked out, leaving the blue. They ranged from the Artic to the Antartic, from Norfolk to the Mediterranean.

"Everything we've got is looking for those boats,'' Nelson said. "Mr. Dean, Safari Bravo.''

Most of the symbols disappeared from the screen. The chief groups were located in four task forces off the coast.

"That's the primary hunt group," Nelson said. *"Prebble* and *Mitscher* are the two destroyers directly east of us."

"Isn't *Prebble* the destroyer with the anti-stealth gear?"

"Right. We're trying to keep her centrally located. Northwest of them is a six-ship task force headed by the frigate *Knox*. Down near the Bahamas is a task force under command of the *Oliver H. Perry*. The carrier *America* and her Task Force 22 has been recalled from the Caribbean. That's it, coming through the Straits of Florida."

"You're not showing Coast Guard vessels?"

"Not on the screen. They're Safari Alpha, and right now, we've got them canvassing the ports."

"You don't think the *Sea Spectre*s have left the area," Monahàn said.

Nelson grimaced. "Hell, Jim, I don't know. Admiral Clay and I have gone over this a dozen times. By now, those boats could be entering the Med. But to answer your question, I don't think so, not yet."

"Why?"

"With two boats travelling together, one or the other should have been seen by someone's naked eye by now. Clay thinks they might have been loaded aboard some transport to hide them, and I tend to agree with him."

"And the transports are slower."

"Right. Mr. Dean, let me see Safari Target Two."

The screen blinked, and several dozen small rectangles appeared, each of them shown in orange. They were spread up and down the Atlantic, some of them halfway across it. Many were clustered near the West Indies.

"Target One are the boats themselves, Jim. Target Two are suspicious vessels, primarily of Third World registry, with the capability of transporting one or both *Sea Spectre*s. Freighters, tankers, container ships. We can't exactly board these ships on the high seas, so we're tracking them with choppers and other aircraft from the task forces, with subs and with land-based AWACS aircraft. As they make port, we'll be able to begin eliminating them.''

''The ships you're showing are all outbound.''

''Right,'' Nelson said. ''The premise was based on finding vessels that could have had a sea rendezvous with the stealth boats, then headed for somewhere else.''

''What about inbound ships?''

''What for?''

''Something Aaron Stein mentioned is sticking with me,'' Monahan said. ''The Persian Gulf is not the only place terrorists could operate those boats. We've got a lot of shoreline and shipping right here. Why pollute the Gulf when you can sink a supertanker off Houston or in New York harbor?''

Nelson looked stricken. ''Goddamn. You don't mean it?''

''I'd hate to overlook the possibility, Aubrey. Hell, who's to say one of those ships out there didn't pick up the boats, steam out a ways, then turn around before we got our search grid set up?''

''That'll damn near double the vessels we'll have to keep an eye on.''

''The CIA may have to shift the orbits of some satellites. In fact, that should have been done by now.''

''Ah, hell.'' Nelson reached out and pressed the key on an intercom.

''Sir?''

''Go down to Admiral Clay's office, and ask him if he can step in here, will you?''

1635 hours, 35° 37' North, 71° 9' West

The Combat Information Center (CIC) was lit with red light. Captain Barry Norman entered through the light trap and stood for a moment, letting his eyes adjust. On the bulkhead directly in front of him, someone had taped a picture of the *Sea Spectre,* like a postwar Betty Grable pinup. The picture had been sent to all ships of the Atlantic Fleet. It was somewhat superfluous to the men aboard the *Prebble,* since they had been involved in search-and-capture games with the boat for months.

Lieutenant Commander Al Perkins saw him and strode across the room. "Hello, Captain."

"Al. What have we got?"

"Deuce Two just made a pass near that freighter we picked up an hour ago." Deuce Two was one of the Seasprite helicopters. "She's Albanian and looks to be bound for Bristol. The decks are stacked with cargo, and Deuce Two doesn't think they'd have been able to shift it enough to load a forty-foot boat."

"You pass the information to CINCLANT?"

"Yes sir, I did."

"Okay. We've got some new orders," Norman said. "CINCLANT wants to look at vessels inbound, also. You still have tracks on the container ships we passed?"

"I can get 'em back, sir."

"Do that, and send Deuce Three out to have a look."

"Aye aye sir."

Norman took a moment to look over the electronic plot. *Mitscher* was five miles off their starboard flank. Half a dozen other ships within sixty miles were currently under observation.

"I wish one of them was our bogey, sir."

"Do you, Al?"

"I'd like to blow the son of a bitch out of the water."

Perkins's red hair and intense anger made Norman remember a chief petty officer who had been assigned to Norman's first command, a maintenance section at Pensacola. Norman had been a fresh lieutenant (j.g.). A hundred years ago, it seemed.

Devlin McCory had not been an easy man to forget, since he and Norman had corresponded a few times a year for several decades. In fact, when he thought about it, he remembered that McCory had had a few ideas, and good ones, about boat and ship construction. Had one of those Christmas letters mentioned a stealth boat?

McCory would probably find it ironic that the Navy had built a boat so stealthy that they could not find it themselves.

Norman could hear the Irish laughter.

1840 hours, Edgewater

McCory drove a 1966 Chevrolet step-side pickup. Like his older boats, it was in fully restored condition. The 327 cubic-inch V-8 hummed. It was painted a metallic blue, and "Marina Kathleen" was lettered in flowing script on the doors.

He parked it in front of John Barley's dry dock and shut off the engine. Before he could get around to the other side to open the door, Ginger Adams was out and on the ground. She was independent that way.

She was wearing running shoes, jeans, and a gray-and-green plaid cotton blouse. Her blonde hair was fluffed out casually. McCory stopped to enjoy the view.

"What are you looking at?"

"You don't look like a bank vice president."

"Now you want me to look like a vice president?"

"Of course not. I'm just glad I came to you for a loan."

"Loans. Plural. Over a third of a million, and now in jeopardy. I'll probably lose my job," she said.

"You'd better not go in there, then," McCory told her, being serious. "There's something about accessory after the fact."

Ginger slipped her arm inside his. "I've thought about it, Kevin, and I'll take my chances."

He studied her face.

"I'm being serious. This could mean big trouble for you."

"I said I'd thought about it."

"Your boss might not like seeing your name in the papers again."

"He didn't say anything when I was arrested at the zoo in Miami."

"This is slightly different," he said.

She went up on her toes to kiss him. "It's going to be all right. I mean it."

Over the years, McCory had been involved with a number of women. In some cases, infatuated. After a few months, however, the relationships had dissipated. With Ginger, however, the bond seemed to be growing stronger after almost a year.

It was strange in a way because, though they had some common ground—Florida natives, degrees in business, an affection for some of the same authors, and a faith in the Miami Dolphins, they frequently disagreed on food, recreation, politics, and national issues. She accused him of being romantic and impulsive. Ginger thought his planning processes were, if not nonexistent, then chaotic. McCory had told her that, despite her personal appearance and activism, she was a conservative.

Thinking about that, he said, "This really isn't something that you should get involved in, hon."

"There is that element of danger, isn't there? Beyond that, there is also an element of injustice that intrigues me. So quit worrying about it, McCory, and show me the damned boat!"

He walked her up to the door and unlocked it. Pushed it open and turned on the lights.

"My God!"

"That's about what Ted thought, too, only he was a little more profane."

They slipped inside, and McCory locked the door. His security measures weren't intensive, but he was more conscious of them than he had ever been.

Ginger crossed the dockhead and went down the side dock, dodging the dry dock's cradle timbers. She reached out and ran her hand over the smooth surface.

"Nice lines, huh?" he said.

"It's beautiful. You're sure Devlin designed it?"

"I'm positive. I'll show you."

McCory opened the hatch and helped her inside. Leading the way forward, he turned on overhead lights, using the white lights, rather than the red. The notes from his clipboard and Devlin's drawings were spread out on the banquette table. Ginger slid onto the bench seat, and McCory sat beside her.

She was patient as he went through the dozen sheets of paper on which he had scrawled notes, pointing out the details on the drawings. On the drawings, he had used red ink to write numbers in small circles that corresponded to the number of the comparison note.

"She's exactly forty-four feet, six inches long. The beam is thirteen feet, ten inches. The keel is cast in carbon-impregnated plastic, and the dimensions match the drawings exactly. Every rib is spaced as Devlin planned it. In the structure itself, the only differences are the cabin layout and the absence of a foredeck hatch. Here? See this? The same damned rotary engines Devlin proposed."

Ginger pored over the drawings intently, then said, "It seems conclusive enough to me. What are you going to do about it?"

McCory snorted. "I was going to hold a mammoth press conference. It doesn't seem like such a hot idea, under the circumstances."

She turned her head to look at him. "I'd agree with that. What does Ted say?"

"To wait it out, see if they find the other boat. Then find a way to open negotiations with both the Navy and Advanced Marine Development."

"I don't think you're that patient."

"It's difficult," he agreed.

Ginger leafed through his notes. "This is a mess."

"Are you a critic? I can read it."

"But no one else can. I'll type it up for you."

"That will definitely make you an accessory."

"And then we'll make copies of the notes and drawings. I'll put the originals in the vault."

"That's a good idea," he said, wondering why he hadn't considered the precaution.

"Of course it is. Now, show me the rest of it."

He stood and led her to the helm. Powering up the instrument panel, he demonstrated some of what he had learned from reading the operations manuals. He explained the navigation system and the computer. Showed her the normal, the night-vision, and the infrared modes on the bow and stern cameras.

"They're telescopic, too." McCory punched a code into the keyboard, and the main screen immediately zoomed in on the dockhead. Wood splinters became steeples. In the upper right corner of the CRT, a green "10" appeared.

"That's a magnification of ten," he told her.

At the radar console, after powering up, he went active for one sweep. The ground clutter return along the shore almost whited out the screen, but dozens of blurry blips indicated ships and boats moving on the waterway or sitting at docks in Edgewater and New Smyrna Beach. Vehicles on coastal streets also returned an echo.

He showed her the communications console.

"What are these?" she asked, tapping the black boxes that were almost devoid of controls.

"Those are a problem."

"In what way?"

"I've experimented with most of the radio sets, and I'm pretty sure those three are encryption and scrambling devices. They'll have top secret classifications, and there aren't any manuals aboard for them. I expect the Navy would like to have them back."

"As if they don't want the whole damn boat back?"

"I'm going to negotiate that."

"Uh-huh. What else?"

"Well, there are the missiles."

"Missiles! Shit."

He took her back and showed her the cargo bay.

"Now, for the first time, I think you're in real trouble," Ginger said. She moved around the bay, caressing the missile cases with persimmon-tipped fingers.

"Think so?"

She spun toward him and smiled.

"What now?" he asked.

"Let's go shoot one."

2235 hours, Sarasota, Florida

Chambers checked into the Holiday Inn, then moved his rented Ford to the parking place in front of room 118. He got out of the car, stretched his back muscles by rolling his shoulders, then reached back inside for his portfolio and carry-on bag.

There was a stiff breeze coming in off the Gulf. Down on the beach, the palm trees swayed. It was a warm wind, and it only served to drive the mosquitoes inland.

He locked the car, unlocked the room, entered, and

tossed the bag on the bed. Slapping a mosquito attacking his neck, he closed the door and turned on the lights.

Standard room, hot.

He found the air conditioning controls and reset the thermostat. The blower came on and drowned out the sound of traffic on Highway 41.

Slipping out of the silver-gray suit jacket, Chambers hung it on a hanger. It looked as if he had slept in it for two days. He shrugged out of the shoulder holster harness, wrapped the straps around the holster clamping the nine millimeter Beretta, and put it in the drawer of the night-stand. Then he unpacked the bag, hanging up his spare suit and shirts, taking the Dopp kit into the bath, and finally reaching one of his two bottles of Jack Daniels.

Carrying the plastic bucket, he went back outside and found the ice machine. Only after he had his drink in hand—two cubes of ice, long slug of whiskey, dash of water—did he pick up the phone and dial the number in Glen Burnie. While the phone clicked at him, he took a long swig from the plastic glass, then sat on the edge of the bed.

"Justin Malgard."

"Chambers."

"What did you find, Rick?"

"I haven't found a damn thing yet, Justin. Not much, anyway."

Malgard preferred to be called *Mr.* Malgard, but after his first mission for AMDI, Chambers started calling him by his first name. It irritated the man, but he didn't make an issue of it. Chambers had had enough of rank distinctions in the damned peacetime army.

"Tell me about it."

Chambers drank from his glass. "First of all, there ain't a Marina Kathleen in Fort Walton Beach. I found the address, all right, but the name's been changed, and there's an old couple runnin' the place, managin' it for some conglomerate. The corporation bought the marina from an insurance company, they said, and the managers didn't know anythin' about Devlin or Kevin McCory.''

''Bought it from the insurance company, huh?''

''Yeah. I nosed around the whole damned bay, talkin' to a lot of people. After the old man died, I guess there was a hell of a fight between the insurance outfit and the kid. Nobody seemed to know for sure, but it could still be in the courts. The kid, Kevin, just walked. Or sailed, I guess. He took some boat, and one guy said the ownership of the boat is still in dispute.

''Disappeared?''

''Not entirely, Justin. I got a lead to Port St. Joe and drove down there, found out he'd worked in a marine shop for a couple months, then took off again. Shit, I've been back to Panama City, then down to Cedar Key, Tarpon Springs, and St. Petersburg. The son of a bitch keeps on movin'.''

''Where are you now, Rick?''

''Sarasota. I've got to check the marinas in the morning. What I'm thinkin', though, is that we ought to find out whatever insurance company was involved. If they're still debatin' it, the company might have an address on him.''

''No.''

''No?''

''We're not involving anyone else, Rick. It's just you and me, like it always has been.''

''That's really dumb, Justin. We could be savin' a lot of time.''

''Hey, Rick. I pay you fifty grand a year to do what you're told to do.''

''Plus bonuses,'' Chambers got in. He didn't want Malgard forgetting the bonuses.

''Plus bonuses. For fifty thousand, you get to sit on your

ass all year. For the bonus, you do what I want you to do. Got that?''

"I got it." Hell, the guy was right, after all, Chambers admitted to himself.

"So you keep following the trail. And you call me a little more often."

"I got that, too."

2340 hours, Washington, D.C.

"Ted, this is Kevin."

"I recognize the voice," Daimler said dryly. "You know it's almost midnight here?"

"Almost midnight here, too. I had a thought."

"That's troublesome."

"From the papers, the Navy's out there looking for terrorists with two boats."

"That is true, my friend."

"When, in actuality, the terrorists have only one boat."

"The Navy's still looking for two."

"Well, their search strategy might change if they knew they were only looking for one."

Daimler thought about that. He did not know what the Pentagon was doing, of course, but McCory might have a point. Astoundingly, he sometimes did. Hell, Kevin had kept him from dropping out of undergraduate school at one time, had hauled him on his back for six miles after Daimler broke an ankle during night jump. The points added up.

"I was thinking," McCory said, "of placing an anonymous call to the Navy."

"They're never anonymous for long."

"Maybe just let Norfolk know they were only looking for one *SeaGhost*."

"Incorrect, Mac. They're looking for two, though I admit they're probably expected to find them in the same place. You'd just confuse them."

"Well, hell. I want to do something to help."

"This is a hell of a time for you to get all patriotic again," Daimler said. "The two of us have already done our time. Keep in mind that you're a thief, please."

"Only for the moment. I have a good motive."

"From your point of view, you mean? Oh, hell, probably from mine, too. Did you finish examining the boat against Devlin's drawings?"

"It matches, point for point. It's Devlin's boat, all right, Ted."

"Okay. I have to admit that I thought you were right all along. Let me think about this for a couple more days before you do anything."

"I hear your fee meter clicking," McCory told him.

"It's a nonstop meter. Don't do anything."

"As long as you're charging me, do some work, will you? Check on Advanced Marine Development."

"I'll see what I can find out about them," Daimler said. "You talk to Ginger?"

"Showed her the boat."

"Jesus Christ!" McCory's attitudes sometimes alarmed Daimler, made him wish the man was not the best friend he'd ever had, or probably would have. "You'd better get hot on composing a marriage proposal."

"That might be tough. You don't know her as well as I do."

"I hope she doesn't know you as well as I do."

"Why?"

"I'd never marry you," Daimler said, and hung up.

7

Chief Petty Officer Devlin McCory's face was a mottled red, confused between anger and frustration. He did not know where to direct his anger.

The tears streamed unabashedly down his cheeks, streaking the dirt caked on his right jaw. His red hair was messy, a glob of grease caught in it on the left rear side. His eyes stared at the wall opposite the one he leaned against.

He was in uniform, but it was stained with oil and tar and paint splotches. The polish on his left shoe was eradicated by gasoline. He had come right from the docks.

People moving down the bridge corridor gave him plenty of leeway. There seemed to be a lot of people. Back and forth. Going nowhere in a hurry.

At the far end of the corridor, a chrome-plated floor polisher whirled on the linoleum. If it got much closer, McCory was going to kick the damned thing into small pieces.

The odors. Medicinal. Chloroform. Antiseptic. Iodine?

"Chief?"

He looked up, bleary-eyed.

93

The man floated in front of him, all furry-edged and green.

"I'm Commander Hartford, Chief. I'm sorry as hell."

"Jesus."

"We did our best. It wasn't enough."

"Oh, Jesus Christ!"

"You all right, Chief? Maybe I can get you something?"

McCory pushed off the wall, coming to his full six feet. *"Where's the son of a bitch who killed her?"*

"He died at the scene of the accident," the doctor said.

McCory's shoulders sagged in defeat.

He felt entirely deflated. At Pusan, and earlier, at Guadalcanal and Bougainville and Midway, there had always been someone to strike out at when the ones you liked died.

"Can I see her?"

"You don't want to, Chief. Believe me."

He just nodded. The tears continued to stream down his face. McCory had never been beaten before.

He turned away and walked down the hall toward the nurse's station, leaving Commander Hartford standing by himself.

The nurses who had been tending and playing with his six-month-old son looked up as he approached. Their faces went carefully slack.

McCory leaned over and picked Kevin up from the two chairs that had been shoved together. *"Come on, ol' son. Time to go home."*

The boy's blue eyes stared back at him, searching his own.

For what?

McCory pulled Kevin close to his chest and pressed his head against his shoulder.

The nurse smiled grimly.

*And McCory and his son walked on down the long cor-
ridor looking for a door.*

Kevin started to cry, too.

0145 hours, 28° 41' North, 79° 50' West

"Pretty late in the game for you to get so adventure-
some, isn't it, lady?"

"No one's going to see us, right? That's what you told
me." Ginger's eyes shone in the dim haze of red-blue light
from the instrument panel.

"That's the theory," McCory said.

She was having a grand old time. Since leaving
Ponce de Leon Inlet, Ginger Adams had taken over the
helm. The speed seemed to thrill her, and while she managed an almost easterly course, she spent more time
playing with the bow and stern cameras and with the
computer than with the automatic pilot. The automatic
pilot bored her.

For the past hour, McCory had played a little himself.
Carrying operating manuals back and forth, he had experimented with the various consoles. He figured out the sonar, wearing the headset that hung on the bulkhead. At
their speed of nearly sixty knots, though, he mostly got
feedback from the rotary engines. When he rested his
forehead against the screen's hood, he found that the screen
was primarily one pale green blip. He estimated that the
SeaGhost would have to be below ten knots in order to get
a decent interpretation. Even then, it might require an ex-
perienced and master sonarman to read the ocean's sounds.
There was a computer link with the sonar set that he hadn't
been able to work out yet. He suspected that the computer
could identify and match screw signatures, but he didn't
know how large the data base aboard might be. Or perhaps

there was a data link through a satellite to a shore-based data center.

He had set the radar on automatic and random scan at thirty miles of range. The alarm had sounded off several times, jolting Ginger the first time, but the marine traffic was miles away from them.

McCory also figured out the range of the *SeaGhost*. Before leaving Edgewater, he had brought the *Kathleen* in alongside the dry dock, snaked a hose under the sea door, and used an electric pump to siphon diesel fuel off the cruiser into the *SeaGhost*'s bladders. Fortunately, the rotaries used diesel.

Based on topping off an empty cell of the four fuel bladders, he determined that the capacity was 880 gallons. His fuel consumption on the trip down from the Chesapeake had varied between 9.8 and 12.6 gallons per hour. Figuring a cruise speed of forty-five knots and a consumption of around eleven gallons per hour, the boat had a 4000 mile range. At sixty knots, while he was teaching Ginger the computer code, the consumption rose to 18.2 gallons per hour, which dropped the range to around 3300 miles.

It was still respectable.

The interior was dimly lit from a single red bulb recessed in the overhead and from the screens and readouts of the helm, radar, and communications panels. The AM radio was locked on a Tampa station, playing Billy Vaughn's "Blue Tomorrow." A compromise. McCory liked country and old rock. Ginger Adams liked jazz, classic and new wave.

They had provisioned the galley with peanut butter, bread, orange juice, coffee, and few pieces of china from the *Kathleen*. McCory got a couple of mugs from the cabinet and poured coffee. The coffeepot was made of some kind of plastic with a ceramic base. It sat in a three-inch-deep recess in the countertop, so it wouldn't slide around in heavy seas. McCory guessed the Navy paid a couple thousand for it.

He carried Ginger's mug to her.

"Thanks, Kevin."

"You tired?"

"How could I be? This is just fantastic."

"I recall your telling me that you're not a morning person. Several hundred times. You're supposed to be asleep now."

"Are you kidding? And miss this?"

The fingers of her right hand gripped the wheel almost lovingly. Her eyes scanned the panel even as she sipped from her mug. The monitors displayed front and rear views in the night-vision mode, but only a dim, dark green sea and lighter green sky were visible. Through the windscreen, there was only blackness, with an occasional whitecap reflecting the moon's light. Long swells were running, but the *SeaGhost* skimmed them, with only a slight up and down motion.

McCory went to the bunk room and found the toolbox he had brought aboard. He got a battery-powered electric drill and loaded it with a quarter-inch bit. Carrying it back to the commander's desk, he put his coffee on the desk, then sat on the deck. He had to move his head to the side to keep a shadow from the overhead light off the drawer locks. Setting the tip of the bit against the top lock, he squeezed the trigger.

"What are you doing?" Ginger called over her shoulder.

"Breaking and entering."

It took ten minutes to drill all three locks. There was nothing in the bottom drawer. The middle drawer contained two nine-millimeter Browning automatics and a dozen loaded magazines. The armory. The top drawer contained a ring of keys and several thin books, and

McCory rose to sit in the captain's chair. He turned on a goose-necked reading lamp and leafed through the books.

Uh-oh.

"What'd you find?" Ginger asked.

"Some books I wish I didn't have."

"Like what?"

"Like call signs and frequencies. Codes. Instructions for the black boxes back there."

"Top secret stuff."

"Very."

"Maybe we should burn them? Or throw them overboard?"

"You're quite right," McCory said, but intrigued, got up and went to sit at the communications console. Flipping the pages of the first book, he found a VHF frequency for CINCLANTFLT operations, along with a series of numbers. He powered up the transceiver and punched the buttons until the digital readout gave him the frequency listed.

The speaker in the panel jabbered in gibberish.

He turned the volume down.

On the scrambler box marked "ONE," he punched mode two.

Still gibberish, but clearer gibberish.

On the encryption box, he tapped mode four.

". . . ask Force Two-Two, CINCLANT authorizes movement to Safari Sector Five."

"Copy that, Diamond Head. Safari Sector Five. Two-Two out."

The frequency went silent. McCory didn't know what he had, but he did know that he ought to hang onto the books for a while. He couldn't go around throwing away important documents.

He experimented with more frequencies and scrambling modes. When he didn't get silence, he got what he thought were ships talking to each other or to aircraft. He had been out of the Navy long enough that the radio lingo had lapsed for him, but parts of it came back slowly.

He finally left the set tuned to CINCLANT, turned it down low, and brought Tampa back on another speaker. Chet Atkins doing "Faded Love." That was better.

Moving over behind Ginger, he rested his hands on her shoulders and asked, "Any idea where we are?"

"Should I know?"

"It's sometimes helpful. On the computer keypad, on the top row, press the square marked 'NAV MAP.' "

She found the touch-sensitive pad and pressed it.

"Now, press 3084."

"What's that?"

"That's the latitude and longitude of the top left corner of the map grid you want."

"Sure it is."

"Now, press 2575."

"Bottom right?"

"That's correct. Now execute."

She pressed the pad labeled "EXC."

Ginger scanned the panel. "Nothing happened."

"The computer's working on it. Finding the grid coordinates in the data base and checking with the NavStar satellite network. Press the number four pad under the main CRT."

There were eight numbered pads under each screen. McCory had learned that they selected camera views in normal, night-vision, and infrared modes, navigation maps, radar repeater, and a gunsight for the forward-mounted cannon. The last two buttons always came up blank. Either he had not determined their usage, or they were reserved for future enhancements.

As Ginger pressed the keypad, the screen flickered, then changed to a map. Coördinate lines were shown in light green spaced at every ten minutes. A large orange dot was

in the upper left corner. She reached out and tapped it
with a clear-polished fingernail. "That's us?"

"That's us."

"Neat."

"I thought so, too. Watch this."

McCory stepped to the radar console and switched it to
active. Immediately, the interface between the radar and
the mapping system put four yellow dots on her screen.

"Those are other boats?"

"Or ships, maybe. I don't have the antennaes aimed up
very high, but that one to the far right might be a low-
flying airplane, judging by its speed. The closest one is
over fifteen miles away from us. And we're about ninety-
seven miles off the coast."

He flipped to the 220-mile range. Dozens of yellow dots
came to life on the monitor.

"That's at two hundred and twenty miles of range," he
told her.

"I can't believe there are that many ships out here."

"Several of them are aircraft. We're kind of in the track
between South America and New York."

He shut down the radar, just in case some of those yellow dots belonged to Task Force 22, headed for Safari
Sector Five. The Navy would be looking for active radar,
especially an active radar that appeared where there was
no other return.

"Are we far enough out?" Ginger asked.

"I suppose. There isn't any traffic in the immediate
neighborhood, anyway."

McCory was feeling a little anxious about this, like a
kid with a fistful of firecrackers, scanning the alley for a
place where the adults wouldn't hear them go off.

"Well, let's do it!"

McCory sighed. "The Navy will probably charge me
fifty thousand dollars for expended ordnance. Probably
more than that."

"They're not going to miss just one."

"They keep careful count," he insisted.

"You don't know how to make it work. Is that it?"

He assumed she was pressing his male ego button, but said, "I think I can figure it out. I'm pretty mechanically minded, you know."

"Sure."

"Okay. Bring her back to around five knots and maintain headway. There's a headset hanging under the instrument panel. You might see if it's fashionable."

While Ginger slowed the boat, McCory went aft to the cargo bay. Outside the door was a headset on a long coiled cord. He put it on.

"Can you hear me, hon?"

"Aren't you supposed to use some kind of jargon, like, 'Missile man reporting in, Captain?' "

"When did you get promoted?" he asked.

It took him ten minutes to load a missile into the sling of the crane, position it over the launcher, and slide it onto the upper left launch rail. The connections were simple. A wire cable and multi-pronged plug hanging from the missile body plugged directly into a receptacle on the launcher.

Forward on the base of the launcher was a small door marked, "POWER." McCory opened it to find several switches and digital readouts. Knowing the Navy was super-conscious about safety, he thought there would be a disabling system that prevented missiles from being fired while the launcher was in the down position. He hoped that was the case.

He flipped the switch for launcher power. Above it, a green LED came one.

A switch for missile power. He threw it, also, and digital readout promptly came to life with numbers that were meaningless to him.

GUIDANCE LINK. What the hell, he switched it on. Green light-emitting diode there, too.

"Did you see anything happening up there?" McCory asked on the intercom.

"I didn't know I was supposed to be watching for something. I don't think so, though."

McCory closed the small door, left the cargo bay, and closed that door. On the deck of the port cross-corridor was a small bundle. He bent down to open the duffle and pull out an old rubber raft.

"Okay, Ginger, all stop."

She pulled the throttles back.

McCory opened the hatchway, slid the raft outside, and while holding its line, pulled the CO_2 cartridge. The raft inflated quickly, and he dropped it over the side. He leaned back for the duffle bag and dug around in it for the two rolls of aluminum foil he'd brought along. Ripping off long sheets, he wrinkled them and tossed them in the raft. When the bottom of the raft was full of crumpled foil, he let go of the painter.

He thought it looked like a pretty good target.

"All right, full ahead."

The boat leapt forward before he could get the hatch closed.

Replacing the headset on its hook, McCory went back to the main cabin and sat in the radarman's seat.

"You think it's going to work?"

"Of course it's going to work," he told her, mentally crossing his fingers.

Between the helm and radar positions on the bulkhead was a small control panel. It was contained in a box about three inches deep, as if it had been added as an afterthought. The face was flat black, translucent plastic except for one red switch. He tried it, but it wouldn't move.

Leaning forward, he examined the box more closely and discovered a key slot on the side.

Ah, hah.

He went to the captain's desk, found the key ring, and brought it back. The second key he tried in the slot fit, and he turned it.

Nothing happened.

He tried the red switch button again.

The panel lit up. Blue lettering.

On top, it read: "ARMAMENT: ACTIVE." Next to the designation "AVAILABLE," was one green LED.

He had a guidance selection. Radar, infrared, or optical. He pressed the pad for radar.

Missiles were not new to McCory. He had observed firings of several types while aboard naval ships. Personally, he had used the handheld Stingers and Redeyes a number of times.

He had a choice of computer-controlled or manual launch and tracking. He selected the former.

In the middle of the panel was a set of five pads, the center one marked "CNTR" and the others marked with arrows for the four cardinal compass points. It was obviously used for manual control of a missile in flight.

Below the direction controls were four more buttons, and he assumed they were all interlocked with one another. One controlled the opening of the cargo hatch, another the elevation of the launcher. The third armed the missile, and the fourth was ominously named "LAUNCH."

He went back and selected optical as the guidance system, then pressed the number seven pad under his monitor. He had a sudden view of the front of the cargo bay.

"Try number seven on your CRT, Ginger."

"All right! That's a view from the missile?"

"Yes, but we're not going to use it now. I'm just experimenting. Bring her back to thirty knots."

There was no way to select one of four missiles that could be mounted on the launcher, so McCory presumed that, due to stresses on the launcher itself and maybe the mounting to the boat, only one could be launched at a time.

As the boat slowed and steadied in the water, McCory went back to the radar mode on the missile, then opened the cargo doors and pressed the button to raise the launcher.

He was rewarded with two green LED's. Which he didn't trust, so he got up and went aft to check for himself. Opening the cargo hatch, he found the doors retracted and the launcher fully extended. The missile head was about five feet above the upper deck. It looked menacing as hell. The cool night air poured into the bay.

He went back to the cabin.

"It's up."

"Great! Shoot it."

"Don't get antsy."

On the radar panel, he selected the radar mode for the monitor, then found a switch for armaments-to-radar link and activated it.

An orange target circle appeared on the screen. He found that it was controlled by a set of keypads similar to the guidance pads on the armaments panel.

He went active on the thirty-mile scan.

On the screen a dim blip showed him his target about four miles behind them. He moved the orange circle until its cross-hairs were centered on the target, then pressed a pad labeled, "TARGET LOCK."

The sound of electric motors came through the deck. The launcher was rotating, aiming the missile aft.

Blue letters appeared in the upper right corner of the screen, "LOCK-ON."

McCory heard something droning, looked under the instrument panel, and saw another headset. He put it on and heard the long-ago sound of a missile's message to its operator. The low tone sounding in his earphones told him the missile's brain had locked onto the target selected by the radar.

"Ready?" he asked.

"I'm ready."

McCory looked to the armaments panel and pressed the launch keypad.

Nothing happened.

For one second.

All he had done was commit the launch. The computer selected the optimum launch time.

WHOOSH!

The ignition and launch could be heard through the skin of the *SeaGhost*.

But only for an instant. Outside the windows, the night went white for a second, then winked back to black.

The missile was gone, gone, gone.

"Look, look, look!" Ginger shouted.

McCory glanced at her primary CRT, still on the optical view. All he saw were dancing stars.

Back to his own screen. Close in, the radar sweep left two blips behind it. Four miles away was his poor rubber boat. A mile away was a streaking dot.

Two miles away.

Three.

"God! Look!"

McCory flicked his eyes to the helm screen. Out of the night, a yellow blur appeared.

Grew.

And grew into a real yellow rubber boat.

Expanded.

And disappeared into blackness.

On the rearview screen, he saw a momentary blossom of red-yellow light. The image remained on his retina for several seconds.

"We got it!" Ginger said.

"Yeah. Maybe we did." He had no way of knowing if

he'd hit the target. From the optical view delivered by the missile, it seemed certain, however.

It seemed like a puny explosion on the direct rearview screen, but then it was over four miles away.

Ginger sighed. "Now, I'm tired. Us night people have to get our sleep."

"Did you want to sleep alone?"

"Of course not."

McCory retracted the launcher and cargo doors, then supervised as Ginger set up a course for the mainland on the automatic pilot. She left the throttle settings for thirty knots of speed.

He set up the radar computer for random search and alarm.

And they went aft to the port bunk cabin to see if they both fit in one bunk.

They did.

1000 hours, Washington, D.C.

At moments like this, making phone calls like this, Ted Daimler remembered going to Harvard Law School. He and McCory were just out of the Navy, and McCory was going back to Fort Walton Beach to work with his father. Daimler had been accepted to several law schools, and he very much wanted Harvard. His accumulated Navy education benefits, however, were insufficient for Harvard. He told McCory about it.

"When my mother died, she left me an insurance policy worth a thousand dollars," McCory had said. "Devlin put it in a savings account for me. There's about five thousand in the account now."

"You haven't touched it?"

"No. I'll loan it to you."

"I can't do that, Mac."

"Sure you can. As long as you have a chance at Harvard, take it. I want interest, though."

"Nine percent?" Daimler had offered.

"Call it seven," McCory had said.

Daimler had long ago repaid the loan, but the offer itself was just one of the things he owed McCory.

He heard the phone ringing.

"Advanced Marine Development."

"Justin Malgard, please."

"May I say who is calling?"

"Weirgard, Amos, Havelock, and Moses," Daimler made up on the spot.

"Please hold on."

While he held on, he thought about the information his paralegal had dug up on Malgard. From the time he had taken over AMDI, it was apparent that Malgard wanted to be a big-time defense industry wheeler-dealer. He had drastically expanded his plant facilities located in Baltimore, at the cost of some heavy-duty loans. He and his wife had moved into an upscale house in Glen Burnie and purchased matching Mercedes 550 SEC's. He was laying out stiff rentals for the office suite on New Hampshire Avenue. He could have operated out of the factory offices, but Malgard wanted to be in the thick of Washington intrigues.

"Hello. This is Justin Malgard."

Without offering a name, Daimler said, "Mr. Malgard, I represent a person who has a special and personal interest in the XMC-22."

"What! What are you talking about?"

"Let's just say this person is possibly interested in seeing that the boat is returned to your control."

"You're saying you know who stole the *Sea Spectres*?"

"I'm saying that maybe we should discuss the problems."

"Bullshit! You're asking a ransom."

"No. But we'd like to discuss the history of the boat and its design. With proper compensation . . ."

Malgard hung up on him.

Which was about what Daimler might have expected.

1222 hours, 35° 29' North, 68° 7' West

For almost ten hours, the *Prebble* had been making flank speed to the south. She had left the *Mitscher* to keep tabs on the plethora of freighters and tankers working into and out of the northeast sector.

CINCLANT had ordered Barry Norman to join with Task Force 22 coming up from the Caribbean. The order had come twenty minutes after one of *America*'s AWACS aircraft had spotted what it believed to be a missile launch.

Short-lived, but a missile launch.

Coming out of nowhere.

No source identified.

No target identified.

CINCLANT was convinced the event suggested one of the stealth boats was experimenting with the Mini-Harpoon.

Norman was on the bridge, listening in on Task Force 22's command net. According to the navigator, they were still eleven hours away from joining the task force. He was urging the clock to go faster.

When they ran down that boat, Norman wanted to be there. In fact, utilizing the gear aboard the *Prebble* was probably the only way they would corner the *Sea Spectre*.

His executive officer entered the bridge.

"Commander?"

"We've completed the drill, sir. It went very well."

"Do it again, XO."

"Sir?"

"I want these guys sharp as hell on that equipment.

When we have to use it, there may be lives hanging in the balance.''

''Aye aye sir. We'll do it again.''

Norman had read the coded cables describing the Warriors of Allah and their leader, Ibrahim Badr. That son of a bitch was someone he would like to get his hands on, personally.

1240 hours, 28° 6' North, 72° 21' West

Ibrahim Badr had compromised with Captain Abdul Hakim. The *Hormuz* had to appear as if it were going somewhere if it were picked up on someone's radar, or by the Americans' aerial reconnaissance. Circling about in the western Atlantic would be suspicious, although a breakdown of the vessel's single steam turbine engine could be faked at some point, if necessary. Judging by the ship's appearance, in fact, a breakdown could be expected.

At the moment, they were about 300 miles from the Bahamas, after fifty hours of steaming to the west, and were again headed north. They could have been transporting Venezuelan crude to Nova Scotia, creeping along at the *Hormuz*'s standard twelve knots of speed.

It was hot on the deck, just forward of the tanker's superstructure, when Badr gathered his Warriors for a short meeting. The heat brought out the worst odors from the deck—acrid oil, spoiling garbage.

Badr leaned against a ventilator and surveyed his men.

Omar Heusseini's eyes were dark and baggy. He had been studying radar and sonar manuals for four days almost without break. Heusseini was somewhere in his fifties—he had never been certain of his birthdate. There was a great deal of gray in his dark brown hair, and his eyes had a washed appearance. The desert had lined his face heavily and brought a slope to his shoulders, making him stoop a little. Heusseini had learned the trade of radar operation and maintenance as a member of the Shah's armed forces and had fled Iran a few days after the Shah had been deposed.

"Omar?" Badr asked.

"I am ready, my colonel."

When he had formed the Warriors of Allah, Badr had promoted himself to colonel. The rank seemed appropriate and not as self-serving as that of general.

The drone of airplane engines could be heard to the west, and Badr turned to look but could not see the aircraft.

"We will lift the boat from the tank again tonight, so that you may practice," Badr told him. Within the steel hull of the tanker, the *Sea Spectre*'s electronics performed dismally.

"That is good," Heusseini agreed. "There are some new computer routines I need to rehearse. It is truly magnificent equipment."

Badr felt comfortable with Heusseini's expertise. He was less comfortable with Amin Kadar, who would operate the radios and the sonar system. Kadar was in his early twenties, a very intent and focused young man. His gaze was clear, but as often as not, concentrated on some unknown objective just beyond the bounds of reality. A dreamer.

"Amin?"

Kadar turned away from his study of the sea and said, "Yes, Colonel?"

"The sonar?"

"It is fine. Much better than I have used in the merchant marines."

"And the radios?"

Kadar shrugged. "Who will we talk to?"

"I am less interested in talking to anyone than I am in listening."

The young revolutionary smiled. "The manuals in the

desk were invaluable. I have given you the locations of the
American naval forces, have I not?''

"That is true."

When the *Sea Spectre* rested above the deck at night,
suspended from the crane, Kadar scanned the naval frequencies, using the encryption and scrambling devices.
He estimated that they had intercepted perhaps twenty percent of the Second Fleet's directives to the task forces
searching for the *Sea Spectre*s. The search effort was called
Safari, and the search area had been broken up into sectors, but they had not been able to determine where, or
what size, the sectors were. Heusseini had charted many
of the ships that might belong to one search force or another. He had used active radar with some impunity, since
its use could be attributed to the *Hormuz*.

Badr was still bothered by the missing second boat.
From the Navy intercepts and the newscasts, it, too, had
disappeared from the face of the earth.

The aircraft engines became louder, and low on the horizon, Badr saw the amphibian approaching. It was a twin-
engined Canadair CL-215.

''Ahmed?''

Ahmed Rahman had been a missile specialist in the Iraqi
army. He was thirty-four years old and appeared somewhat studious behind thick spectacles and a bushy black
mustache. His fundamentalist Sunni beliefs made him a
dedicated soldier. Badr had brought him along originally
to direct the tanker's defense, with handheld Stinger missiles, in the event that pursuit led to the tanker. With the
acquisition of the *Sea Spectre*'s missiles, Rahman's mission had changed. His task was made difficult by the lack
of manuals regarding the missiles, their launcher, and their
relationship to the other systems on board.

"From the missile that I have disassembled, I suspect
that it is a small copy of the McDonnell Douglas RGM-
84A Harpoon, Colonel. The electronics are miniaturized

beyond belief. There is a solid boost motor for launch and a small turbojet for cruise. The warhead consists of a depleted uranium armor penetrator and approximately two hundred pounds of high explosives.''

"We can make it work?'' Badr asked.

"I will know that only after I am able to try it. Target acquisition is accomplished from the boat, but I do not know the effective range or speed. Once airborne, the missile either follows active radar or infrared emissions to the target or may be guided from the boat by way of the electro-optical scanner or radar targeting. It will be interesting,'' Rahman concluded.

"Yes. It will be interesting.''

The amphibious airplane had circled the ship, then settled to the sea and was approaching the ship quickly.

Badr signaled el-Ziam, and the two of them crossed the deck to the railing where Hakim's sailors had attached a transfer basket to the crane.

Ibn el-Ziam was a Bedouin, and looked uncomfortable in his western clothes and newly smooth-shaven face. His discomfort, however was more likely derived from his role as a sailor. El-Ziam was quite at home in the west. He wore Levi's, running shoes, a plaid shirt, and a heavy cast on his arm. The cast contained the tools he would need on his mission and provided the cover story. Injured at sea, he was being transferred to the Bahamas for medical attention. He carried a small valise.

"Do you have your papers?'' Badr asked.

"Yes, Colonel. I am Francisco Cordilla. I have American dollars and Spanish *pesetas*.''

Badr held the valise while el-Ziam scrambled into the basket.

"You know what you must do?''

"Of course. As soon as I reach Washington, I will seek out this manufacturer, this Advanced Marine Development, Incorporated.''

"You must find the other boat."

"I will find it, Colonel. Do not fear."

Of all his men, Badr trusted el-Ziam the most. The man had proven over and over again his ability to slip unnoticed into foreign countries—Germany, France, Britain, Italy, and others—and deliver lethal parcels.

The man enjoyed his tasks, and he smiled at Badr as the crane groaned and the basket lifted from the deck.

8

McCory didn't get up until almost noon, worrying that he was falling into Ginger's habit of sleeping late. He liked being a morning person.

He crawled out of the queen-sized bed in *Kathleen*'s master cabin, located under the stern deck, made the bed, then slipped into the small head to shower and shave. He dressed in Levi's, deck shoes, and a blue T-shirt with a Dolphin's logo on the left breast.

Taking the short companionway up to the salon, he started the pot with four cups of real caffeine, flipped on the stereo to catch the news, then got two strips of bacon, one egg, and two pieces of rye toast underway.

When his breakfast was ready, he scooped it all onto a plate, set it on the dinette table, and slid open the big window over the table. Windless day, temperature climbing. It felt good. His newspaper was resting on the side deck next to the window. He tipped the paperboy well for that service.

McCory took his time with breakfast, leafing through the paper, listening to Randy Travis, Reba McIntyre, and Ricky Van Shelton issuing from the Marantz stereo receiver. Nashville had a whole new generation of names

114

attached to it, and he lamented the absence of Cash, Haggard, and Lynn from regular inclusion on the top forty.

From his vantage point in Slip 1, McCory could survey most of his minikingdom, primarily down the main dock. Bob Weston was fueling his sport fisherman, the *Prime Mover,* down at the fuel dock. Among his residents, McCory had an honor system of fueling. They topped off their tanks, listed the quantity on a clipboard, and signed it. He billed them. The inventory hadn't come up a gallon short in a year.

Try that in Miami or New York.

His residents were a continual renewal of his faith in people.

Mimi Kuntzman came up the dock, whistling some song he didn't know. She was seventy-one years old, looked fifty, and wore shorts and a pink-and-blue striped blouse. Strong, muscled, chorus girl's legs. Ann Miller. Juliet Prouse. As she came alongside the *Kathleen,* she stopped and peered in his window.

"That smells suspiciously like breakfast."

McCory leaned close to the window. "It is. Want some, Mimi?"

"I had mine at seven. You didn't work so late, you could get up like normal people. It's not good for you, Kevin, all that work."

"I'll try to slow down."

"It's another big boat, isn't it? Like *Mimosa*?"

"What is?"

"The one you're working on over at John Barley's. Monte Harris saw the *Kathleen* tied up over there last night. And you didn't get back until nearly six this morning."

Mimi was what McCory imagined having a mother would be like. "I promise. I'll slow down."

"And I want you over for dinner on Saturday night. Six sharp. Bring your friend."

She turned and went on down the dock.

McCory watched her through the front windshield until she started up the ramp. Shook his head. Secrets were difficult to keep around here. He was going to have to be more careful. And for the first time, he began to wonder what the reaction would be among his friends if they found out he'd stolen a Navy boat. They read the papers and watched TV. They weren't stupid, and there was always the chance that a Mimi Kuntzman or a Monte Harris or a Bob Weston might start putting two and two together and come up with XMC-22. None of them had ever known Devlin, but he had mentioned his father to them from time to time.

He worried a little about firing the missile. The news media had yet to notify the public that missiles were missing from Navy inventories. What if one of his friends found out how McCory and Ginger spent their nights?

He didn't want to lose any friends.

The dishes were almost done when the phone rang. He crossed the salon to the built-in desk—every tenon and mortise hand fitted by Devlin—and picked up.

"Kevin." Gravelly voice.

"Yes, Marge."

"There's a couple gentlemen here would like to rent the *Starshine*. Two days."

"What do they look like?'

"I can't answer that."

"Because they're right there?"

"Yes."

"Ages over thirty?"

"More than that," she said.

"Clean and sober?"

"Yes."

"How do you feel about them?"

"Well, now . . . pretty good, I guess."

"You think drugs?"

"Oh, no!"

"Go ahead, then. Standard rate. Ask Ben to check her over and top off the tanks."

He went back to the galley, picked up a towel and a plate, and the phone rang.

Back at the desk, he lifted the receiver again.

"McCory."

"Mac, you know Air Force General Mark Aspin?"

"No, Ted. Should I?"

"I had breakfast with him. He's a client. Works at the Pentagon in some planning function."

"You supposed to be telling me this?"

"I wouldn't reveal anything of a professional nature, you know that. We small-talked about the news of the day."

"And the news behind the news?"

"That, too. There's a lot of pressure building up on the other side of the river. The White House and the Secretary of Defense are putting the screws on the Navy people. Jobs could hang in the balance."

"I'd think so," McCory said. "Losing a whole class of boat just isn't done."

"It may be to our advantage, come negotiation time," Daimler said.

"I've been thinking about that."

"Getting anxious?"

"Yeah. People around here might start catching on."

"Well, there are some other things," Daimler said. "One, I called Malgard."

"Who's Malgard?"

"I sent you a package. He's the CEO of AMDI. I didn't identify myself, but I suggested a deal for getting his boats back. Not boat. I implied the plural."

"And?"

"He didn't buy it."

"What's he like?"

"Instinctively, I didn't like him," Daimler said. "But then, I'd just read the background package myself. He's an ambitious bastard."

"The kind who'd steal a boat design?"

"Perhaps, but we're going to have to prove it."

"Ginger's going to type up my notes. I'll send them to you when she's done."

"Does she know that women's prisons are separate from men's prisons?"

McCory didn't respond. He figured she knew.

"Then," Daimler went on, "the primary reason for this call. Apparently, the Air Force had some of its recon planes involved in the search. I get the impression from Mark Aspin that the Air Force is trying to stay an arm's length away from the debacle, but they're contributing a little. They're kind of laughing at the Navy, buy only in private. How-some-ever, Mac, he tells me that the Navy has narrowed the search to one particular area of ocean."

"How in hell did they do that?"

"Well, you and I know the boats have missiles aboard. I acted totally surprised, naturally, when Aspin told me about that."

That was pure Washington. Secrets were only vague aspirations.

"What about the missiles?"

"That terrorist, Ibrahim Badr? He fired a missile last night. Some search plane picked up the active radar and the missile track."

All McCory could say was, "No shit?"

"No shit, *compadre.* Cross your fingers, and hope for the best. If the Navy gets that boat back from Badr, our time has come"

"I do see a problem," McCory said.

"Problem? What problem?"

"I don't know if you want to hear about it."

"Try me."

McCory was right. Daimler didn't want to hear about it.

1710 hours, Washington, D.C.

Justin Malgard's Washington office was just as comfortable as the one in his home. Thick, plushy carpet in rust tones. Dark woods, heavy leather. There was a wall of bound books. Four hundred square feet supporting two couches and an oversize desk. A pedestal was topped with a computer terminal, to show he was state of the art. Next door was his matching conference room, with the bar built into the end wall. From the corner windows, he had a view down New Hampshire to Dupont Circle. He entertained senators, representatives, and important staffers in the suite.

The sun was starting a downward trek, and he had slanted his blinds against it. The office had a gloomy air about it, and he had turned on the overhead lights to wash it away.

His secretary stuck her head inside the doorway. "Okay if I leave now, Mr. Malgard?"

"Sure. See you in the morning, Cheryl."

"Sorry I couldn't raise Mr. Chambers for you."

"That's all right. He's bound to call in."

As soon as he heard the outer door close, Malgard went back to his pacing. He was going to wear a large circle in his rust carpet.

All afternoon, Cheryl had been calling up and down the Gulf Coast of Florida, looking for any motel that had a Richard Chambers registered.

Nothing.

He kept glancing at his telephone, willing the light for the private line to start blinking.

Nothing.

He had searched all of his telephone books, as well as telephone information for surrounding cities, looking for some law firm called Weirgard, Amos, Havelock, and Moses.

Nothing.

A probe, that's all it was.

But it confirmed what he had been thinking all along. Kevin McCory had his boats. The damned Navy was off searching the world for wild geese, but McCory had the boats.

He sure as hell couldn't tell the Navy about it. There was no way in hell that he could allow a Navy investigation to involve McCory.

All he could do is wait for that phone to ring and then shove a stick up Chamber's ass.

1815 hours

Ibn el-Ziam no longer wore his arm cast.

He had abandoned it at Dulles International Airport, after four and a half hours of flights and waiting time, when he changed from his jeans and sport shirt to a conservatively cut blue-gray suit, white shirt, maroon tie, and highly polished black wing tip shoes. He detested ties but was convinced they helped make him invisible. In busy airports, people paid very little attention to yet another businessman in pursuit of American dollars.

He did get a few appreciative glances from several women, ranging from a blonde, blue-eyed young lady in designer jeans and a short fur jacket to a well-kept and stylish woman in her sixties. That kind of attention was expected, for el-Ziam had always been attractive to women. He was only 178 centimeters tall, but his body was well proportioned. His hair was dark and moderately long, combed back over the ears, with a forelock allowed to drape over his forehead. His skin was smooth, and his smile was white and frequent. He suspected that his eyes were his best feature, laughing eyes with a hint of adventure, and perhaps violence, in them. Set slightly wide to either side of a fine, straight nose, they were a limpid brown. Various women had described them as sensuous, sympathetic, or bedroom.

Quite often, the women he met on his travels for the Warriors of Allah had been quite useful. On his arm, they got him through security checkpoints or into restaurants and hotels that contained his targets.

Immediately after changing clothes in the men's room, el-Ziam had gone to a telephone booth and looked up Advanced Marine Development, Incorporated. There was an address for a manufacturing facility in Baltimore, Maryland, and an address for an office in the District of Columbia.

He chose the District of Columbia.

Outside the terminal, the heat had been oppressive, much more humid than that to which he was accustomed. He had flagged a taxi and told the driver in flawless English that he wished to be taken into the District, to the address on New Hampshire Avenue.

He spoke Arabic, Farsi, English, French, German, and Italian with ease. He could get by in Spanish and Greek, also. His facility with languages was what had first drawn the attention of Colonel Ibrahim Badr.

The highways were choked with noisy, erratic traffic, and the taxi driver fought and cursed his way into the city, taking the Key Bridge north to Theodore Roosevelt Island to cross the Potomac River.

It was almost seven o'clock by the time the taxi driver let el-Ziam and his suitcase out in front of the office building. It appeared nearly deserted, the workers gone home for the day. A few people were running late, emerging from the twin glass doors with harried expressions on their faces. El-Ziam entered, looked about, and sauntered over to the directory.

There was a security desk in front of the elevators with a uniformed man, who did not seem exceptionally busy. He was only checking those who were coming into the building.

El-Ziam scanned the directory. Advanced Marine was on the fifth floor. He chose a message service on the second floor, crossed to the security desk, and said, "I am to meet the manager of Capitol Convenience Services."

"Just sign the log, there, mister."

El-Ziam signed Francisco Cordilla's name with a flourish, then added the time. He passed around the desk and entered an open elevator.

After the short ride, he stepped out on the second floor, found the nearby stairway door, then descended to the basement. He had to use picks to open the lock of the steel door into the basement, but it only took him two minutes.

And then it only took twelve minutes to locate the telephone panel, find the leads for Suite 510, and connect the transmitter to the first of several sets of telephone terminals. El-Ziam was back on New Hampshire Avenue shortly after that, looking for a nearby restaurant.

1940 hours, Edgewater

It was becoming compulsive behavior. Every time he had a few straight hours of free time, McCory found himself in Dry Dock One of Barley's Refitters.

He would sit at the banquet table, studying manuals. He would wander around the boat cabin, touching. He would stand near the forward bulkhead, staring through the windshield at nothing, at the sea door.

I see, I feel, your dream, Devlin.

Just being aboard the *SeaGhost* made him feel closer to his father. When he was at the helm, feeling the slight vibration of the rotary engines in his fingertips, it was as if he had contact with . . . the soul of his father. It was the same sensation he found with the *Kathleen*. Or maybe it was Kathleen Moran McCory with whom he shared an illusive contact. Many, many times, McCory had wished he had known his mother beyond the image in old photographs.

Ginger was right, of course. McCory was something of a romantic and a dreamer. He liked old things. Old boats, old desks, old pictures, old books, old morals. True craftsmanship and integrity seemed to wither with each passing year. He wanted to hold onto it for as long as he could.

There were ironies. The *SeaGhost* was as high tech as could be found, and it hadn't even been built by Devlin McCory, but the essence of his thought, his craftsmanship, and his thoroughness were in her. Devlin's rough and tender hands might as well have smoothed her beautiful hull.

McCory had stocked the pantry and the refrigerator, then eaten a dinner of home fries and a chopped sirloin steak. The refrigerator contained twelve bottles of Dos Equis. He was making a home out of her, becoming familiar.

The interior lights of the dry dock were extinguished. There was only blackness outside the *SeaGhost*'s windows. The cabin lights were turned low. McCory had left the hatches open and had a ventilator operating. Warm, slightly salty air permeated the cabin.

He got a bottle of beer out of the refrigerator and went forward to sit in the sonar operator's seat. Propped his Top Siders on top of the instrument panel.

"Shit," he said aloud to himself and maybe the *Sea-Ghost*. "I'm hooked."

He had been intent upon righting a few wrongs, then relinquishing the boat. If he were halfway smart, he'd do it within the next few days, before too many of the local people started catching on. He had even driven over in the truck that evening, so Monte Harris or someone wouldn't spot one of his boats tied up alongside the dock.

Now, he didn't want to give her up.

Daimler was going to squawk.

Hell. I can't even take you out in public, girlie.

Not too many pleasure boats were outfitted with scramblers, targeting rader, cannon, and missiles.

Strip it all out and ship it to Norfolk.

Anonymously.

C.O.D.

Damned missiles would get him in trouble, yet. In his mind, he could see several fleets of battlewagons converging on that four-mile stretch of Atlantic where he and Ginger had sunk a tattered rubber boat.

He was really screwing it up. By showing off for the girlfriend, he had aimed the Navy in his own direction.

While the bad guys slipped over the horizon with *SeaGhost II.* It was like having Devlin held hostage.

Christ, Devlin. You taught me better.

0212 hours, New River Inlet, North Carolina

New River Inlet slipped by unseen except for the buoys marking the passage. Only an occasional light marked dwellings of some kind on the coastal islands. The moon had set over an hour before. It was a clear night, and the stars were hard points overhead.

The *Sea Spectre* barely whispered. Her engines could not be heard at her speed of fifteen knots. In the rearview screen on the panel, Ibrahim Badr could see only the mild twin-legged vee of the wake designating her trail, the water not churned enough to create a damning whiteness.

Any small noises within the cabin were dampened by the cushioned earphones he wore.

To his left, Omar Heusseini sat at the radar console. He looked more haggard than he should have, and Badr suspected he had not been sleeping well. The green glow of the screen tinted the unshaven whiskers on his face sickly gray.

To the left of Heusseini, at the sonar position, Amin Kadar sat rigidly in his seat, his tension betrayed by the set of his shoulders. He was leaning forward, his head resting against the hood of the sonar screen. His hand rested on the control panel, his thumb poised over a keypad, ready to switch his headset from the sonar-listening mode to the intercom.

Ahmed Rahman was back in the missile bay. The times that he had spoken to Badr in the past few hours, he had sounded completely at ease, fully relaxed. Rahman was comfortable with his missiles and his role.

A click sounded in the headset.

"I have a contact," Kadar said, his voice squeaky with his fear.

"Location?" Badr asked.

"Ahead, to the left. You had better bear to the right, Colonel."

Badr eased the helm slightly to the right.

"Do not go too far," Heusseini warned. "The depths are deceptive. I will need an active radar, soon."

Heusseini had learned about the mapping system available in the *Sea Spectre*'s computer but had also discovered some limitations. The maps of a few major harbors and bays were stored in the computer, but small waterways inland were not. The New River Bay in North Carolina was not. In fact, only the northern Atlantic and the Caribbean maps were accessible. Heusseini suspected that only the maps for the boat's planned area of operations were input to the machine. The computer mapping function would have been useless to them in the Arabian Gulf without access to the appropriate software.

It was also useless for most waterways inside the American continent. Badr had told them that the Americans had not planned on attacking their own installations with the boat. It brought a laugh.

"How large is the contact?" Badr asked.

"A medium-sized boat," Kadar relied. "Two propellers."

"Range?"

"Two thousand meters. Yards. This equipment thinks in yards. I do not."

Badr studied the night-vision screen. Soon, a set of running lights appeared, moving slowing toward them, but on the other side of the stream. They would clear each other by half a kilometer.

Without permission, Heusseini went active on the radar, using only the forward antenna. He shut it off within seconds.

"I see no other traffic," he said.

Badr thought it unwise to chastise the man about following orders at the moment. An argument would only disrupt the concentration of them all.

Give me strength, Allah.

"You must turn now," Heusseini said.

Badr could see for himself. The river took a ninety-degree turn to the right, past a point littered with trees. The shore on his right appeared swampy. The camera lens did not provide him with a decent view of the opposite shore. Through the windshield, the river's edge was only a band of dense shadows against blackness.

He made the turn, maintaining a steady speed of fifteen knots. Four kilometers later, he made a left turn, continu-

ing inland. Ten minutes after that, the lights of the Camp
Lejeune Marine Corps Base appeared.

It was a large base located at the head of the bay. Ge-
ometric lines of streetlights defined it well, and a glow of
more lights beyond would be the city of Jacksonville. As
they closed with the base, the night-vision lens gave Badr
a view of barracks, training fields, large maintenance-type
buildings, and other unknown structures.

He slowed the speed of the *Sea Spectre* three kilometers
away from the base and glanced down at the armaments
panel. It was active, its blue letters clear in the darkness
of the cabin. Four green indicators at the top of the panel
suggested that four missiles were in place on the launcher
and that they were prepared for ignition.

"Ahmed?"

The confident voice responded at once. "Four missiles
available, Colonel Badr. I have two more on the cranes,
ready for reloading. I am clear of the missile bay."

"Omar?"

"I am ready, Colonel. Targets?"

"Choose large buildings. There is a truck park."

"Opening missile bay doors." Heusseini touched a
keypad.

A green light.

"Doors clear," Rahman reported.

Badr pulled the throttles all the way back. The boat
slewed to the side a little as it slowed.

Heusseini pressed another pad.

"Launcher elevating. Locked in place," Rahman said.

"I am using electro-optical targeting," Heusseini said.

"You may fire when you are ready," Badr told him.

He switched his primary screen to the optical-tracking
function. A green view of the Marine base appeared on
the monitor, low on the screen, seen from the nose cone
of the missile. A pair of automobile headlights snaked
along one of the streets.

WHOOSH!

The missile launched directly ahead, the white-hot trail of its exhaust attacking his eyes through the windshield. He blinked his eyes, and when he opened them, the missile was a white dot dancing in the sky far ahead.

He looked down at the screen. The view was jumping all about. Flashing lights sliding. Sky. Water. Lights again.

Heusseini was having difficulty directing the missile with the directional keypads on the armaments panel. His fingers frolicked on the keys, pressing one, then another, as he sought to stabilize and direct the missile. He kept his eyes on his own screen.

"You must relax, Omar," Badr said.

He heard the man take a deep breath.

The picture steadied. An equipment park. Badr had a fleeting glimpse of large military trucks, personnel carriers, fuel tankers, and jeeps.

The words "LOCK-ON" appeared in the upper right corner of the screen.

The screen abruptly blinked to black, then to a new view from another missile as Heusseini abandoned his control of the first.

WHOOSH!

The second missile launched.

Badr closed his eyes just in time.

When he opened them, it took a half-second to locate the missile trail.

The first missile drew his attention to it when it exploded. There was a brilliant yellow-red flash that was soundless in the night.

The dull *whump* of the detonation followed a second later, very likely heard only because of the open missile bay doors. Most others sounds were filtered out by insulation and the headsets.

He looked at his screen. A large building with a peaked roof.

LOCK-ON.

Blackness.

WHOOSH!

White-out through the windows.

Another yellow-red flash on the shore as the second missile struck.

At the truck park, orange-blue flames were starting to rise high. Smaller explosions peppered the view and the windshield as automotive gasoline tanks exploded.

On the screen, another building. A barracks?

LOCK-ON.

Blank screen.

New view.

WHOOSH!

"Retracting launcher," Heusseini said. His voice was steady now, calm with the knowledge that he had met the challenge.

"Launcher retracted," Rahman reported. "I will reload with two missiles."

Badr felt the pride welling in himself. This was magnificent!

The fourth missile slammed into a building and detonated. Four fires were raging around the base, spread across a three-kilometer arc. Heusseini's accuracy was nothing he should boast about. He had merely locked his missiles onto whatever happened to be in view. Badr suspected that the first target, the truck park, was either a lucky fluke or had been under the guidance of Allah.

He quickly switched his primary screen to the boat's video camera view and eased the throttles forward to gain headway and control over the camera. Manipulating the computer keys, he found the formula to magnify the view by seven.

In the enhanced view, he could see that dozens of trucks, jeeps, and personnel carriers were on fire. More of them exploded as he watched. Hoods and doors leaped into the air. The canvas coverings on troop carriers were a flame.

Most of the buildings were made of wood, and structures adjacent to targeted buildings began to catch fire. The skyline was taking on a rosy hue.

Panicked men were running everywhere. They were dressed in white underwear, streaking across the streets, around the corners of buildings. Lights were coming on in most of the buildings. A few of the men pulled fire hoses behind them.

It was all very quiet. Within the insulated cabin of the *Sea Spectre*, with the headsets in place, they could not hear the screams and the agony. That much was disappointing.

"Missiles in place," Rahman reported.

"Raising launcher," Heusseini said.

Within three minutes, the last two missiles detonated in yet two more areas of the base.

There was fire everywhere. Fire trucks were now responding. Red and blue strobe lights blinked against the six separate infernos.

"Retract the launcher, and close the doors," Badr ordered. "We will now go see if Abdul Hakim has deserted us."

9

0241 hours, CINCLANT

The activity in the Operations Center was considerably more controlled than what was taking place in Camp Lejeune, Monahan thought.

He had made the trip from his home to the Center in record time, arriving a few minutes before Admiral Clay. Fortunately, he had had fresh khakis on hand, and he felt and looked better than either of the admirals. Matthew Andrews had had his last Chivas and water not too long before he had received his call. He appeared a bit unsteady in his chair at the table, talking earnestly to someone in North Carolina.

Bingham Clay came into the Center under full steam, tossing a briefcase toward one corner of the room. He came to a stop against the table, leaning into it, staring at the plotting board.

"Tell me, Jim."

Monahan had come to his feet as soon as Clay appeared. "Not good, Admiral. The reports are still coming in, but it looks like they were hit with six missiles."

"Casualties?"

Andrews, with a telephone pressed against the side of his face, responded. "I've got the hospital on the line,

131

Bing. Ambulances are still coming in, but so far, we're counting forty-two dead and one hundred and twelve wounded. Some of those are damned serious. The fatality count is going to climb. I've ordered aircraft to transport burn cases to San Antonio.''

''Son of a bitch!'' Clay snorted.

One of the things that Monahan had always respected about Bingham Clay was the man's concern for people. He worried about the men and women assigned to his command first and everything else second.

''Matt,'' the admiral said to the intelligence deputy, ''you see if they need more medical help down there. If they do, you get it to them.''

''Aye, aye,'' Andrews said, and went back to the phone.

''We got Washington in on this?'' Clay asked.

Monahan nodded. ''Lieutenant Commander Horan is the duty officer. He called the CNO's office right away, and they're monitoring our board.''

Monahan had a mental picture of the staff cars converging on the Pentagon. Someone would have gotten the President out of bed by now.

''Targets, Jim?''

''From what I've got right now,'' Monahan waved the telex he was holding, ''it looks sporadic. One wing of the headquarters building; a warehouse full of soft goods—bedding, uniforms, and the like; and a motor pool—fifty-six vehicles damaged at last count. Three barracks buildings were hit, and that's where we took most of the casualties.''

''Shit, shit, shit! Any doubt in your mind that it was the *Sea Spectres*?''

''No sir,'' Monahan said. ''I think, though, that only one of the boats was involved.''

''Why?''

''Elapsed time of the attack. With both boats, we'd have had eight missiles launched in the first wave. There were only six total, and there was almost a five-minute pause from the first salvo to the second.''

"They're holding one of the boats in reserve, then?"

"Yes. Or they've sent the other boat on to the Persian Gulf."

"Give me an impression, Jim."

Monahan took a minute to sift through the images in his mind. "I think the primary objective was shock value, sir. They didn't go in with preset targets. The impact pattern is too random. There were other targets available that would have been more spectacular. Fuel and ammunition storage sites, for example."

"Matt?" Clay looked to Andrews.

Andrews nodded while continuing to talk on the phone. His expression said he did not necessarily want to agree with Monahan but did not have a better alternative prepared at the moment.

Clay pointed at the plotting board. There were so many symbols converging on the coast of North Carolina that it was difficult to read. "What the hell's going on there?"

"Task Force 22 is three hundred miles southeast. *America* has sent Tomcats and Intruders. Langley Air Base has put up F-15's. There's some Coast Guard cutters in the area. Every naval installation within four hundred miles has scrambled air and sea search craft."

"Who in the fuck ordered that?"

Monahan held off on an answer, and Andrews finally spoke up, "I did, Bing. We've got to pin that SOB down while we've got him in a known sector."

Clay frowned, slipped out of his uniform blouse, and tossed it on the chair next to him. He sat down.

"Well, let's get some order injected into it. Commander Horan, get a headset and stand by. Jim, you go find an airplane and get down to Lejeune."

0250 hours, 30° 19' North, 74° 12' West

The *Prebble* had joined up with Task Force 22 just after midnight. The flagship had stationed her three miles ahead and one mile to the port side of *America.*

Since 0220 hours, Barry Norman had been pacing his bridge, pausing frequently to watch the flights of aircraft taking off from the carrier. Their afterburners streaked the horizon behind the destroyer.

He was angry and frustrated. He was mad as hell about the success of the attack on the Marine Corps base. It made a statement, not only about the value of the *Sea Spectre* as an assault craft, but also about the complacency of American troops in a peacetime garrison.

His frustration was a result of being stationed within the task force, when he should be closer to the scene. The *Prebble* had the best, if not the only, chance of locating Badr.

"Bridge, CIC."

Norman recognized Perkins's voice and crossed the deck to the intercom mounted on the bulkhead. "Bridge. Go ahead, Commander."

"Message just in, Captain. CINCLANT's suggesting that only one boat was involved in the attack. All Safari elements are to continue observation of commercial vessels while simultaneously mounting the search in the North Carolina sector."

Norman had figured out sometime before that only one boat was involved. It was about time the commands figured it out, too. On the task force radio net, broadcast from the overhead speakers, he heard the flagship detaching some ships to continue surveillance of the tankers and freighters they had been dogging. The rest of the task force was given a new course heading.

"Commander Perkins, send a message to CINCLANT, copy CINC TF22. 'Commander, *Prebble* recommends her detachment at flank speed to scene of crisis. Rationale, *Prebble* mounts anti-stealth gear.' "

"Right away, sir."

Twelve minutes later, Perkins called him back, unsuccessfully disguising the jubilation he felt. "Captain! We've been released from the task force! We're now Safari Echo."

"It's about damn time somebody started thinking," Norman said. "Instructions?"

"Wide open, sir. 'Proceed at best possible speed. Engage search at your discretion.' "

"Thank you, Commander." Norman turned to the second mate, who had the watch. "Susan, give us a course for Onslow Bay. And we want every knot we can get out of her."

"Aye aye sir."

Norman went below to his quarters to catch a few hours of sleep but found himself spread out on his bunk, eyes closed, wide awake.

He felt the vibrations as the turbines met the challenge of full power. The chief engineer would have all of his people on duty, watching those shafts.

He kept thinking about that one boat.

A damned terrorist could cause a lot more havoc using both boats. Since when did someone like this Ibrahim Badr think rationally?

He did not want to underestimate Badr or anyone like him. As far as Arabic logic went, Norman was the first to admit he did not fathom it, but still . . .

Terrorist groups were not known for holding back. Hell, if Norman was directing a similar operation and had both boats available, he would have used them.

Devlin McCory.

Norman had looked up his old correspondence with Devlin. Clear back in 1985, he had mentioned a design he was working on for a stealth boat. Twice more, in later letters, he had referred to it. There was nothing specific, but he had sounded excited about it.

But Devlin was gone. Only the boy was left, and Norman had no idea what had become of him. Kevin, that was the name. From the tone of Devlin's letters, he suspected that father and son had been close.

Maybe Kevin had Devlin's drawings? Could he be helpful in tracking down the *Sea Spectre*?

No.

But Norman could not let go of it. He ought to tell someone.

He sat up on the edge of his bunk and pressed the intercom button. "Comm, this is the Captain."

"Comm, Captain."

"Find me someone to talk to at CINCLANT. Somebody who's working on Safari."

1413 hours, Miami, Florida

Rick Chambers had driven the full length of Florida, on the Gulf side, and he was getting tired. He hoped to hell that Malgard was right about this. By the time he found Kevin McCory, he was going to be in a mean mood.

Since February of 1987, when the old man died, McCory had worked, or holed up, in six different marinas. So far.

He was living aboard an old home-built cruiser named the *Kathleen,* and he worked a few charters or got himself a job on the docks for a few weeks before moving on.

It hadn't been easy. Chambers had followed a dozen false leads. "Guy named McCory? The *Kathleen*? Damn, seems to me ol' Cap'n Eddie said he'd seen him over 'round Siesta Key. Might try there."

It got so Chambers didn't know whether the good old boys were putting him on or not. Most of them kept their jaws clamped tight. They didn't talk to Northerners who weren't buying a charter. He was certain some of them had sent him on deliberate wild-goose chases.

After a while, though, he learned to chat up the younger women hanging around the marinas. More often than not, Becky or June or Melinda would remember the handsome young master of the *Kathleen* and be happy to talk about him. More often than not, also, Chambers would see the yearning in their eyes. Pissed him off, is what it did.

He took the Tamiami Trail across the city to the Atlantic side, turned north on Biscayne Boulevard, and pulled into the first convenience store he found. He got out of the green Taurus, stretched, and headed across the parking lot for the public telephone.

Chambers had learned to search out the low-end marinas. McCory didn't go for the world-class stuff. The trouble was, the yellow pages didn't tell him what was first class and what was crumbling. Every advertisement pictured or narrated a state of the art marine operation.

He ripped the pertinent pages from the telephone book, folded them, and stuffed them in the pocket of his beige suit jacket. It was pretty wrinkled, he decided. He was going to have to stop somewhere along the way and get both of his suits pressed.

He figured he could reach Malgard in his Washington office that time of the afternoon, so he used his credit card number and dialed the AMDI office number. Malgard didn't often go out to his manufacturing plant. Chambers figured him for being more interested in being a wheel around Washington than in building boats for the Navy.

"Advanced Marine Development."

"Cheryl, this is Rick Chambers. The boss around?"

"Hold on a moment, Rick."

It took nearly four minutes for Malgard to drop whatever he was doing and pick up the phone.

"Where are you at, Rick?"

"Miami."

"Christ! You haven't found him, yet?"

"Hey, I just got here. I've got maybe a hundred marinas to check out. You sure McCory stole your boats?"

"Not on this phone, damn it! Yes, I'm sure."

Chambers sighed and patted the yellow pages in his pocket. "Okay, Justin. I'll get on it."

"Get on it fast, damn it! He's had damn near six days now."

"Maybe he sunk them?"

"He didn't sink them. He's got them somewhere, and he's going to want big bucks for them. I'm not paying."

"Yeah, okay. You can pay me instead."

Chambers hung up the phone and turned around to stare at Biscayne Bay. Jesus, there were a lot of boats.

But what he needed was to find a young lady.

He found her three hours later, in the twelfth marina, up near the northern end of the bay. Her name was Elaine, and she was relaxing in the cockpit of a small sloop named *Lainie's Choice*. She was in her mid-thirties, tanned the color of cashews, and dressed in pink shorts and a man's white shirt. Chambers didn't think there was anything under the shorts and shirt but Elaine.

He leaned on the railing of the dock and looked down at her. A big cruiser moving out of the marina created ripples that rocked the small sailboat.

She looked up at him, frowned.

"You Elaine?" he asked.

"Who're you?"

"Name's Davis. Harold Davis." He pointed his thumb toward the shore end of the dock. "The manager back there said you might know a man named McCory."

There. That little shift in the eyes, thinking back on pleasurable thoughts.

"Why you looking for this McCory?"

"I'm with Marathon Equitable Insurance. We've been

trying to find Kevin McCory so we can pay him a settlement.''

''What kind of settlement?''

''It has to do with his father. Can't say much more than that.''

''I haven't seen him in almost two years,'' she said, her blue eyes remembering every lost day. She used the back of her hand to flip the long, bleached blonde hair away from the side of her face.

''You have any idea where he went?''

''Not really. He talked about Tampa Bay, once.''

Chambers had already been there. ''Anywhere else?''

''Fort Lauderdale, maybe.''

''Has he still got that cruiser? The old one?''

''It's a motor yacht. Custom-built. The *Moran*. Yes, he still had it when he was here.''

That explained a couple of big gaps in McCory's itinerary. He'd changed the name of the boat.

''Well, thanks, Elaine.''

''Sure. I hope you find him.''

''Oh, I will.''

1721 hours, Chevy Chase

Ted Daimler felt sick, but it was not the flu.

It was the carnage he had viewed on television.

All of the networks had abandoned their scheduled programming, which was not much of a loss, and gone to North Carolina, first with affiliates, then with their own reporters as they arrived on the scene. The twisted wreckage of armored personnel carriers and trucks was a favorite scene. Gaping holes in structures and burned barracks came in second. Subreporters were stationed at the doorways to hospitals in Camp Lejeune, Jacksonville, Wilmington, and Brooke Army Medical Center in San

Antonio, where a number of bad burn cases had been flown.

The government had been noncommittal for most of the day, but finally in the early afternoon, the Navy conceded that the stolen stealth boat was likely behind the attack. Ibrahim Badr was profiled.

The fatality count stood at sixty-one. There were 194 wounded.

Daimler had gone to the office in the morning but was back home by ten o'clock. He called McCory a dozen times but only left a message with Marge Hepburn.

Finally, just as Reba started talking about a dinner he did not feel like eating, McCory called back.

"Worst possible scenario, Ted."

"Do you really think so?" Daimler asked. The sarcasm could not be more evident.

"Shit, I'm aching, man."

"Oh, hell, I know you are." Daimler found himself pushed into his counseling role. For most of the day, his world had been self-centered, knowing that he had a part, however small, in the whole drama. "We have to keep in mind, Mac, that this isn't us. It's not our script."

"I appreciate your use of 'our,' Ted, but it's me. I started this thing."

"Not necessarily. If we hadn't knocked on the door of Pier Nine first, this Badr asshole would have two boats."

"Maybe."

"What surprises the hell out of me," Daimler said, "is that the SOB hung around. I thought he'd be knocking off supertankers in the Persian Gulf by now."

"Which offends your Republican sense of justice."

"Sure, but losing oil is better than losing Marines. But, Mac, what I called about. I think it's time I approached the Navy. We're not going to get anywhere with this Malgard. Let's lay the whole thing out—the drawings and your notes, and give them the boat back."

"There's just one thing, Ted."

"There would be."

"I've decided to keep the boat."

Daimler groaned. McCory did things like that. Always the unexpected. When he was younger, Daimler had been able to take it.

2020 hours, Edgewater

McCory wore his gray slacks and a blue blazer. He wore a white dress shirt and a conservatively striped blue tie. Except for his single suit, it was the best combination in his wardrobe.

Ginger Adams was a knockout in a white sheath that was just a little taut in the right places. She had her hair up in a carefully sculptured style that, counting her three-inch heels, made her over six feet tall. He figured she could stop traffic better than any cop.

It was a festive occasion, the annual summer dinner party for the bank's employees. McCory didn't feel very festive, and he knew that Ginger didn't either. Still, she kept a bright smile in place, and she appeared very comfortable in the company of her tellers and the members of her board of directors. She was good at small talk.

McCory had never been invited into her banking family before, so this was kind of a formalization of their relationship, he supposed. If it hadn't been planned for three weeks, he might have begged off.

The lights in the ballroom of the Adler Hotel had been dimmed to a level that competed with the flickering candles on the tables. A multi-faceted, mirrored ball rotated over the dance floor, like something out of the forties, and the raised bandstand was outlined with white Christmas tree lights. It felt like Tommy Dorsey or Guy Lombardo.

The dinner came off well, with the president and vice

presidents making gratefully short speeches, though McCory could have listened to Ginger for a while longer. They passed out awards to outstanding employees. They served roast beef contributed by a very lean steer. Afterward, a trio of guitar, bass, and piano, fronted by a college-girl singer, played music that had been mostly recorded before the band members were born. They were heavy on Eddy Arnold's stuff, and McCory guessed that Ginger had not been on the selection committee.

She came back to their table from a gab session and said, "Dance with me."

"That didn't sound like a question."

"It wasn't.'

"I'm a terrible dancer."

"I'll judge that."

After he got into the rhythm of "Turn the World Around," feeling her close to him, her fingers keeping time against the back of his neck, he figured he wasn't too bad.

She agreed. "You're only half-terrible."

"That's what all my friends say." He pulled his head back to look into her eyes. There were golden sparkles among the hazel. "I'm afraid I'll spoil your night."

She pulled his head back and rested her forehead against his cheek. "No, you won't. I understand. The Marines."

"I'd like to find the son of a bitch."

"Maybe you will," she said. "Maybe I'll help you find him."

2310 hours, Miami

Ibn el-Ziam deplaned and walked through Miami International's teeming terminal into a hot, moist night. From a dispenser, he bought a copy of *The Miami Herald*. The headlines, and practically the whole front page, were devoted to the terrorist attack on Camp Lejeune. It was all he could do not to throw his arms up and shout, "Rejoice!"

He looked at the first taxi in the line, rethought his needs, and went back inside to rent a car. The lady told him he would like a Pontiac.

He did not like it. Americans were too soft, surrounded themselves with unnecessary luxuries. He had not liked the Mercury he had had to rent in Washington, either. Sitting in a restaurant or hanging around the alley near the office building on New Hampshire Avenue drew too much attention to himself, so he had rented the car and parked it successively in different spots around the block, staying within range of the transmitter attached to the Advanced Marine Development telephone.

The company had a large number of telephone lines coming into it, and el-Ziam had selected the first one. He had almost gone back into the building several times in order to change the tap to another line, because the calls made to the first number were so infrequent.

But finally, in midafternoon of the second day, his patience had been rewarded. He had two names. Rick Chambers and McCory. He did not know what either of them looked like, but he did know that Chambers was searching for McCory among the marinas of Miami. The Justin on the telephone in Washington seemed certain that McCory was responsible for taking the boat. Of interest to Ibrahim Badr, too, would be the fact that this Justin assumed that McCory had taken both boats.

As he pulled into one of the multiple lanes of the Airport Expressway, el-Ziam wondered if the man named Chambers had been exaggerating when he said that he had a hundred marinas to search.

Surely, he must have been.

But then, el-Ziam had never been in Miami before. Even if it were true, it should not take him long to locate someone who had seen Chambers. If the man had asked many questions, he had probably left a broad trail behind him.

A trail that would lead el-Ziam directly to McCory.

Ala bab Allah. Whatever will be, will be; let us leave it to Allah.

10

0135 hours, Intracoastal Waterway, Southern Georgia

Ibrahim Badr was enjoying himself immensely. Allah was on the side of the righteous. The news reports on the radio of the consternation in the American military were gratifying. The Marine Commandant had demanded, in front of some reporter, the right to invade the Middle East and had subsequently been reprimanded by the Secretary of Defense.

The success of yesterday's raid on the Marine base was with them all. Heusseini had slept all day, sweating in the heat of the day and the cargo tank, in one of the bunks. Amin Kadar was a little more relaxed, his eyes focused upon this world for a change. Ahmed Rahman had prepared himself—shaving, trimming his full mustache, cleaning his glasses—as if he were to meet a beautiful woman.

The cabin was almost totally dark, but Badr could feel the changes vibrating in the air. It was optimism. It was invincibility.

"They will expect us," Omar Heusseini said.

"Yes," Badr replied over the headset. "I expect the American president has ordered his bases to the highest state of alert."

Through the windshield, he could see that the submarine base was lit with every available light. It was six kilometers away to the south. Badr had brought the *Sea Spectre* into the Intracoastal Waterway near the head of Cumberland Island and threaded it silently southward down the waterway.

Small boats crisscrossed the nighttime bay, their probing searchlights rotating about, skipping across the surface of the water.

The *Sea Spectre* was making ten knots, riding smoothly on waveless water.

"Launcher deployed," Rahman said.

"I have too many targets," Kadar said from his sonar position. "At least six small boats. I think a submarine is moving south."

"On the surface?" Badr asked.

"I cannot tell. Perhaps. Probably."

"Omar?"

"I may go active?"

"In one minute. Amin, you will go to the back now and assist Ahmed."

They had practiced the new procedure several times that afternoon, using Kadar as an assistant to Rahman in reloading the launcher.

As Kadar left his seat at the sonar, Badr said to Heusseini, "You may go active."

Badr switched in the radio. Kadar had used the manuals to locate the frequencies, as well as the scrambler and encryption modes, for several channels utilized by the Kings Bay Submarine Base operations center. Kadar programmed the radios to scan all of the channels. There had been very little activity on the radio. Occasionally, some of the small boats patrolling the outreaches of the submarine pens had reported in.

The frequency was quiet then, until Heusseini let the radar make three full sweeps.

"I see only two submarines in the docks," Heusseini said.

"Proceed," Badr told him.

"Boxer!" burst over the radio. "Mickey Three. I've got a hot radar in the north."

"Pinpoint it, Three."

"It's gone now."

"Mickey Three and Six, Boxer. Investigate radar radiation source."

Badr eased the throttles in, picking up speed. "Is the missile bay clear?" he asked.

"Clear," Rahman reported.

"You may fire when you are ready, Omar."

With targets as clearly defined and as defenseless as submarines on the surface, Badr had elected to use the radar-targeting mode of the missiles.

He glanced at the green-tinged video image in the screen, set for a magnification of five. Two small patrol boats were rising to the plane, headed toward him.

Heusseini went active on the radar again, manipulating his radar-targeting circle with the controls on the panel. Badr watched his thumb as it pressed the arming, then the launch keypads.

The computer decided.

A half-second.

Several voices screamed on the radio. "Active! He's gone active!"

The missile launched with a bright scream of fire. A second later, the second missile ignited.

"Incoming! We've got incoming missiles. Two of them!"

Badr slammed the throttles forward, and the *SeaGhost* lifted out of the water, racing toward the southeast as Badr shut down the radar.

Two kilometers away, he pulled the throttles back. He had lost the camera view of the patrol boats, but through the side window, he saw their running lights streaking toward where they had been. Aboard one of them, an impatient finger triggered a stream of green machine-gun tracers, all useless.

He could not hear it.

The first two missiles had detonated. At that distance from the base, Badr could not tell what they had hit, but it was in the port area.

Heusseini went active again. Within four seconds, two more missiles launched, and Badr again moved the throttles forward. He turned the wheel slightly to the right and headed directly south, bypassing the base by several kilometers.

"Retracting launcher," Heusseini said quietly.

The patrol boats had swung in their direction. They were now within three kilometers.

Two more of the patrol boats raced toward them from the port.

Missiles three and four found their targets. Bright flashes of yellow-red fire erupted in the night.

He was making fifty knots. The voices on the radio were panicky, overlapping one another. The radio scanner jumped from channel to channel. Someone was asking for damage assessments. Someone else confirmed for Badr that both docked submarines had been hit. Watertight doors were closing off compartments. One of the submarines was taking water.

"Boxer, this is *Memphis*."

"Go ahead, *Memphis*."

"We've got him on sonar. Making five-two knots, bearing one-seven-seven. Coming directly at us, five thousand yards."

"Take him out, *Memphis*."

"I have permission to free weapons?" the man on the submarine asked.

"Go. I'll take responsibility."

The conversation had to be between the base and the submarine underway for the Atlantic, now ahead of the *Sea Spectre.*

In the rearview screen, Badr saw that two of the patrol boats had lined up directly behind the *Sea Spectre.* They may have seen the wake the stealth boat was creating, but he did not think they could catch him. Machine-gun muzzles on the foredecks winked whitely.

"Reloaded," Rahman called on the intercom.

"Raising launcher," Heusseini said. "I am going to the active mode."

"Aim first for the pursuit boats," Badr said.

Heusseini worked his controls, pressed the launch key once, then a second time.

The darkness ahead was erased twice as first one missile, then the second, launched toward the rear.

"Incoming!" screamed the radio.

In the rearview screen, he saw both boats veer off as they took evasive action.

Two white trails of exhaust.

WHOOMP!

WHOOMP!

The two detonations came within two seconds of each other.

Both boats disappeared in the middle of white, then yellow-red fireballs.

Allah, Allah, Allah. This we do for you. The infidels will no longer rule our world.

"The submarine is in the middle of the channel," Heusseini said. "It is two thousand meters from us."

"Launch," Badr ordered.

Two missiles ignited.

The first missile went bad for some reason. It spiraled wildly, then crashed into the surface of the water a thousand meters ahead. It exploded under the surface, raising a waterspout that rose hundreds of meters in the air.

Badr spun the wheel to the left to avoid it.

A large cannon on the deck of the submarine began firing at him.

The second missile hit the conning tower of the submarine, exploding in a fireball. Badr could not see the damage from where he was, and the bow camera was not lined up.

More frantic voices chattered on the radio.

Stormy water from the waterspout splashed down, peppering the foredeck like hail, streaking over the windshield.

Small geysers from cannon shells erupted off the right side, in range, but far from their target.

He retarded the throttles as he heard Heusseini and Rahman securing the launcher and the missile bay doors.

At ten or twelve knots, he would disappear from all of their sensing devices.

And slip out to the sea, dancing on their graves.

"Allah Akbar," Kadar said.

0830 hours, Glen Burnie

Justin Malgard got the news on the early morning telecast. He kept the remote control handy, switching between networks, looking for the best coverage.

One submarine had been sunk. Two others had suffered heavy damage. Two patrol boats had been lost in the waterway, and they were still looking for crew members. Seven hours after the attack, they were reporting sixteen dead, twenty-one wounded, and seven missing in action.

Missing in action. At a base within the United States. Unthinkable.

And yet . . .

And yet, he thought about the substantially changed position he was in. His boat was proving invincible. The

Navy should double the order. Congress would have only to refer to the newspapers for support of the appropriation.

He was nervous all through breakfast, trying to settle on a course of action. Trish noticed his agitation but did not say anything. Patty and Jason sniped away at each other with sarcastic comments as though there were no earthquakes, or even tremors, in their world.

As usual, Trish was running late. She left the dishes and rushed around the house, looking for the precisely right clothes to take Patty to her piano lesson and Jason to baseball practice.

As soon as Trish's Mercedes had backed out of the drive, Malgard went to the den and started making phone calls. The admirals were too busy to talk to him. Commander Rosse at procurement was not in his office.

Finally, he was given a phone number for the commander he had met on Sunday morning, the one he did not like. Monahan was at Kings Bay.

"Yes, Mr. Malgard. What can I do for you?"

"I wanted to see if there was some way in which I could help." Being helpful now might lead to larger contracts later, and God knew he needed some large contracts.

"I don't know that there's any way in which you can help," Monahan said. "The Navy's taking care of it."

"And not very well, from what I see on the news. Look, I built the damn boats. I know what they can do."

"As does Admiral Stein. We have the Ship R&D people available."

Malgard restrained his temper. "Still, something might have slipped through the cracks. Hell, man, I want this stopped as much as you do."

"Very well, Mr. Malgard. Why don't you fly down to Norfolk? Report to Rear Admiral Matthew Andrews."

"I'll do that."

"And while I've got you on the line, Mr. Malgard, I do have a question."

"Shoot."

"I had a discussion with one of our ship captains, a man named Norman. He had an interesting story. Have you ever heard the name Devlin McCory?"

Shit!

"No, I haven't. Is it important?"

"Perhaps not. Thank you, Mr. Malgard."

Malgard missed the cradle when he slapped the phone down. He had his eyes closed.

0925 hours, Kings Bag Submarine Support Base

"I'm just checking in, Admiral," Monahan said into the phone.

"What's the picture down there, Jim?" Admiral Bingham Clay asked.

"We've recovered all the bodies, sir. Fatalities stand at twenty-four now."

"Goddamn."

"You knew Captain Torrey, I think."

"Oh, Christ! He had the *Pogy.*"

"Yes, sir. He was killed aboard her when the first missile hit."

Clay sighed deeply. "I'll call Janice myself. Damage assessment?"

"The *Pogy* sank in position at her dock, but she's salvageable, and the reactor's secure. *Sargo* and *Lipscomb* are both heavily damaged. The first estimate suggests three to four months for repairs."

"This is a real son of a bitch, Jim. Anything else?"

"Not here. I talked to Malgard, and he thinks he can help us out."

"Right."

"I sicced him on Admiral Andrews."

"Okay. I'll warn Matt. Speaking of warnings, Jim, the

CNO and the SecDef went to the president. All East Coast installations are now on full alert, including Air Force and Army.''

"I hope that helps," Monahan said.

"So do I.''

"One other thing, Admiral. Do you know Captain Norman on the *Prebble*?''

"Barry? Sure do. A fine officer, but he doesn't have the temperament for flag rank. I think I promised him a battlewagon before he retires. In fact, Jim, we've moved the *Prebble* down your way, because she's got some equipment that might help out. What about Norman?''

"He called me. It's a long story, but way back when, he knew a CPO named McCory, helped him out in some crisis, and they've corresponded over the years. McCory claimed to have designed a stealth boat.''

"Is that right? What does Barry Norman want us to do about it?''

"Well, McCory is dead, but Captain Norman thought maybe the son would know something that could be beneficial.''

"Did you reach McCory? The son?''

"His name is Kevin. But no, the last address Norman had is a bummer. I wanted to know if you thought it was worth pursuing.''

"If Barry Norman says it's worth a shot," Clay told him, "it probably is. And let's not fuck around finding him. Put the FBI on it. Better yet, I'll call the Bureau.''

"That'll probably get faster action, Admiral.''

"And you get back up here, Jim. I have a feeling I'm going to need you.''

"Uh, Admiral, would you mind if I stayed here a while?''

"What for?''

"I've got a feeling of my own.''

"Share it.''

"Badr's moving south."

"He strikes twice, and you're reading his mind?" Clay asked.

"It's just a gut reaction, I know."

"Stay there. I'll put out a notice to the South Carolina, Georgia, and Florida installations."

0605 hours 28Aug72, Fort Walton Beach, Florida

Another few days, the fourteenth of September, and it would be the nineteenth anniversary of the marina. The time went by so damn fast.

Marina Kathleen was located near the eastern end of Santa Rosa Island, on a stubby promontory facing Choctawhatchee Bay, and was not a large enterprise. McCory had two hundred slips, over half of them occupied by permanent live-aboard residents. The place was nearly fifty years old now and was not the most modern facility in the area. It had been thirty years old when he bought it, using Kathleen's $2000 insurance policy payment, and most of the $5000 settlement he had wheedled and threatened out of the estate of the drunk who had killed her for the down payment.

It had been a struggle all the way, but the marina was clean, the paint of the buildings and docks kept fresh. The slip rentals met the debt service, and most of McCory's livelihood came from the maintenance end. He kept five full-time employees off the Fort Walton Beach unemployment rolls, and the three maintenance buildings were usually humming with engine overhauls and hull rebuilding. Generally, he had a runabout, ski boat, or small cruiser of his own design under construction, using finely fitted exotic woods in the earlier years, then more recently, fiberglass. He had a local reputation as a craftsman of the first order, and he loved the work. But more important, the marina kept him and Kevin together. When he was not in school, Kevin could be found close on his father's heels.

Kathy's folks had offered to take care of Kevin after she died, but McCory would have none of it. He took a hardship discharge from the Navy, his application greased along the way by his commander, Lieutenant (j.g.) Barry Norman. Though he loved the Navy, he loved his son more, and he was not going to take a chance on losing him.

Until now.

The two of them sat at the kitchen table in the apartment above the marina office, the only home Kevin had ever consciously known. It was small—two bedrooms and a living room—but it was ship-shape. Everything in place, from the out-dated, fifties, overstuffed couch upholstered in chartreuse to the walnut secretary that had been Kathy's grandmother's. There were six framed pictures of Kathleen Moran McCory grouped on the wall in McCory's bedroom, two in the living room, and one above the banquette in the kitchen. There were a dozen similar pictures of Devlin and Kevin McCory, usually with a boat or a fish in the background. Kevin's high school swimming awards were hung over the secretary.

Through the window overlooking the main dock, McCory saw the Childress kid fueling Dag Wither's Trojan sportfisherman. He checked his watch. It was five minutes after six.

Kevin reached for the counter behind him, grabbed the coffeepot, and refilled both of their mugs.

McCory found the manila envelope on the leatherette bench beside him and shoved it across the table.

"What's this, Pop?" Kevin frowned.

Sometimes, it was like looking in the mirror. His own eyes looking back at him.

"For you." He tried not to sound as gruff as he knew he frequently sounded.

"Ah, hell." Kevin pulled the flap and dumped the contents of the envelope on the table.

Counted the cash. *"Three hundred dollars, Pop? You can't afford that."*

"Sure I can. Gainesville's goin' to be expensive. You'll need it. Next semester, I'll come up with a little more."

"I've saved some of my own."

"Yeah, I know. And the Navy's payin' part of it. But I want you to enjoy it a little, too, Kev. Don't work your ass off all the time."

"And these?" Kevin picked up the key chain and twirled the keys.

"That's the sixty-six Chevy. Billy sanded the signs off the doors and repainted them."

"Damn it, Pop. That's your newest truck."

McCory had never owned a new vehicle and had not owned a passenger car since the '47 Ford sedan, which had been totalled when Kathy was killed.

"You need some wheels."

"I've got a bus ticket."

"Cash it in."

They went down the outside stairs together, each of them carrying one of Kevin's beat-up suitcases, and crossed the parking lot to where the marina vehicles were parked. Three pickups, two forklifts, and three small tractors. The fresh blue paint on the doors of the '66 pickup did not quite match the oxidized paint of the rest of the truck.

McCory opened the passenger door, and they put the suitcases inside.

"Don't mind tellin' you, Kev, I ain't been lookin' forward to this day."

"Me either, Pop."

"Bullshit. Every kid's got to get out and kick the world in the ass a little. Let the SOBs know you're alive and you're not takin' their crap."

They walked around to the other side, and Kevin got in behind the wheel.

"Do me proud, son."

2145 hours, Edgewater

McCory knew it was way too early in the night to be moving the *SeaGhost,* but he shoved the dry dock door upward, then went back and boarded the boat. Closing the hatch, he went forward, flipped switches to warm up the radar and computers, then settled behind the helm.

The rotary engines started right away. He shifted to reverse and backed slowly out of the building. After circling back to the south, he shifted to forward, then advanced the throttles.

The *SeaGhost* advanced silently across the waterway. A number of boats were moving around to the north, apparently putting into Edgewater and New Smyrna. McCory didn't hurry it. He drifted along at ten knots while the engine temperatures climbed to normal operating levels.

Once he was out of the usual traffic lanes, he turned north and activated the video cameras for night vision, fore and aft. He experimented with his speed, seeing how fast he could go before the wake tattled on him. Fifteen or sixteen knots seemed to be the maximum, and he held that speed.

Swerving the bow toward New Smyrna, he punched the third keypad under the monitor, switching it to the infrared tracking function. What he got was a kaleidoscopic mishmash of reds, oranges, yellows, greens, and blues. The red seemed to indicate the hot spots of exhausts and lights, both marine and automotive. He didn't think the infrared was of much use, aimed at a beach.

He put the bow back on a northerly course until he reached Ponce de Leon Inlet, then turned eastward. Three miles offshore, he opened the throttles to the forward stops.

The *SeaGhost* responded immediately, leaping forward, the momentum holding him securely in his wrap-around seat. Within two minutes, he was making sixty-two knots. That was seventy-one miles per hour. On the highway, Florida State Trooper Mickey Myers would have pulled him over.

Myers kept a nineteen-foot Baja cuddy cabin at Marina Kathleen and had stopped McCory in his pickup a couple of times, offering mild warnings.

McCory tried some maneuvers. Sharp left and right turns, getting a feel for what abuse the *SeaGhost* would accept at various speeds.

She was exhilarating. There was a light chop to the seas, maybe two-foot troughs, and she skipped across the wave tops with ballerinalike ease. The turns at high speed were a little sloppy, but under fifty knots, she was as agile as Devlin might have dreamed.

She could stop on a dollar, if not a dime. To the right of the throttle handles were two levers that, when depressed, dropped curved paddles over the jet exhaust, deflecting the water stream forward. McCory tried using them at various speeds.

He devoted two hours to learning her characteristics, thinking occasionally that, if he had done the same with some of the women he had known, he'd probably be married, offspring underfoot, and the TV in permanent on-mode.

Just after one in the morning, some sixty miles off the coast, McCory set the automatic pilot and switched his attention to the sonar, radar, and radio sets. He spent two hours familiarizing himself further with the electronics.

The radio messages he listened to were a little baffling. CINCLANT and other operations centers seemed to be using code words. Some of the frequencies, and many of the scrambler modes, had been changed. Perhaps they had figured out that the terrorist boat had the ability to listen in on their scrambled conversations.

He practiced setting up the scanner, which allowed the monitoring of a dozen channels in all of the frequency bands.

There was a Task Force 22 in the area, somewhere to the north of him. By the number, he knew it was a task force of the Second Fleet. Normally, it would probably have operated in the Caribbean. He also figured out the TF22 was part of Safari Bravo. There was a Safari Alpha, also, but he didn't determine what class of ships were included in the designation.

Safari Echo seemed to be a single ship. He heard coordinates and, after checking them on his chart, decided Safari Echo was fifty miles offshore from Kings Bay. Safari, McCory deduced, was the overall code for the search effort.

He resisted the impulse to go on the air and identify himself as Safari Zebra.

Last of the alphabet.

The last chance.

McCory had decided, independently of Ted and Ginger, that he and the *SeaGhost* had a better chance than anyone else of finding another *SeaGhost*.

If he wasn't going to give her back to the Navy, he might as well use her. Devlin would have.

Do me proud, son.

So far, Kevin McCory wasn't very proud of what he'd done. Or if he had been, he'd changed his mind.

What he could do, though, was monitor the Navy's frequencies and be ready to step in. He was damn sure he could stop Ibrahim Badr.

If he could just handle all of the control stations by himself.

Ginger had said she'd help him, but there was no way in hell that he was going to further involve her.

All he had to do was learn the boat and her systems as well as he could, provision her, and be ready if he saw his chance.

Being ready meant learning to use the cannon and having the missiles prepared for launch.

McCory went aft to the cargo bay to load the launcher.

11

"Mr. Malgard, Admiral Bingham Clay," Matthew Andrews said, introducing them for the first time.

Malgard leaned forward slightly to shake the admiral's hand and offered his best smile. Despite the man's miniature stature, his hand was hard as steel, and his grip was firm. "Happy to meet you, Admiral."

"Mr. Malgard." Clay's voice was neutral.

Why was it that every Navy man he met lately treated him like a distant, uninvited cousin? Damn it, he was a patriot and a defense contractor who had given them a state of the art weapons system. He held contracts worth millions. He was getting tired of the sneers.

"No attack last night, Admiral?" he asked.

"No. Have a seat, Mr. Malgard."

Clay went around his gargantuan desk and sat in a swivel chair. Malgard and Andrews took seats on the sofa.

Both Clay and Andrews looked haggard, and Malgard understood why. He had spent the night on the sofa in his den with the TV on, sleeping fitfully, waiting for a news alert. His thinking was muddied by tendrils of fatigue.

His internal conviction that McCory had taken the *Sea Spectre*s had been shaken by the events at Camp Lejeune and Kings Bay. At first, he could not imagine McCory having either the guts or the emotional drive to attack naval defense installations with the boats. The Navy must be right, this Badr was behind it.

Then, the longer it took Chambers to run McCory down, he drifted back to his original theory. McCory had the boats, and out of some revenge-driven scenario, he was telling the Navy what he thought of it. Malgard kept thinking back to that phone call he had received from the pseudo attorney. If he had been willing to deal, maybe a couple hundred Marines would still be alive.

It was a heavy load to carry. He had to keep telling himself that he was not at fault. He had not made the fatal decisions.

Besides, he did not have the cash necessary to make deals with anyone. AMDI was up to its neck in loans.

Clay was waiting expectantly.

Malgard said, "I'm here to help in any way I can, Admiral. I'd like to be brought up-to-date on what you know, and perhaps I'll think of something that will assist in capturing the boats."

"Right now," Clay said, "we're worried less about regaining the boats than we are about blowing them out of the water."

"You are certain that the *Sea Spectre* is involved?"

Clay nodded toward Andrews. "Matt."

The intelligence chief leaned forward on the couch, his elbows resting on his knees. "The damage analysis is consistent with the use of the Mini-Harpoon missile. Those are available only at the testing ground, the Ship R&D Center, and aboard the *Sea Spectre*s. Except for the missiles aboard the stealth boats, the rest are accounted for. At Kings Bay, we had a sonar contact with the attack boat. It was making fifty knots. It was the *Sea Spectre*."

"There haven't been any radar contacts?" Malgard asked.

"Should there be?"

"I mean, was the boat's radar radiating?"

"Yes. A couple minimal contacts. At Kings Bay, the missiles were radar guided."

"Suggesting that someone who knows both radar and missiles was operating it."

"Badr has those specialties available to him," Andrews said.

"No one saw the boat?"

"Not as far as we know. We had two boats pursuing, but lost them and the ten men aboard them."

"You don't think the boat was being operated by one person, Admiral?"

Andrews shook his head. "There were at least two, one tending the helm and radar, and one manning the missile launcher. The speed with which the missiles were reloaded suggests a third man assisting. There may be a fourth man on the radar."

That was about what Malgard had thought. McCory had friends. Maybe he had hired Arabs. That would certainly account for the dead man at Pier Nine.

Where was Chambers?

"How about communications from the terrorists, Admiral? They usually have to brag."

Clay intervened. "That point has bothered us to some extent, Mr. Malgard. We suspect, however, that they're waiting until they're done."

"In a way," Andrews said, "we'd like to get the message, to feel like there's an end to it. Unfortunately, they have another seventy missiles."

The papers and TV had not mentioned the number of missiles fired. "Where's the *Prebble*?" Malgard asked.

"She has the counterstrike systems."

"She's in the area," Clay said. Malgard thought he could have been more specific.

"So," Andrews said, "any ideas, Mr. Malgard?"

"There are two vulnerabilities. Sonar and highly sensitive infrared detectors can pick up the *Sea Spectre* when she's at speed. If, during the next attack, we can concentrate enough sea and air power to force a high-speed escape, we can follow her."

"You're not telling us anything we don't already know," Andrews told him.

"We know the advantages and the limitations of the technology," Clay said. "What's more important here are the people involved. We've got fifty people from the CIA, the FBI, and the Navy examining the way Ibrahim Badr thinks. If we can pin down a pattern in his strategy or tactics, we can be waiting for him the next time."

Malgard felt a twinge of guilt race down his spine. He almost told them about McCory.

"We were damned certain," Clay went on, "that he was going to attack an installation early this morning, perhaps further south on the coast. But he didn't."

"Why were you so certain?"

"Badr likes symbolism, and this is the Fourth of July."

1030 hours, Kings Bay Submarine Support Base

Monahan stood at the dock head and watched the activity aboard the two salvage barges that had been maneuvered alongside the slip where *Pogy* had gone down. The upper four feet and antenna heads of her conning tower were above the water. The rubber-clad heads of divers emerged from the oily waters, then disappeared as they worked at getting temporary patches over the six-foot hole in her side. Air hoses snaked across the water, up the conning tower, then disappeared inside the submarine. They were already pumping air into some of her ballast tanks and sealed compartments.

Except for the clatter of machinery aboard the barges,

it was a morguelike atmosphere. People seemed to whisper, careful of disturbing the dead.

Monahan turned and walked along the quay, back toward the operations building.

He was feeling morose. He had called Mona earlier to
apologize for missing the picnic. Being a Navy wife, she
had understood, but Geoffrey and Mark, aged nine and
ten, had been less forgiving.

His khakis were rumpled from sleeping on a borrowed
cot the night before. He had only taken his shoes off,
expecting to be called at any moment, when Badr hit some
base in Florida.

The absence of an attack was almost frustrating, because it seemed like the only way he would be able to find
an enemy he couldn't see.

Inside the operations center, he checked the plotting
board. Bingham Clay was apparently giving some consid-
eration to Monahan's suggestion. Ships that had been further at sea were drawing closer to the coast. TF22 was
moving south now, a cluster of blue symbols off the
northern Florida coast. The *Prebble* was also continuing
southward.

The men at the communications consoles all had blue-
covered code books on the desks in front of them, flipping
through them as they conversed. With Badr in control of
a radio scrambler, and possibly scanning all the naval frequencies, they had been forced to encode messages man-
ually.

He picked up a phone and dialed the FBI headquarters
in Washington, asking for a deputy director named Bulwark, the man who had been assigned to Clay's request.

After identifying himself, he asked, ''Have you located
Kevin McCory?''

''Well, no, not just yet.''

How hard can it be to find a responsible citizen? ''What
seems to be the problem?''

"The address that Admiral Clay gave us was that of a marina in Fort Walton Beach. At one time, it was owned by Devlin McCory."

Barry Norman had told him all of that. "And?"

"Back in January of '87, something happened, and it was taken over by an insurance company. Kevin McCory left the area at about that time."

"So ask the insurance company where he is."

"Commander, it's the Fourth of July. Everything's closed for the day."

"Director Bulwark, people are dying whether it's a holiday or not. Start calling people at home."

1120 hours, Fort Pierce, Florida

"Harold Davis, huh? You have a card?"

He did have. Chambers used the Davis name frequently, and he had a variety of occupations listed on a variety of business cards. He gave Bernice the appropriate card.

Bernice was almost six feet tall, supporting a ton of white-gold hair. She was tanned the color of a Seminole and had black hawk eyes filled with suspicion.

"Wrong insurance company," she said.

"What?"

"Mac told me all about the shithead company that ripped off his daddy's marina. It wasn't Marathon Equitable."

"Well, no. We weren't the primary insuror. We had the secondary underwriting."

"And when those assholes finally settled last year, it liked to kill Mac."

The plastic nameplate taped to the front of the cash register read: Bernice Gold—Owner-Operator. Like a damned independent semi truck driver.

"Mrs. Gold, I don't know anythin' about the litigation.

My company carried a supplemental policy and, as I understand it, was just waitin' for the first company to reach agreement. All I know is that I'm supposed to find McCory and give him a check."

"How much?"

"I'm not at liberty to discuss that, Mrs. Gold."

Bernice Gold took a long swig from her tall, frosty can of Budweiser. Chambers was thirsty, but she didn't offer him a beer.

Bernice Gold eyed him for a long time, certainly with disfavor, then said, "Edgewater."

"Edgewater?"

"Mac bought a marina up there."

Chambers smiled at her.

1122 hours

Green had not been a popular color for automobiles for some time, Ibn el-Ziam thought. A lot of older cars were green, but very few of the newer models were painted green. It had helped him immensely in spotting the Ford Taurus that Rick Chambers was driving. A large number of people around the Miami marinas had remembered a man some of them called Davis, very tall and big, and driving a green Ford.

He had caught up with the green Ford and its driver in Fort Lauderdale, and he had been following him since. It was a boring existence. He had eaten nothing but American fast food. He had slept in the Pontiac's front seat outside of motels when Chambers stopped for the night.

Now it was Fort Pierce.

There seemed to be no end to the small towns along the eastern Florida coast. No end, also, to the marinas, salvage operations, and marine repair businesses that Chambers entered and left. And el-Ziam had been looking at an endless Atlantic Ocean for what felt like days.

So much useless water depressed him. He was ready to return to his homeland.

Chambers came out of the marina office, paused, and looked up at the sign that was lettered, "Gold and Silver." He was grinning widely as he threaded his way through the parking lot to his Ford.

There had been some sort of breakthrough, el-Ziam thought. He started the engine of the Pontiac, waited until Chambers had turned out of the lot, then backed out of his space and followed.

The city of Fort Pierce was draped in red and white bunting. A parade of bands, automobiles, horses and decorated trailers was assembling on a side street. Throngs of people dashed about, laughing and smiling. One day, el-Ziam would have an independence of his own to celebrate.

Chambers went right to a gas station.

El-Ziam drove on for a block, then stopped at another station and filled his own tank. He had the feeling that a long drive was ahead of him.

It was. When Chambers passed again, he drove only two blocks before turning inland, ignoring the coastal highway. He took the northbound on-ramp for Highway 95, and in seconds, had settled in at a steady seventy miles per hour.

El-Ziam stayed a mile back, driving the same speed, but keeping six or seven cars between the two of them. The man named Rick Chambers was a simpleton who thought himself invincible. He seemed intent upon what was ahead of him, and he never once looked back.

El-Ziam wondered how much farther, and how much longer, it would be before Chambers did whatever it was that he was supposed to do.

He assumed that Rick Chambers would kill the man named McCory.

Before or after Chambers located the boat?

The fate of McCory did not matter to el-Ziam. The fate of the boat did.

2040 hours, Edgewater

Ginger stacked cardboard boxes on the stern deck of *Kathleen,* hauling them up from the salon. She had come dressed to work, wearing Levi's and an old, faded blue shirt of McCory's, with a button-down collar.

McCory had backed the motor yacht partway into the dry dock, stern-to-stern with *SeaGhost,* and the pumps were transferring diesel fuel at 150 gallons per minute. He was aboard the stealth boat, manning the fuel nozzle.

One more tank to go.

While he waited, kneeling on the smooth afterdeck, head drawn back to avoid the fumes, he dreaded the next billing from his bulk fuel supplier.

The nozzle clicked off.

McCory withdrew the nozzle, replaced the filler cap, disconnected the grounding strap, and pressed the filler panel back into place. The panel hid all four filler tubes, blending in with the rest of the deck.

Sliding off the *SeaGhost* onto the stern platform of the *Kathleen,* he climbed the boarding ladder to the stern deck and shut down the pump. It took him five minutes to coil and stow the hose and pump, then remove the rest of the grounding straps.

"Last box, Captain, sir."

"This is not a good idea, Ginger. Why don't you take *Kathleen* back to the marina?"

"Not on your life."

"It could mean *your* life. I don't like that."

She moved up close to him in the dark, gripped his forearm, and looked up at him. "I haven't done anything meaningful since university environmental protests, Kevin, and those were kind of hollow. Don't deny me this."

Her voice was throaty, and her tone sincere.

"Ginger . . ."

"Please. I'll get off if you tell me to get off, but I'll hate you for it."

"Ah, damn."

"No, I won't hate you, but I'll be disappointed that I had the chance to contribute something and blew it."

"Even if it goes smoothly, you could lose your job. Ted tells me you could go to prison, along with me."

"There are better things than being a bank manager."

"Like what?"

"Like being with you."

"I'm broke."

"You just need a financial advisor."

"Back to the point," he told her. "I don't want you at risk."

"I don't want you at risk," she said.

"It's different."

"Bullshit."

"All I'm going to do is patrol the area. Probably, nothing will come of it."

"Then the risk is less."

"Go home, Ginger."

"I am home."

He gave up for the moment and descended to the side dock to take the cardboard boxes she shoved through the boarding gate. When they were stacked on the dock, he climbed back aboard the yacht, cranked up the engines, and moved her out to the finger pier. Together, they secured the hatches, then walked around to the dry dock. He went out the side dock and shut the sea door, then turned on the lights.

It took twenty minutes to load, then unpack the boxes. He'd brought linen, pillows, and blankets for a couple of the bunks, more coffee, a couple cases of beer and Coke, bread, condiments, hamburger, hot dogs, frozen potatoes, bacon, eggs. He was half afraid he'd be caught off-coast in daylight and have to hide out for a day.

Additionally, he added to his store of tools and repair items—epoxy glues and powder, fiberglass cloth, engine and pump seals and bearings, oil, and grease. There was a portable electric pump, wiring cables, hoses. McCory liked to be prepared for anything, and he liked to have it stowed away neatly.

He had also brought additional maps and charts for inland waterways. From the classified code book, he had made up a sheet of frequencies and encryption and scrambler modes for the naval and air force installations in the immediate vicinity. He taped the sheet to the bulkhead next to the communications console.

At 9:15, he opened the sea door and backed the *Sea-Ghost* out into the waterway.

Ginger sat down in the radar seat next to him. "Thank you."

"I still don't like it."

"But we're a team. You'd never get a missile off by yourself."

As they crept down the waterway, the night's fireworks displays erupted at Edgewater and New Smyrna Beach. Exploding star shells cascaded rivers of white fire, violet blossoms, and red and blue clusters.

"Pretty," Ginger said.

"Unless you get in real close," McCory told her.

12

Badr thought that his strategy was working well. It was evident in the radio traffic that had not been encoded between the Second Fleet headquarters and the ships of the task forces seeking him.

The United States Navy was converging on the southern coast of the continent, as they were expected to do.

The *Hormuz*, commanded by a reluctantly admiring Abdul Hakim, was still steaming steadily to the north. Hakim had faked breakdowns of his steam turbine twice in order to slow his pace, but he was now several hundred kilometers to the north and nearly a hundred kilometers off the coast.

Ibrahim Badr had ranged far ahead of the tanker, beginning his attacks in North Carolina, then working his way south. He had set up a direction for the United States Navy, and they were following it. They were so predictable. He judged the main task force to be about 150 kilometers north of them.

Now, there was the naval air station in Florida. This one did not even require that they move in close.

In the dark of the night, the *Sea Spectre* was ten kilometers from the coast, at rest. The sea swells were heavy,

172

suggesting an oncoming storm, and the boat bobbed up and down, rising several meters, then dropping. Amin Kadar sat at the dining table, gnawing on chunks of lamb left over from their meal. He stared out the window at the night, looking for whatever it was he longed for.

Heusseini and Kadar, after their assessments of the previous attacks, were certain that the small missiles had a range far greater than ten kilometers.

Because the search was concentrating toward the south, a great many Navy and Air Force search aircraft had been deployed from their normal bases into the area. Many of them were parked on the tarmac at the Mayport Naval Station.

Omar Heusseini sat at the commander's desk, grinning to himself.

Badr said, "Are we clear on the sequence?"

"Of course," Heusseini said. "We will launch eight missiles, utilizing the electro-optical targeting. At this distance, I will have the time I need to line up a missile visually, lock it on, then launch the next. After four missiles have been launched, we will move to another position, then launch four more. Then we will make our triumphant return to the *Hormuz*."

"Allah willing," Rahman said.

"Allah has been more than willing," Ibrahim Badr reminded him.

"But now we have dozens of hostile vessels and aircraft all around us."

"If they should get in our way, we will sink them," Badr said.

Kadar swung around from his view of the night and whatever was out there in it. "I would like that."

"Perhaps we will have the opportunity," Badr said. "Still, we must be careful. A confrontation with a major warship is not in my plans."

"Planning!" Kadar snorted. "It is planning that gets in the way of our cause. There is too much planning."

Like so many of his followers, the young Kadar was too accustomed to reaction. Violent reaction, of course, but unthinking.

"There are a great many targets available to us. Targets that do not shoot back. We serve Allah far better by seeking out such targets, Amin."

The young man frowned and turned back to his contemplation of the sea.

Badr waited a moment, nodding to himself, then said, "Let us begin."

The first four missiles launched without a single problem. American weapons had far fewer mechanical and electronic problems than did those of the Soviets.

Ibrahim Badr particularly enjoyed watching the video monitor as it gave him a view of the first missile homing in on an Air Force E-3 Sentry parked on the base. That was one Airborne Warning and Control craft that would never be loaned to the Saudis or the Israelis.

As a hundred million dollars disappeared into blackness, he thought that the American taxpayer should be screaming loudly. The admirals and generals should face offensives from without and from within.

Allah worked in countless ways.

0222 hours, 29° 20' North, 80° 15' West

The radio traffic out of CINCLANT had been hectic for the last minute. McCory hunched over the desk with headphones on, trying to decipher messages with coded words.

"Safari Bravo, Safari Echo to Safari Sector Four, code Pearl-Four-Six. Repeating. Jackhandle under attack, target reference grid Baker Two, two-four, nine-eight."

Shit.

They were using a distinctive map grid overlay to determine their coordinates, and it wouldn't correspond to anything McCory had on a chart or in the computer.

"Ginger, let's go north. See how fast you can go."

"Got it, Kevin."

He felt the *SeaGhost* heel over as she made the turn. The thrum of the rotary engines vibrating in the deck picked up tempo.

McCory scanned the sheet he had copied and taped to the bulkhead.

No Jackhandle.

He flipped through the pages of the frequency listings. There wasn't a Jackhandle identified there, either.

The sheet on the bulkhead listed all of the major Georgia and Florida naval installations. The target could have been Air Force or Coast Guard, but he didn't have information on them. He picked the southern Georgia and northern, east coast Florida bases and began entering the digits for their radio frequencies into the radio, tapping away almost feverishly.

Mostly gibberish.

The scrambling and encryption modes had all been changed, and it took time to try each of the four modes on his black boxes. Anytime something came in clear, that he could identify with some certainty, he entered the new modes and codes on his cheat sheet.

From his momentary contacts, he figured out that aircraft were being scrambled all over the Eastern Seaboard.

He found Safari Echo talking to Safari Bravo. ". . . all three Deuces ranging at seventy miles."

The Deuces were probably helicopters. ASW, he guessed, sowing sonar buoys.

Twenty minutes later, he found Jackhandle. The code names and the modes for the encryption machines were different, but the frequency was for the Mayport Naval Station. He jotted the new data on his chart.

The excited, almost nonstop chatter also gave them away as the target site. The radio operator couldn't keep the tension and adrenaline out of his voice.

McCory pulled the headphones off, dropped them on the desktop, and went forward to stand behind Ginger. Looking at the back of her platinum head, watching the intensity with which she peered through the windshield or scanned the instrument panel, he damned himself for letting her become involved.

"Well, do something," she said. "Find the bastard."

"We're looking," McCory said, though he was thinking that he wouldn't look too hard.

Leaning over her right shoulder, he tapped the "NAV MAP" pad on the keyboard, then entered upper left and lower right coordinates. Pressed "EXC."

Ginger automatically hit the monitor's number four selection, and the map came up on the screen. She was getting pretty good with the systems.

Along the gray-shaded coast, Jacksonville was shown, but Mayport was not. He reached out and tapped the city with his forefinger.

"They've attacked Jacksonville?" Ginger asked.

"Mayport. It's a Navy base. I don't know what the damages are, but it sounds as if they were hit by eight missiles."

"It's what? Eighty miles away?"

"About that, hon. But we don't know where Badr launched from. He could be fifty miles out."

McCory scanned the seas ahead. They were thirty miles off the coast in a clear, starry night. Running lights on the right oblique suggested a ship of some size, maybe six or seven miles away. The sea was choppy, but the *SeaGhost* leveled it. She was riding smoothly, the visual sensation of her speed of sixty knots difficult to pin down.

In the far distance, he saw the lights of a few aircraft.

As they neared the scene, he thought the air traffic would become congested.

Moving over to the radar/fire control station, McCory settled into the seat and studied Ginger by the glow of the panel lights. She gripped the wheel with determination. Her face and long throat were in profile, and though she seemed very intent, she also appeared particularly vulnerable.

Jesus, this is stupid.

"You know, Ginger, when we reach Mayport, about all that's going to happen is that fifty or sixty ships and aircraft looking for a terrorist will have a chance to spot us. We happen to look exactly like the terrorist."

She jerked her head toward him. "You don't think they'd shoot at us?"

"I suspect they're mad enough."

"But you said we have the best chance of catching Badr."

"I did say that. We can match him for speed and weaponry, if we locate him. In my zeal, however, I overlooked the fact that the Navy won't care who's driving the boat, as long as it's a *SeaGhost*."

"If they can't see him, they can't see us," she said logically.

"Maybe. But they've got an awful lot of people looking."

"What's the body count now?" she asked.

McCory sighed. His resolve was wavering. "The risks are damned high, hon."

"Go see if you can pick up a newscast."

0246 hours, 31° 9' North, 79° 12' West

In the CIC, the plotting screen had the grid code-named Baker Two overlaid on it, the thin green lines identifying the coordinates they were working from. Norman studied the plot, copying the new positions of ships to the picture he maintained in his mind.

Prebble had a slight lead over the rest of TF22. *America* and her escorts were nine miles behind them. From the south, the *Oliver H. Perry* and her task force were moving toward them at flank speed, but they were over three hundred miles away.

A steadily expanding yellow stain was centered on the plot.

A P-3 Orion out of Mayport, flying the coast at 30,000 feet, had observed the missile launch. Backtracking the tapes of their infrared sensors, they had identified the ignition points, located some nine miles off the coast of Mayport. That was the starting point, the center of the pale yellow area on the plot.

In the twenty-five minutes since the missiles were launched, figuring the *Sea Spectre*'s speed of sixty-five knots, the target boat could have moved almost twenty-nine miles in any direction, except inland. And maybe even that, Norman thought. The *Sea Spectre* seemed to have too damned many outrageous capabilities.

Already, the search area covered around 150 square miles. Within the yellow half-circle were two Coast Guard cutters and fifteen search aircraft, including the *Prebble*'s helicopters. The *Prebble* herself was still sixty miles north of the search area.

Albert Perkins shook his head in resignation as he crossed the CIC from a communications console. His red hair absorbed the red light of the center.

"Commander?"

"Twenty-two aircraft damaged or destroyed, Captain. They hit a fuel depot, and the fires are still out of control. No firm numbers on fatalities yet, but they expect it to go over fifty."

One goddamned boat, Norman thought. In the hands of a madman.

Perkins looked at the plot, and his face exuded his sadness. "We're going to miss him again, aren't we?"

"We'll intercept the target area in another hour, Al, but by then we'll have over three hundred square miles of possibility. It'll be up to the choppers."

Perkins checked his watch. "We'll have to bring them back for refueling in another hour and a half."

Norman nodded absently, thinking about something else.

"Al, we had early morning strikes on the second, third, and fifth. He skipped the fourth for some reason."

"Yes, sir."

"Lejeune, Kings Bay, and now Mayport. It's three hundred and fifty miles from Lejeune to Kings Bay, but only about fifty between Kings Bay and Mayport. There's no pattern in the distance between targets. Not yet, anyway."

"No, sir. Random selection."

"Except that they tend to go south," Norman said. "That's a mild trend. The only other pattern is that he goes away somewhere during the day and hides, then makes his move in the early morning."

"Perhaps, Captain, Badr wants us to feel the randomness, yet focus on the time and the southern movement. That's why he skips a day, that's why he makes a big jump, then a small one."

"What would you do next, Al? If you were Badr?"

"Southern Florida, sir? Even around into the Caribbean?"

"Keep in mind we've set up a mild pattern. We're leading the U.S. Navy into our thinking."

Perkins closed his eyes for a moment. "Maybe I'd shoot back to the north."

"Uh-huh. Me, too, Al. Then's there's one other thing."

"Yes, sir. Where does he go during the day?"

Norman studied the plot. There were vast, empty spaces available to Badr. "That boat could park on the surface somewhere lonely and go unnoticed during daylight hours, Al. But, at minimum, with the distance he's covered since June twenty-seventh, he'd have used half his fuel load. I'd think it was more than that, unless he's alternating the use of the two boats. And unless that sunken Zodiak had a few floating containers of' food, Badr and his buddies would be damned hungry by now."

"He's got a support ship somewhere."

"What we need to do, Al, is find us a suitable ship that's been in the area since June twenty-seventh."

"I could request the plot tapes from CINCLANT, Captain."

"Good idea, Al. Do that."

2215 hours 16Jan87, Fort Walton Beach

Kevin had taken the Colleen, *a forty-foot fiberglass sportfisherman that McCory had designed and built in 1982 on a week-long fishing cruise into the Gulf. He had two well-heeled couples on board, who McCory suspected were less interested in fishing than in other games.*

It wasn't until after Kevin came home from the Navy that they got into chartering. McCory preferred being around the marina, working on the boats, to putting up with novice fisherman, but Kevin seemed to like it. So McCory had turned the Kathleen *over to him until the new boat was finished.*

Kevin wanted to build a couple more boats and hire some captains to run them, but McCory was resisting. He didn't want to infringe unduly on the trade of the charter boats that home-ported in Marina Kathleen.

As was his custom, McCory took a late turn through the marina, checking the locks on the maintenance buildings, making certain kids hadn't gotten into the boats sitting on cradles in the storage yard and cautioning the party boats to keep the noise within limits.

The new floating docks were complete on the west end, jutting out from the central, raised dock, and most of the permanent residents had been re-installed in their old slips. The crane had been moved to the east side of the marina, and the barge tied alongside it was piled high with old planks, piers, and railings.

The renovation was expensive as hell, more than he'd first guessed, and he'd had to float a couple large loans. Still, the results would keep Marina Kathleen in competition with the bigger outfits. He'd had four or five offers for the marina, since good beach-front property was sky-rocketing in price, but he'd turned them all down. McCory didn't want money, he wanted the freedom to be himself.

McCory walked along the new central dock, patting the steel railing with his hand. It didn't have the character of the old two-by-four railings, but it didn't have the splinters either. Out at the end of the "E" floating dock—McCory had placed the younger, louder crowd on "E"—the Darkins were hosting thirty or forty of their neighbors aboard their fifty-foot Hatteras. Tinkly laughter and the guitar of Chet Atkins wafted on the air.

As he walked by the base of "C" dock, McCory looked down to see Jefferson, a young black writer, sitting in the cockpit of his elderly sloop, Muse. He had a yellow light hung from the boom, and he was drinking wine and writing in a legal-size tablet.

McCory stopped and leaned on the railing. "Hope you're not writin' about me, Jeff."

"Oh, hi, Devlin. I'd like to write about you."

"No, you wouldn't. Not enough flash."

"Bet there's more than you let on. How'd you get that Navy Cross?"

"Short story. My destroyer went out from under me at Midway."

"That's it?"

"Well, the lifeboat me and twenty other guys were in was holed pretty bad, and the engine wouldn't run. I just fixed it before it sank completely. That was my job, that's all."

"Hell, Devlin, I think there's a whole novel in that. Why don't you and I . . ."

McCory was suddenly aware of red-yellow light behind him. He spun around and looked toward shore.

Maintenance Building One was on fire.

The flames leaped from the windows, licked at the old siding, climbing high. Strange shadows flickered on the ground.

"Jesus Christ!" Jefferson yelled.

McCory pushed off the railing and ran toward shore. Damn, there were flammables. . . .

The explosion rocked the marina. The structure disappeared in a yellow holocaust. The concussion knocked McCory into the railing. He rebounded off the steel and landed on his side on the dock.

Shaking his head, trying to clear it.

Up onto his hands and knees.

The flames roared, surprisingly loud, fed by drums of solvents and paint. He could feel the heat.

He regained his feet and stumbled toward the office, thinking telephone.

At the end of the dock, he reached for the screen door handle.

The whole screen door came off as the office exploded.

McCory saw a microsecond of white flash before the door handle imbedded itself deep in his chest.

The *SeaGhost* rocked a little, from side to side, as she cruised eastward at an angle to the swells of the sea. She was making twenty-five knots.

The radio was set to Safari Bravo's command net, and the chatter between vessels and aircraft was heavy, but terse and vague as a result of all the coded words. McCory had gone active on the radar for one sweep, freezing the screen picture into computer memory. That one sweep on active had intensified the radio traffic. He interpreted some of it to mean that aircraft were moving in on them and had told Ginger to go to top speed for five minutes, removing them from the scene of his radar emanation.

Within minutes, there were three airplanes overhead, but the search pattern drifted away from them after a while.

He put the computer-stored image on the screen and studied it. Thirty miles to the north were at least a dozen ships. Two hundred and fifty miles to the south were another half dozen in a cluster. Sporadically aligned to the east were independent ships, probably commercial, in the normal sea-lanes. Again, he had not had the antenna aimed upward, so he had probably missed most of the aircraft. Along the coast, the ground clutter feedback obscured what were probably additional ships. Coast Guard, maybe.

If he were able to identify a couple of those blips as specific ships, then pinpoint their coordinates by radio reports, he might have been able to recreate the Baker Two map grid. He didn't, however, think that it was going to happen in this lifetime.

They cruised eastward, again at twenty knots.

McCory had a vision of his sonar signature being picked up by some submarine in the region. Conning tower rising suddenly from the sea, water sluicing off it. Gun crews spilling out of the hatches.

He got up and went to the sonar station, which was set on passive. Pulling the headset on, he listened for a while to sea noises. Big fish, maybe. Nothing that he could identify as man-made.

When he took the earphones off, Ginger asked, "Getting nervous?"

"Hell, yes. You?"

"I've been nervous since Ponce de Leon. You want to take the helm while I try out your bathroom?"

They switched places. McCory tried all of the modes on the primary screen. Night-vision video showed him a lot of sea. A few running lights and anti-collision strobe lights on aircraft in the distance. Infrared was cool, except for distant hot spots which he suspected were generated by aircraft exhaust pipes.

There was nothing of particular interest out there.

Badr could be, and probably was, sixty miles away. Getting further away.

The only thing closing in was the United States Navy. If they spotted the *SeaGhost,* they would probably shoot first and talk later, if there was anything left to which they could talk. If he was in a listening condition, he would be listening to charges of treason.

Ginger came back as he was turning to a heading of 190 degrees. Moving into the swells, the ride evened out.

"Trying another direction?"

"Yes. A direction for home."

She sat in the radar operator's seat. He didn't think there was any disappointment showing in her face.

"It does seem a little futile," she said.

"If I'm going to do this, I'm going to have to plan a little better," McCory said. "Racing off to where Badr was doesn't do much good."

He shoved the throttles in, felt the *SeaGhost* rise to the power.

"Should I make some coffee?"

"It's almost breakfasttime, why not?" McCory said.

Ginger moved back to the galley, and McCory half-concentrated on the empty sea ahead. The star shine gleamed on wave caps.

He wasn't paying much attention to the radio, which was channeled through a speaker in the bulkhead next to his right shoulder. Only the excitement in the voice jarred him awake.

"Safari Echo, Deuce Three. I've got a hot target."

"Three, this is Echo. Target coordinates?"

The pilot read off some Baker Two numbers. "I'm not getting a radar return on the target, but the infrared's screaming. It's the same picture we've had during sea trials up north."

"Let's have some sonobuoys as soon as you get in close, Deuce Three. And go to Tac-Two. Let's get off the command net."

The voices disappeared as they moved to another frequency, replaced by cryptic messages among ships of the task force.

From what McCory could deduce, Safari Bravo had themselves a target.

Ginger had been listening. "They found him!"

"They found us."

"No!"

"Yes."

McCory pulled the throttles back as he made a 180-degree turn. He didn't know where the helicopter was, but he thought it would be tracking on the heading he had shown them.

He settled on a heading of 355 degrees. The speed came down to twelve knots, and he held it there.

Two minutes later, he saw the helicopter sliding by on his left. It was several hundred feet high and a half mile away, and it obviously didn't see him as it went by. A minute after that, he picked up its lights on the rearview screen.

He sighed.

Ginger came up behind him and rested her hands on his shoulders. "That was close, I guess."

"Yeah. It may take us a while to get home."

"I thought this thing was invisible."

"So did I, but apparently we leave an infrared trail at speed."

"What speed?"

"I wish I knew."

McCory waited another five minutes, then turned to a heading of 270 degrees. He would hold that for ten minutes before again aiming toward the south.

Through the left-side windows, he saw the dance of the strobe light as the helicopter began circling.

All around them, in fact, he could see more aircraft lights approaching.

1845 hours, Edgewater

Rick Chambers was wearing his silver-gray suit. He hadn't had a chance to have it dry-cleaned, and it was wrinkled badly, though not as badly as his only other choice. The shirt was fresh, a blue cotton with a spread collar.

He was tired, and he was getting hungry again, though he didn't feel like having another hamburger. He'd grabbed one yesterday, after getting into town. It was probably the reason why he'd missed McCory.

The girl in the office hadn't known where he'd gone, only that he taken his boat, now renamed the *Kathleen*, and gone somewhere. She had no idea in the world when he'd be back.

He'd had another hamburger for breakfast, when he

called Malgard. He called the office and got referred to a Virginia number.

"I found him, Justin."

"It's about damned time. Where?"

"He's got a marina in Edgewater. Funny thing, it's named the Marina Kathleen, just like the old man's was."

"You find the boats?"

"No. In fact, though, McCory's not around. He left sometime last night and wasn't back when I checked at five this mornin'."

"Well, you hang around until he shows up."

'And then?"

"Just what we discussed."

"I can do it like I did the first one. Accidents will happen."

"No, damn it! That turned out to be a hell of a mess. The newspapers didn't let it die for a long time. You just locate the boats, then take him out. Very clean, now, Rick. He just disappears."

"Gotcha, chief. Write out my bonus check."

When he'd gotten back to the marina, the *Kathleen* was back in its slip. Chambers parked across the street, down half a block from the marina office, under a stand of palm trees, and waited.

He waited forever.

He fumbled with his binoculars from time to time but saw no movement aboard the boat.

He pulled the Beretta from its holster and double-checked the nine millimeter loads in the magazine.

He fidgeted.

At eleven, he left the car and walked down the street to buy two hamburgers, fries, and a milkshake.

At 11:40, McCory appeared on the deck of his boat. He messed around for a while, hosing it off and polishing some of the chromework.

A little after noon, he went up to the office and disappeared inside. He didn't reappear until after five, going back down to his boat. Chambers left the car several times, taking walks along the street, but staying close to the marina.

Boring, boring, boring.

Chambers had another pair of hamburgers.

At a quarter of seven, McCory left the boat, dressed in Levi's and a blue T-shirt. He walked up the ramp, bypassed the office, and got into an old pickup in the parking lot.

Chambers started the Ford.

McCory left the lot, headed south.

Chambers let a Volkswagen and a Camaro get between them before he pulled away from the curb.

It was a short trip, maybe four or five miles.

He almost missed it. As he went by a place called Barley's Marine Refitters, a conglomeration of old boats and old structures, he saw the blue pickup pulling up to a dilapidated building on the shore.

He drove on by and, a mile later, found a place to make a U-turn.

Coming back, he stopped short of his destination by a quarter-mile, pulling off the road to park in a clump of palmetto.

He checked the Beretta again, then got out of the car and walked along the road verge.

There was a gate in the chain-link fence at the refitting place, but it was open.

Chambers scanned the yard but didn't see any movement inside. The pickup sat nosed up to the boat house. He couldn't see any lights on inside, then noticed that all of the windows were filled with plywood.

Good place to hide a stolen boat. There were a couple more of the boat houses to the south, also.

He looked up and down the road. A few cars moved

along it, ignoring him as they shot by. Down the way, a pizza joint was doing a brisk business. Hot rods and custom trucks were parked all around it.

He walked through the gate and started down the slope toward the boat house. It was still light out, but he figured, what the hell? It was isolated, and if Malgard's boats were inside, it was as good a place as any other.

13

1847 hours, Mayport

Except for the disaster on the tarmac, Mayport Naval
Station appeared secure. The fire at the fuel depot had
been quenched in midmorning. A hazy pall hung over the
base, and the odor of burnt rubber and paint drifted in the
still air.

Jim Monahan had spent most of the day in the operations center, following the search tracking sequence of
TF22, Safari Bravo.

Safari Echo was no longer with them.

At four in the morning, shortly after he had arrived, he
had talked to Admiral Clay in Norfolk.

He had provided a concise damage report. "The same
story as the first two, Admiral."

"You really think we should be in the defense business,
Jim?" Clay asked. His tone was less sarcastic than it was
disgusted.

"We're going to get them, Admiral."

"I have a request from Norman. He wants to steam
northward, fifty miles off the coast."

"Perhaps he knows something we don't," Monahan
said.

"At this point, everyone seems to know something I don't know," the admiral said.

"The pattern, if there is one, suggests Badr is headed south."

"Norman thinks that's intentional. He tells me that, even if Badr hits an installation in southern Florida, he's going to switch on us, go north, and do it abruptly. What do you think, Jim?"

Monahan didn't like command decisions, suddenly. He knew he wasn't making this one, but Clay liked sounding boards. His response skipped around the edge. "You know Captain Norman, sir. My impression is that he's got some savvy."

"He does that. I'm going to give him his way, but only with the *Prebble*. We'll keep TF22 down your way. I'm going to divert the *Oliver H. Perry* slightly north and about a hundred miles offshore. Norman's certain there's a support ship we should be picking up on."

"I agree with Captain Norman in that respect, sir."

"All right, then. You call me if you get any intuitive ideas."

"Are we down to that? To intuition?"

"Nothing else is working. What's my casualty count, Jim?"

"Fifty-four, Admiral. Most of them resulted from the explosion at the fueling depot. They had been going all night, turning aircraft around."

"It's a damned sorry business," Bingham Clay said, and hung up.

Monahan took a nap for a couple of hours, then shaved and spent the rest of the day reviewing damage reports and following the progress, or lack of it, of the search efforts.

Clay called him back just before seven.

"Jim, I've got a report from the FBI here. Kevin McCory's got himself a marina in Edgewater, Florida. I think they finally called the IRS and got the address. The insurance company provided some additional data, and there are copies of some court papers.''

"Edgewater? That's just down the coast from here. I thought he was on the Gulf Coast.''

"He might have wanted to be. From what I've got here, Kevin McCory was more or less run out of town after Devlin McCory was killed.''

"Killed? What was that?''

"Hold on,'' Clay said. "It's in here somewhere. Yes. Devlin McCory died in an explosion which all but destroyed his marina in Fort Walton Beach. There was some brouhaha with the bank and insurance company. At the time of the accident, the older McCory was heavily into some bank for cash to renovate the place. Apparently, the insurance policy rider didn't cover the costs as it was supposed to, and the bank foreclosed, with the insurance company buying up the pieces. Kevin McCory disagreed and brought suit. He also took off with the company's files and some boat his father had built, but which the insurance outfit claimed. The insurance company treated him like a fugitive, but the local sheriff apparently didn't agree.''

"Jesus. Was it ever settled?'' Monahan asked.

"Yes, about eighteen months ago. This doesn't say what the settlement was, I don't think. Hang on.''

Monahan waited, listening to the sound of rustling paper.

"Yes. There's a court order here, an agreement signed by the insurance company and McCory's lawyer. The company paid off a quarter million and let him keep the boat. I don't . . . son of a bitch!''

"What's the matter, Admiral?''

"Guess who the attorney was?''

"I don't know, sir.''

"Daimler. Theodore Daimler.''

Monahan knew the name from somewhere. It flitted

around for a bit before he grabbed it. "The guy up on the Chesapeake who had his boat stolen."

"That's it, Jim."

"I was going to call McCory, but I think I'll grab a chopper and fly down there," Monahan said.

"Go."

1850 hours, Edgewater

McCory heard someone banging on the door.

Ginger.

Damn.

He had been planning to slip away earlier tonight, leaving her behind. She'd be mad as hell, but he had decided that half of his anxiety was having her in harm's way.

All of the lights inside the dry dock were on, as well as the standard lights in the cabin and cargo bay of the *SeaGhost*. It still felt lonely.

He was double-checking the missile connections on the launcher. Resigned to her catching him in the middle of a double-cross, he left the cargo bay, crossed along the corridor, and emerged from the hatchway. Leaping the short chasm to the side dock, he walked to the door.

Flipping the dead bolt, he pulled the door open.

It wasn't Ginger.

The man appeared hard. Angles and planes in his face. Military haircut. Death in his eyes. In his hand, too.

He gestured with the automatic. "Back it up. Slow. Keep your hands in sight."

Navy? How'd they figure it out?

McCory took a few steps backward and kept his hands out in front of him. He was dismayed that they had found him so easily, that he and Daimler hadn't even opened negotiations.

"Hey, we can talk about this."

The man ignored him, stepped inside, and closed the door. He didn't lock it.

He looked around the lighted dry dock, nodded as if to himself, and said, "Where's the other one?"

"The other one?"

"The *Sea Spectre*."

"Got me. I understand some terrorist got it."

"You have it hidden in one of these other boat houses?" He used the automatic to point south.

"As far as I know, they're empty."

He stood there, thinking. He wasn't happy, and the expression on his face hardened, if that were possible.

"Where are the cops? The FBI?" McCory asked.

The hard eyes refocused on him. "There won't be any. You and me, we're going to wait a few hours until full dark, then we'll take a little trip in that boat."

What the hell?

McCory couldn't figure it. Who *was* this guy?

Then he had it.

"You work for AMDI, right?"

"I work for myself."

Advanced Marine, or Malgard, or whatever his name was, wouldn't want the boat connected in any way with McCory. That might make the Navy investigate. For that matter, they wouldn't want McCory found, at all.

"You got some rope around here?" The man backed away a couple of feet, kept his gun trained on McCory's midsection, and let his eyes dart around the dock head. He spotted the coils of marine line hanging on a nail driven into one of the cradle timbers on the side dock.

"Over there. Come on, move."

McCory led the way down the side dock and stopped in front of the lines. The man pulled up behind him.

"Hand me one of those ropes over your shoulder. Real easy, now."

McCory lifted a heavy thirty-foot coil off the nail and tossed it over his shoulder.

"Hey!"

He spun to his left, crouching, whipping his right leg out, and swinging it.

It worked for Chuck Norris every time, but not for McCory. His ankle caught the man in the knee but didn't topple him or sweep his legs out from under him.

He went off balance, though, shuffling his feet to regain equilibrium. Several coils of the rope hung on the wrist of his gun hand, and McCory grabbed the line and jerked as hard as he could.

The line clamped tight around his wrist and the hammer of the automatic, pulling it forward and aiming the muzzle down.

The gun went off.

Loud in the confined space, startling McCory.

The asshole dropped it.

McCory turned for the open hatch of the *SeaGhost,* took five running steps, and leaped headfirst through the hatch. He tucked his chin down, landed on the back of his neck and shoulders in the cross-corridor, and rolled over onto his feet. He grabbed the corner of the central corridor and pulled himself around it.

It took him five seconds to reach the commander's desk, paw at the drawer, and find one of the Brownings. He slapped a magazine in and thumbed the safety off.

Pulled the slide back to inject the first round.

The boat rocked slightly as the man came aboard.

"Come on, McCory. You ain't goin' nowhere."

McCory moved aft toward the communications console and slid along the bulkhead until he reached the central corridor.

"Where you at?"

McCory peeked around the corner. The man was standing in the juncture of the corridors, his gun held out in front of him. The light of the cargo bay defined him in the doorway. He saw McCory's head and shifted his gun hand.

"Just step . . ."

McCory shot him.

The report numbed his ears.

The cabin filled with the stink of cordite.

McCory wasn't a marksman, but his target was large and close. The slug caught him high in the chest and slammed him backward into the doorjamb of the cargo bay.

He was propped against the wall for a full two seconds as his knees wobbled. The gun tumbled from his hand and hit the deck. His eyes held total surprise.

Then he collapsed and died.

Or maybe it was the other way around.

McCory was numb, his ears ringing.

1854 hours

Ibn el-Ziam had heard both shots. The spacing was awkward, perhaps a minute and a half apart.

He sidled along the front of the building to the door and tried the handle. It turned easily, and he pushed it open a few centimeters.

Inside, it was brightly lit. He leaned close to the gap and scanned a narrow area. Seeing no movement, he edged the door open a little further.

Still, he saw no one.

But there was the boat. Ibrahim Badr had been correct. He frequently was.

El-Ziam stepped inside.

The boat moved.

A head appeared in the hatchway near the dock, and el-Ziam slipped back outside and pulled the door nearly shut.

It was not Chambers.

He assumed it was McCory.

He watched for another minute, then saw Chambers. McCory was dragging his body out of the boat.

Softly, he closed the door. Obviously, McCory was going to be busy for a little while.

While scanning the empty boat yard, he pondered his moves. Colonel Badr wanted the boat, and el-Ziam had a memorized list of approximate positions for the *Hormuz*. He was certain he could operate the boat. The only unknown was the fuel state. If there was enough fuel, he would take the boat out late at night. If the fuel was low, he would simply blow it up, drive to Miami, and fly to Beirut. He would no longer be needed.

From inside his waistband, el-Ziam withdrew the .22 caliber Bernadelli, found the silencer in his pocket, and screwed it in place. It was already cocked, and he slid the safety off.

Again, he turned the door handle slowly and eased it open.

McCory was less than five meters away, his arms wrapped around the chest of the dead man, dragging him toward the door. McCory held an automatic pistol in his right hand for some reason.

El-Ziam shoved the door fully open.

It squeaked.

McCory looked up. "Oh, shit!"

El-Ziam raised the pistol and fired.

Unfortunately, he shot the dead man again as McCory pushed the body aside and dove toward the floor.

McCory fired as he fell, and the bullet whined past el-Ziam's head. He dodged sideways, lining the Bernadelli once again.

He had McCory sighted perfectly.

When McCory's second shot hit him in the right cheekbone.

His vision blurred, then blacked out entirely.

Allah.

1951 hours

The Sikorsky Sea King set down in the middle of the street, amazing a few drivers who had been forced to a stop. They clambered out of their cars and stared. Dust and paper litter swirled away from the rotor blast.

Monahan slid the door back and dropped to the pavement. He waved off the copilot as he ran for the curb, and the helicopter lifted off immediately.

He looked around, spotted the office on the other side of the parking lot, and started toward it.

Down in the marina, people emerged from their boat cabins to check on the ruckus. Two women stood outside the office, the door open behind them. Monahan strode purposefully across the lot and up to them.

"I'm looking for Kevin McCory."

One of the women, a girl really, said, "What are you? A captain?"

He smiled at her. "Commander Monahan. Is McCory around?"

"No," the girl told him. "He left an hour ago."

"Do you know where he went? It's important."

"He was supposed to come to my boat for dinner tonight, but he had to work," the older woman said. It was difficult to tell her age. In retirement, certainly, but she had damned nice legs under the shorts.

"Do you know where he's working, Mrs. . . . ?"

"Kuntzman. But people call me Mimi. What's the Navy want with Kevin?"

"It's . . . kind of like consulting."

"Well, I'm pretty sure he went up to Barley's place. He's got a big boat he's working on."

"Where is this Barley place?" Monahan asked.

The girl smiled at him. Perhaps she liked uniforms. She was examining his hand. Looking for a ring?

"Five miles down the coast," Kuntzman said.

Monahan sighed and looked around. "Is there someplace where I could rent a car?"

"Ah, you don't need to do that, Commander. I'll take you down," Kuntzman said.

"I'd really appreciate that."

"Debbie, I'm going to take the *Camrose*."

"Don't scratch it," Debbie said. "He'll dock my pay, and there isn't that much left to dock."

"C'mon, Commander. We'll go this way."

Monahan followed her around the office, through a chain-link gate, and down a ramp. She sure had nice legs.

2012 hours

An hour after he had killed two men, McCory was still in shock.

That made three in a week. Little over a week.

They were going to put him away forever.

He didn't know what the hell he was doing.

There had been some thought of loading the body of Chambers into the back of the truck, driving somewhere remote, and dumping it.

He had been right about Chambers. The man's wallet held two driver's licenses, one in the name of Richard Chambers and one in the name of Harold Davis. He decided the correct name was Chambers when he found an ID card listing Chambers as an assistant vice president of Advanced Marine Development, Incorporated.

For a moment there, his shock had been overcome by his rage. The bastards would have killed him to protect the secret of the *SeaGhost*'s origins. For the ten-thousandth time, he again questioned whether or not the explosions in Fort Walton Beach were accidental or not. He would have Daimler look into Chambers's history, see how long he had been working for Malgard.

McCory sat there on the deck in the corridor for a couple of minutes, holding his Browning in one hand and the dead man's wallet in the other. Finally, he had roused himself, shoved the wallet back into the man's coat pocket, and picked up his gun from the deck. He didn't even think about fingerprints. He inserted the gun back into the holster under Chambers's armpit, then got up and wrestled the body upright, dragging it to the hatchway.

The body was heavy, and it took some time to get it back onto the dock.

Where in hell will I dump it?

He knew he wasn't thinking too clearly, but he didn't worry about it. There was blood on his hands from the chest wound, though it hadn't really bled profusely. He was still gripping the Browning tightly in his hand.

Why?

The smoking gun. The killer weapon.

Jesus. They'll fry me.

Damn, the body was heavy. The limp feet dragged on the chipped concrete of the dock head.

He should just call the cops, explain his way out of this thing. AMDI sent a hired killer, after all.

The door squeaked.

McCory looked up and saw a handsome, well-dressed man with a long gun standing in the doorway.

The gun moved, and McCory didn't even think. He pushed the body away and fell down, squeezing the trigger twice.

And then he had two bodies.

His first reaction was to abandon everything and run for the truck. He'd successfully hidden himself and the *Kath-*

leen from the insurance company for years. He'd do it again.

Then he pulled the other body out of the doorway, closed the door, and locked it. He shoved the Browning into the waistband of his jeans. Though he felt as if he might gag, he knelt beside the body and patted the pockets until he found a wallet and a passport.

Francisco Cordilla? Who in hell is Francisco Cordilla? My God, they're coming out of the woodwork.

There was nothing to identify him beyond a Spanish name and address in either his wallet or passport. He was carrying a lot of money, both U.S. and Spanish bills.

Leaving the bodies sprawled on the dock head, McCory went back to the *SeaGhost,* stumbled inside, and got himself a Dos Equis from the refrigerator. He sat in the banquette and took deep breaths and deep draughts of the dark ale.

Time slipped by jerkily, the minutes racing, then dragging their feet.

Christ, call the cops, you jerk.

An AMDI assassin would strengthen McCory's case against the company.

Or would it? AMDI was just trying to get its boat back, and its repo man was iced by the thief.

Who was the other one?

He thought about the bodies.

Looked at his watch.

Didn't want to touch the bodies. Not again.

Had to do something.

And McCory finally decided to go chase Ibrahim Badr. He had worked out a feasible plan earlier in the day. He needed to make an early start, though, before Ginger caught up with him.

Ginger.

Thinking about her forced him into action. She might show up at any moment. Taking one last gulp from the bottle, he went up to the dock and devoted ten minutes to loading the bodies back aboard the *SeaGhost*. He laid them out, side by side, in an aft corner of the cargo bay, then tossed a tarp over them.

He would drop them over the side on his way north. At the moment, it didn't seem as if he had anything else to lose. He could devote his whole being to the task of running Badr down.

McCory activated the instrument, radar, and sonar consoles. He started the engines.

Climbing back to the dock, he went to the front of the building and shut off the lights. The interior lights of the *SeaGhost*, in the standard white mode, appeared spooky through the bronzed windows. A white glare from the open hatch bathed the side dock.

He walked out to the end of the dock and raised the sea door by hand.

Heard the deep gurgling of a V-8 marine engine.

It sounded suspiciously like *Camrose*.

While he stood there, the bow of his aged Chris Craft nosed inside the dry dock.

Mimi Kuntzman said, "Hi, there, Kevin!"

0340 hours, Norfolk

Ibrahim Badr had not thought that he would see the Chesapeake Bay Bridge ever again, and in reality, he did not see it clearly. It was very dark, and the skies were hung with low clouds.

Through the windshield, the bridge lights were visible, as were the unceasing strobe lights that warned aircraft. In the video monitor, it was a ghostly structure that quickly passed out of the camera's vision as the *Sea Spectre* raced beneath it at fifty knots.

To the north were the running lights of several ships

moving up the bay. Amin Kadar had identified their passive sonar signatures as those of medium-sized commercial craft.

"Twin screws, three thousand meters, almost directly ahead of us," Kadar said over the intercom.

Badr turned the boat slightly to the right but did not decrease speed. He was becoming very confident of the *Sea Spectre*'s ability to go where it wished, invisible to the normal world. They were, in fact, proceeding head-on in the middle of the outbound traffic lanes, hugging the southern coast. He did not think the Coast Guard would stop him for that illegality. The lights of Virginia Beach gleamed through the left-hand windows like the well-rubbed beads of a tangled set of worry beads.

Ahead were the lights of the Hampton Bridge. Like the bridge behind them, very little traffic moved on it at this time of the morning. In the magnified bow video, he counted seven pairs of headlights.

Then the running lights of a naval vessel. Perhaps a frigate of some kind. It passed a kilometer to their left as he circled wide around it.

There were no alarms, not a visible alert aboard the ship, nor excited radio messages. Kadar had set the radios to the frequencies used by the Commander in Chief of the Atlantic Fleet, and though they frequently heard messages or intercepted telex traffic, both forms of communication were now indecipherable. Someone had realized that the *Sea Spectre* could eavesdrop and begun to employ some code. Kadar had been unable to make sense of it but felt assured that most of the warships were still searching for them far to the south.

It was the Christian Sabbath, an appropriate day to launch his largest offensive yet, Badr thought. He would wreak upon the Atlantic Fleet headquarters the same kind of chaos the Japanese had delivered to the Pacific Fleet headquarters in Pearl Harbor on another Sunday.

Once the bridge was visible in his rearview screen, Badr reduced his speed to fifteen knots. The telltale whiteness disappeared from the wake.

The U.S. Naval Shipyard passed on his left, and he turned left around its point, moving into the Hampton Roads. There were ships of various descriptions and unknown purposes anchored in the Roads. He ignored them and concentrated on the naval base on his left.

When he reached the confluence of the Lafayette and Elizabeth Rivers, fighting to join the James River, Badr slowed and reversed the boat, heading back to the north.

The lights of the naval base were now on his right, sleepy and peaceful.

Unexpectant.

"Omar, you may proceed."

"I am using electro-optical targeting," Heusseini said. "Missile bay doors opening."

"Missile bay clear," Rahman reported.

"Raising launcher."

Badr advanced his throttles until the readout on the panel displayed fifteen knots. He would attempt to hold that speed, moving north back into the Roads, then around the peninsula and east toward the Hampton Bridge as Heusseini launched missiles steadily. Kadar was back in the cross-passage with Rahman, prepared to reload the launcher as quickly as possible. They had settled on twelve missiles.

Badr did not know what land-based defenses were available to the Navy here, but he suspected that within minutes of the first impact, the many naval ships in the area would be alerted.

Their position would easily be determined as the missiles launched. Still, in the four minutes required for reload, he could dart to another location and perhaps disappear for a few moments.

The risk was high, but the rewards were immense. Already, his successful attacks on American continental bases had created consternation within the populace. And in a society that so heavily depended upon justice being served, not to mention a society that was so certain of its definition of justice, his escape would infuriate them further.

Allah would see to it. Wyatt Earp would not get his man.

Or was that a Canadian myth? It was of no moment. Badr thought of the Canadians as American clones.

The *Sea Spectre* was less than a kilometer from the docks when Heusseini said, "We are ready, Colonel."

"Commence firing."

It was a beautiful rhythm. One ignition after another. The third missile was airborne by the time the first impacted somewhere inland. Heusseini selected his targets at random. Large buildings, ships at the docks, warehouses.

As soon as the fourth was launched, Badr slammed the throttles forward, ran toward the Roads, then slowed once again.

Three minutes.

Three and a half.

Fo . . .

"Missiles ready," Rahman reported. "Bay clear."

WHOOSH!

Then another.

Then the seventh and eighth missiles.

Even through the insulated skin of the *Sea Spectre*, Badr could hear the sirens wailing. They were that close to shore. Fires were spotted all over the base, growing in intensity. The morning became artificially light.

A missile struck what Badr thought was a cruiser in a dry dock, possibly rupturing fuel tanks. Yellow flame poured over the hull like fiery molasses.

"Missiles ready. Bay clear."

Badr had swung the helm eastward as they reached the

middle of the James River. They were now two kilometers offshore from the naval base, three kilometers west of the Hampton Bridge.

Four more missiles whisked away.

Half a dozen naval boats and ships were underway, nosing out into the river, aiming in their general direction. Searchlights scanned the waters.

"Load four more," Badr commanded.

To their credit, no one complained about the change in plans. They were totally involved in the operation.

He raced forward at forty knots for three minutes, then slowed once again. The pursuing ships did not alter course to follow him.

"Omar, you must put one of them in the city proper, one on the bridge, and two to the north, aiming for Langley Air Base."

"Allah willing," Heusseini said.

"He does," Badr affirmed.

They had nearly reached the bridge by the time missiles thirteen through sixteen had been loaded.

Heusseini launched them quickly, and Badr watched his repeater screen as if he were mesmerized.

A multistory building with lights in some of the windows, perhaps a sign saying some kind of insurance.

The bridge. A semi truck trailed by two small automobiles. The truck became immense on the screen until it blacked out. He glanced up through the windshield just as the missile erupted, spewing metal, asphalt roadbed, pieces of driver, and structural beams in magnificent confusion. Red and orange and blue flames squirted skyward.

The air base. The missile homed in on a row of parked F-15 Eagles. Blackness. Badr wished he could have seen the actual explosion.

More parked aircraft seen from the camera of the fourth missile, but Heusseini veered from them and centered the missile on the control tower.

Blackness.

American might defenseless against a single boat.

The American ship sinking into oblivion.

While Ibrahim Badr felt his spirit rising against that satan.

Rising, rising, to grasp the hand of the Prophet.

14

McCory thought that the radio messages rattling from the overhead speaker finally changed Monahan's mind.

He had been as stoic as they come for the past seven hours. He was trussed hand and foot on one of the benches of the banquette, the tail end of the rope wrapped around the table support. McCory wasn't taking any chances with the Navy man. He looked competent enough to foul up anyone's plans.

It had been a tense few minutes with Mimi Kuntzman.

She had tapped *Camrose*'s reverse lever momentarily to stop her forward progress and eased in against the side dock, nosed up behind the *SeaGhost*.

"What in the world is that?"

"Experimental, Mimi. Don't tell anyone, huh?"

"You know me, Kevin."

He did. She would hang onto the secret for at least ten or twelve hours.

McCory looked to the officer sitting beside Mimi. The silver oak leaves on his lapel made him a commander. He was peering through the windshield at the assault boat, and he may have been surprised to see it. McCory couldn't tell in the vague twilight.

"Who are you, Commander?"

His eyes left the boat reluctantly, and he looked up at McCory. "The name's Monahan. Jim."

"Come on up here, Jim."

"Well, uh . . ."

"Now."

Monahan eyed the handle of the automatic sticking out of McCory's waistband. He clambered over the seat into the back of the boat and stepped up on the gunwale.

McCory offered him a hand. The commander looked at it for a long moment, then grasped it, and McCory pulled him up onto the dock.

"Thanks, Mimi. I'll see that he gets back."

"Okey doke. We're having dinner next week, remember."

"I won't forget."

"And no last-minute excuses."

She pulled the lever into reverse and backed out of the dry dock. Seconds later, she was gone.

McCory turned to the commander who was once again staring at the *SeaGhost*.

"What do you do, Commander?"

The man laughed, but it sounded as if he had grit in his throat. "For the last nine days, I've been looking for that boat. Where's the other one, McCory?"

"Got me. I think the guys I ran over took it."

Monahan stood there shaking his head, pondering it.

"Come on, get aboard."

His eyes widened in disbelief. "I'm not going anywhere with you."

"Sure you are. You can walk, or I can drag you." McCory tapped the handle of the automatic.

"You wouldn't use that."

"Yesterday, I'd have said the same thing. Go."

Monahan walked toward the hatch and disappeared inside.

McCory released the spring lines, then followed him. He released one of the coiled lines in the cross-corridor from its Velcro strap and carried it with him.

He found Monahan in the cargo bay, and the commander had pulled the tarp back from the bodies. When he looked up at McCory, there was tension pulling the skin of his face tight. His eyes had a new look to them, and McCory didn't think it was respect.

Monahan dropped the tarp back in place and stood up. "Who are they?"

"The big guy worked for Advanced Marine. Wet work, I guess you'd call it. I don't know about the other one, but as a guess, I'd say he's a Warrior of Allah. Retired, now."

"What in the fuck is going on here?"

"I'll tell you something, Commander Jim. I've wondered the same thing."

"You've got missiles loaded." Monahan appeared to have just noticed the collapsed launcher.

"Yeah, I do. But take a count, Monahan. You'll find only one of them missing. Let's go forward and find you a comfortable spot."

McCory used a few varieties of the knots his father had taught him to secure Monahan in the banquette. He had considered leaving him behind, but sure as hell, Ginger would show up and free him.

He needed as many hours as he could get.

It was still twilight when he backed out of the dry dock and crossed the waterway. The *SeaGhost* whispered up the far side of the waterway, past Edgewater and New Smyrna, then through Ponce de Leon Inlet without attracting attention, and as soon as they were clear, McCory shoved the throttles to their forward detents and set the autopilot.

Monahan was sitting in the corner of the banquette, his back resting against the outer bulkhead. He didn't have much freedom of movement.

McCory sat down opposite him.

"Sorry about the bindings, Jim, old boy. But I can't take any chances on you right now."

"Go to hell!"

"Probably, but I'm going to tell you a story, first. You can believe it or not."

It took him almost twenty minutes to get it all out. He went back over Devlin's unsuccessful attempt to sell the *SeaGhost* to the Navy. He detailed his suspicions about Devlin's death in Fort Walton Beach. Told him about his analysis of the boat. Explained what had happened with Chambers and Cordilla.

Monahan didn't say a word, just stared at him.

"What do you think of that, Jim?"

"Fuck you."

"Yeah. You have family?"

The commander wasn't saying.

"You've got a wedding ring. Love your wife? I loved my father, and whatever you might be thinking, that's my whole damned motive."

Monahan didn't even sleep, though McCory stretched out on a bunk for two hours, clutching the Browning in his hand. That was after he had slowed down to pass Safari Bravo. It was still headed south at slow speed, and he worked his way through the task force using passive sonar and without attracting attention. He didn't sleep well.

When he got up, he made himself a bologna sandwich and offered one to Monahan. Monahan wouldn't answer, so McCory figured he wasn't hungry.

From time to time, he checked the sonar and radar consoles, but he didn't go active with either. He scanned different frequencies on the radios, then left the HF set tuned to CINCLANT, switching on the overhead and helm speakers.

He plopped in the helmsman's seat and toyed with the autopilot. Checked his fuel consumption. He still had plenty of fuel.

The primary screen displayed the map function. The dot that was the *SeaGhost* was 103 miles off Cape Hatteras on a heading of sixteen degrees. With the NavStar Global Positioning System, he could bet he was within ten yards of where the computer said he was.

The radio got hot at 0340 hours.

"Listen to that, Jim. Badr's attacking CINCLANTELT."

Monahan struggled to sit up straighter. "Shut up, so I can hear."

They both listened to the transmissions for a few minutes. McCory got lost on some of the code names that were being used, but Monahan appeared to comprehend most of them.

"Shit," he said.

"Bad, isn't it?"

"They hit Langley Air Base, too. Fatalities are high."

"Anyone spot him?" McCory asked.

"I think a couple of them did, but he's gone now."

McCory disengaged the autopilot and swung the helm to the right. Reset the autopilot.

"What are you doing?" Monahan asked.

McCory swung around in his seat to face Monahan. "Going after him. He's using my dad's boat the wrong way, and I'm going to sink the son of a bitch."

"You're headed the wrong way."

"I don't think so. I'm going where he's going, not where he's been."

"You know his destination?"

"Not specifically. But he's got a mother ship somewhere, and she's not invisible."

Monahan pursed his lips. "You know Barry Norman?"

"Norman?"

"Captain Barry Norman."

"Oh. Yeah. That is, not personally. Devlin talked about him a lot."

"Norman thinks the way you do."

McCory grinned. "No one thinks the way I do."

"Do me a favor?"

"What's that?"

"Untie me."

"And what will you do?"

"I'll help. You can't run this SOB by yourself."

0355 hours, 35° 19' North, 73° 2' West

The *Prebble* was making twenty knots, cruising north-easterly. She was 214 miles east-southeast of Norfolk, Virginia.

Barry Norman didn't think he could be in a much better position.

The *Mitscher* was fifteen miles ahead of him, coming his way. She had been joined by another destroyer and a missile frigate. To their east was the frigate *Knox* with four more ships.

Sixty miles to the south-southeast was the *Oliver H. Perry* and four ships in her task force.

Task Force 22 was out of it.

There was an underlying hum of tension and anticipation in the Combat Information Center. Lieutenant Commander Al Perkins was grinning.

Norman had been right.

That did not make it easier for him, listening to the casualty reports coming out of CINCLANT. It only increased his resolve to make the bastards pay dearly.

"Al."

"Sir."

"I'm going up to the bridge now. You keep me aware."

"Aye aye sir."

"And notify the aviator hot dogs that we're going to launch birds in ten minutes."

"Aye aye sir."

Norman left the CIC and made his way up to the bridge.
The first mate, Commander Owen Edwards had the conn.

"Captain's on the bridge," intoned a seaman.

"As you were. You still have the conn, Commander."

"Yes, sir."

Norman stood near the port-side windows and studied
the sea. There were heavy seas running, pushed by thirty-
knot winds out of the southwest. A heavy overcast obscured the stars, though there were a few holes in the
cloud layer.

The intercom sounded. "Bridge, Comm."

Edwards responded, punching the button. "Bridge. Go
ahead, Comm."

"Is the captain there? He's wanted on the Tac-Three."

"I'll take it, Owen," Norman said, replacing the first
mate in front of the intercom.

"Relay it, Comm."

He pressed the Tac-Three button.

"Safari Echo, Captain Norman here."

"Captain, this is Commander Jim Monahan."

"What's up, Commander?"

"You're not going to believe it. Hell, I don't even believe it."

0409 Hours, 34° 59' North, 74° 31' West

"On board a *Sea Spectre*?" Norman's voice was per-
plexed.

"That's right. Only McCory calls it a *SeaGhost*."

"McCory. Devlin McCory's boy?"

Monahan pressed the transmit button and told him the
story in three sentences.

"It sounds like a McCory, all right. What's your intent,
Commander?"

"McCory thinks this boat has a better chance than most

against Badr. He wants to find the support ship and intercept the other *Sea Spectre*."

There was a pause while Norman thought that over. Finally, he said, "Let's keep the two boats straight. You're now code-named Night Light."

"Night Light, copy."

"Now, Night Light, you have reported this to CIN-CLANT?"

"Not yet, Echo."

"Do that. Then get back to me."

Monahan slid back the panel in the desktop to reveal the telex keyboard, spent a moment composing in his mind, then typed out an involved message for CIN-CLANT. He thought it was better that Bingham Clay have something in writing in front of him when he made this decision.

When he was done, he transmitted the message, then turned in the chair. "You have more of that bologna, McCory?"

"Or peanut butter. There's some hamburger in there, too, if you're up to frying it." McCory was still at the helm, studying the map on the screen.

Monahan got up, went to the galley, and made himself a bologna sandwich. He found the Dos Equis in the refrigerator and opened one of those, too. He was starved.

He leaned against the counter and bit large chunks out of the sandwich, chewing fast. Outside, the sea was dark, and no ships were visible. The *Sea Spectre* took the seas well, even though they looked to be roughening. A slight, rhythmic rise and fall was all that betrayed her speed.

"You're buying my story, then?" McCory asked, looking back at him.

"Your tale is pretty damned fantastic. I don't know that I'm buying anything, McCory. It's going to take a hell of a lot of unraveling."

"But you've got some facts."

"Yeah. I don't think you were involved in any of the attacks, simply because you've got the right number of missiles. And you were too damned dumb to dump the bodies."

"I hadn't had the chance."

"You had seven hours."

"Well, I forgot about it."

"Uh-huh."

Monahan didn't know what to think about McCory. The man seemed sincere enough, if misguided. As soon as Monahan had seen the *Sea Spectre* in the dry dock, he had begun to worry. It didn't fit his notion that the boats had both been taken by Badr. When he found the bodies in the carbo bay, he had almost panicked. This was a madman.

He had not liked McCory's story, either. The big, bad Navy, the oppressive financial institutions, the maligned white knight seeking justice. Right out of a paranoid's fantasy.

But he had thought about it in the ensuing hours. Anything was possible, he had decided, though he intended to remain skeptical.

McCory seemed competent at the helm.

"You serve in the Navy, McCory?"

"I've got some SEAL time."

That made Monahan feel a little better. Sometimes, training would tell.

The speaker overhead reported a casualty count at Norfolk.

"What was that?" McCory asked.

"Sixty-four dead, two hundred twelve wounded."

"Shit. Bastards."

By the time he finished his sandwich, the printer began to chatter. He crossed the cabin, waited for it to finish printing, then ripped the message from the printer. He read it with expanding disbelief.

ENCODED, TOP SECRET   MSG 04170607
TO: CMDR J E MONAHAN, NIGHT LIGHT
COPY: SAFARI ECHO, SAFARI CHARLEY,
         SAFARI DELTA
FROM: CINCLANT INTELOFF

SEA SPECTRE UNAUTHORIZED FOR MISSION. *SEA SPECTRE* CONSIDERED FUGITIVE. ADDRESSEE DIRECTED TO PLACE KEVIN MCCORY UNDER ARREST AND PROCEED TO NEAREST PORT ASAP. SAFARIS ECHO, CHARLEY, DELTA INSTRUCTED TO INSURE COMPLIANCE.

He turned around to face McCory. "Looks like your ride is over."

0645 hours, 35° 52' North, 72° 24' West

Admiral Bingham Clay was still out on the base some-where, comforting his casualties in person. By remote control, he was responding to Monahan's and Norman's urgent messages with the reply that he would be in touch soon.

McCory had read the telex right after it came in. "Who's CINCLANT INTEL?"

"Rear Admiral Matthew Andrews."

"He hasn't got much imagination," McCory said.

Monahan didn't disagree, but said, "An order's an or-der."

"Get the big boss. Call the Chief of Naval Operations."

"The CNO isn't going to countermand a fleet order. He never does. Operations are left strictly to fleet command-ers. And I doubt that Bing Clay will reverse it, either. Technically, Andrews is right."

"Who's Bing Clay?"

"He's CINCLANT. My boss."

McCory looked at Monahan with new regard. "You're right up there, aren't you, Commander?"

"I do my job. I'm pretty good at it."

McCory thought it over, then said, "Here's my perspective, Commander. Ownership of the boat is in dispute and not settled by the courts. I've got possession, and damn it, I'm the captain. You try to take my command from me, that's mutiny. Besides, I've got the gun."

"You still want to go after Badr?"

"That's what we're doing, Andrews or no Andrews."

"I'll try to reach Clay."

He tried for a couple of hours while McCory continued on his course, finally altering it slightly northward.

The sea began to lighten after four in the morning, and by 6:45, the day was gray. Choppy, cold, gray sea. Gray overcast. Gray horizons.

There was nothing to be seen on any of McCory's horizons.

The *SeaGhost*'s position was almost directly east of Norfolk, 156 miles off the coast. From the time of the attack and subsequent escape of Badr, the terrorist, if he had gone directly east, could be within twenty-four miles. If he had deviated slightly north or south, the range could be up to fifty miles.

What McCory needed was Badr's support ship.

"Commander, can you operate that radar?"

"Yes."

"Let's go active for a couple sweeps and record it."

Monahan sat down at the console as McCory retarded his throttles. The *SeaGhost* slowed quickly, lost headway, and wallowed in the troughs.

Monahan probably wasn't familiar with that particular radar set, but he looked it over, then did what he was told.

After he had an image stored, he switched to passive, then called the image back up on the screen.

McCory pressed the number four pad on his primary monitor and got a copy of the radar image.

There were ships all around them.

"Jesus Christ!" he said. Checking through the windshield and side windows, he couldn't see a one.

"I'm on ninety-mile scan," Monahan said.

"Can you identify any of those?"

The commander sat back in his chair and closed his eyes, trying to visualize what he knew from the last time he had looked at a plot.

"I'll try. West of us, and slightly north, is a single target. That should be the *Prebble*. Safari Echo."

As he watched the screen, a rectangular square appeared next to the blip, with the letters "PRBL" in it. Monahan's fingers were clicking away at the computer keypad.

"I didn't know you could do that," McCory said. Actually, he had seen something about target identification in the manual but had skipped over it.

"There have been a few advances since you were on active duty," Monahan said.

"How come the *Prebble* is alone?"

"Partly because her captain is Barry Norman. Her choppers are equipped with high-gain infrared sensors."

"They can pick up the stealth boats?"

"They were testing it when you stole the boat."

"It works. They found me Sunday morning."

"But you got away, right?"

"Cut the speed way back. Must have reduced my heat signature."

"Uh-huh. Okay, up north of us, and to the east, is the task force headed by *Mitscher*. That's Safari Charley. To their east is a task force led by the *Knox* and attached to Charley."

"MITS" appeared in a box near the lead ship. On the screen, it looked to be about twenty miles from the *Prebble* and forty miles from the *SeaGhost*.

"PERR" flashed onto the screen next to a cluster of ships to the south.

"One of those, and I don't know which one, is the *Oliver H. Perry*," Monahan told him. "She's heading up Safari Delta."

McCory put his finger on the screen and pointed out about nine blips that seemed independent. "These are commercial vessels?"

"I'd think so. They'll be under observation by either Charley or Delta. We've been dogging most of these ships for six days, McCory."

"Is that right? Then, if Badr didn't make his meet before daylight, he's going to have to hide out until nightfall?"

"That would be my guess. There'll be aircraft watching those ships all day long."

"So we'll just play tag ourselves. Stay out of everyone's way and maybe take a look at those commercial ships."

"Perhaps," Monahan said. "It'll depend on Admiral Clay. And I'm already in defiance of my orders."

The message came soon thereafter.

```
ENCODED, TOP SECRET        MSG 07120607
TO:    CMDR J E MONAHAN, NIGHT LIGHT
COPY:  SAFARI ECHO, SAFARI CHARLEY,
       SAFARI DELTA
FROM: CINCLANT

INSTRUCTIONS MSG O4170607 CONFIRMED.
```

15

Justin Malgard had received a call at his motel in Norfolk at 4:15. A lieutenant asked him to report to the Operations Center.

His taxi arrived at the main gate by five, and he was somewhat excited about being part of the operation. That wore off quickly when the cab was stopped by Navy SP's and Marine guards at the barricaded gate. The base was closed down, and he had to get out of the taxi and wait for an escort.

An ensign in a Navy sedan pulled up a few minutes later, cleared him with the Marines, and put him in the backseat. The ride to the Operations Center relieved him of any excitement he still had.

The destruction was random, and he did not get to see much of it, since it was spread all over the base. In a couple of spots, buildings, vehicles, shrubbery, and landscaping were merged in nearly unrecognizable heaps, still smoking. He could see fires several blocks away that still raged. Ambulances and trucks and jeeps cut around corners and sped down streets in a frenzy. With the window rolled down, he heard the cacophony of sirens, yells, and racing engines. Passing one building on fire, he heard the crackling of flames, the hiss of water directed at it by pumpers standing in the street. Everything was soot covered. Emergency lights were pulsing all around him. A major conflagration near, or on, the Navy docks lit up the early-morning sky.

When he arrived at the door to the Operations Center, Rear Admiral Matthew Andrews passed him by the checkpoint. Inside, Andrews pointed at a chair in the corner.

"Sit there, Mr. Malgard. If we have a question, we want you nearby."

He sat there for almost three hours, drinking coffee and eating donuts passed around by a seaman. He studied the intricate electronic map on the wall and began to identify the movements of some selected ships.

He could not quite figure out what was going on. Messengers came in and left. Console operators talked into their headsets, signaled officers milling around the room, took orders. The dots on the map changed. Andrews seemed to be in charge until around seven o'clock, when Clay came back. Clay's uniform was filthy with soot and dirt, and he and Andrews had a heated exchange on the far side of the room. Malgard guessed that Andrews prevailed, because the intelligence officer was smiling when they broke up the discussion.

Clay barely acknowledged Malgard with a nod. His attitude seemed to have changed significantly. He left the room, and when he returned, he was in a fresh uniform. There was an angry bruise on his forehead, and his eyebrows had been singed.

He came directly across the room to Malgard.

"You sure you don't know a Devlin or a Kevin McCory?" the admiral asked.

"I can't say as I've ever heard of them, Admiral. Is it important?"

"Very. Kevin McCory has a *Sea Spectre* out there." He pointed in the direction of a bunch of blips on the map.

"He's a fucking cowboy who thinks he can take out Ibrahim Badr."

Damn. No wonder he had not heard from Chambers.

"I don't understand, Admiral. This is an American who's been attacking the coastal bases?"

"Not according to my aide, who is on board the boat with McCory."

For Christ's sake! "You've got a man with McCory?"

"I don't believe it was planned that way, but yes."

"So you've got one of the boats back?"

Clay grimaced. "We're not certain. It doesn't look like they're responding to orders."

"Well, can't you force them?"

"You're forgetting, Mr. Malgard. We can't even find them."

Clay spun around and headed for one of the consoles.

Malgard's head felt as if it were spinning. McCory did have a boat, but apparently, so did this terrorist. McCory and some naval officer wanted a confrontation.

He could only hope that Badr would put a missile right up McCory's ass.

1530 hours, 37° 32' North, 71° 15' West

The *Hormuz* had not been where it was supposed to be.

Ibrahim Badr suspected that it had broken down in reality and required repairs. By this time, he thought that Abdul Hakim was frightened enough of him, as well as taking some pride in the accomplishments of the Warriors of Allah, so that he would not abandon them.

If it came down to it, he could abandon Hakim. The stealth boat had been fully fueled before beginning the attack on Norfolk. With conservation, he thought he could make North Africa, perhaps even Tripoli for refueling.

The idiot Colonel would want to take the boat away from him if he did that, of course.

All day long, they had been drifting south, keeping the engines barely idling at six or seven knots. Badr was certain that the *Hormuz* could not be north of them. It was supposed to be on a direct northerly heading along the seventy-one-degree, fifteen-minute track. If he continued south, he would run into it.

Then, one more attack. Against the City of New York. Oh, the panic that would create!

Allah, rejoice!

And then they would return to the camps in southern Lebanon, heroes of the cause. Heroes with a fabulous weapon to be used against the infidels.

"I have a sonar reading," Amin Kadar said from his place at the console. "Twin propellers, ten thousand meters."

"Bearing?"

"I cannot yet tell."

"Let me know if it comes closer. We will alter course to avoid it."

"We should attack it," Kadar said.

"Not just yet," Badr told him.

As he had been doing regularly, Badr scanned the seas through the windows, then glanced down at the rearview screen. For all intent, they were alone on the ocean. The day could not have been better. The overcast had lowered, perhaps to a four hundred meter ceiling. The swells had shortened, the troughs had deepened, and the boat sometimes tilted alarmingly as it drifted. The bouncing was endless and becoming more abrupt. Omar Heusseini had become sick in midmorning.

His vomit was still drying on the back of the dining table bench and the deck. The deck was also littered with candy wrappings, chicken bones, pieces of meat and bread. A plastic water glass wandered back and forth beneath the table. His crew was not a disciplined one.

It did not matter. They were good at what they did. Heusseini had taken active readings on the radar twice during the day. Despite the appearance of emptiness, the sea around them contained a surprising number of ships, many of which he suspected belonged to the United States Navy.

Caution was called for. They would drift, and they would avoid any contact. Soon, the *Hormuz* would come into view.

1450 hours, 36° 12' North, 72° 51' West

Night Light also drifted, but aimlessly. McCory was trying to keep her in the area, while still eluding any probes by the Safaris Charley, Delta, and Echo.

Several times, he had gone aft and opened the hatches to let fresh air enter the cabin. The salt tang tasted good on his tongue. The waves were capping higher, a few washing over the stern deck. Once, he heard a helicopter pass by to the east.

Jim Monahan had apparently accepted his fate. He seemed to have signed on for the duration. He might even use McCory's strained rationale—his claim on the *Sea-Ghost* and his rights as captain—to alibi himself later. McCory had slept for three hours in the afternoon, and when he climbed out of the bunk, he found that Monahan had not taken control and headed for Norfolk.

Monahan had grabbed a couple hours of bunk time in midmorning, but for the better part of the day, he had been listening to the radios, switching frequencies often, jotting notes at the communications desk. He understood the bulk of the code words being utilized.

McCory fried four hamburgers for dinner, stacking them

high with Swiss cheese, onions, and dill pickles. He brought two of them and a bottle of Dos Equis to the communications console.

"Thanks," Monahan said, pulling the right side of his headset back.

"Anything new?"

"Not particularly. I wish we had a copy of the Baker Two map grid. Best guess is that the area is becoming congested. None of the search ships are moving very fast. Safari Echo has identified three ships they're keeping a close eye on."

"What three?"

"A Panamanian container ship named the *Morning Glory*, a Colombian freighter called *Nem Andes*, and a Kuwaiti tanker named *Hormuz*."

"Any particular reason?" McCory asked.

"Damned if I know. Probably, they've been on a track that makes them accessible to the *Sea Spectre* for the past nine days."

"Why don't they just board them?"

"It's called piracy. You should know about that."

"You sound like my lawyer."

"Theodore Daimler?"

"Shit."

"Hey, you didn't think you were going to get away with it, did you?"

"I did. And I still do. This is my boat."

Monahan took a bite out of his hamburger, but his eyes showed his disbelief.

McCory was off his rocker. Short a full deck. One elevator stop from the top floor. McCory thought Monahan was running through all the clichés.

All of them can go to hell, Devlin.

He ate one of his hamburgers while checking the sonar. Nothing. He sat in front of the radar screen, eating and wishing he could go active. He hated being blind.

The *SeaGhost* purred along, climbing the swells, sliding down the other side.

Monahan continued checking the frequencies. CIN-CLANT had tried to contact them a dozen times, but McCory had nixxed any replies.

Once before noon, the *Prebble* had tried to reach them on the frequency Monahan called Tac-Three. They had not responded, but Monahan left the Tac-Three on standby.

When he had finished his second hamburger, McCory said, "I vote we go active on the radar and get a more recent reading."

Monahan got up from his chair and moved forward, bracing himself against the rocking deck.

"You drive. I'll shoot the picture."

McCory slid over behind the wheel, disengaged the autopilot, and rested his hand on the throttles. As soon as Monahan had his sweep, McCory would scoot for a new position.

Two seconds later, Monahan said, "Hit it!"

He slammed the throttles forward.

The speaker beside his shoulder blared, "Safari Echo to all Safaris. We had an active radar at Baker Two, six-one, seven-eight."

As the *SeaGhost* came on plane, McCory said, "Damn, they're fast."

"They want us pretty bad, McCory."

"We're on their side."

"They don't know who they just saw."

"Yeah, I suppose that's right."

1700 hours 36° 15' North, 71° 49' West

It was going to be an early night, Monahan thought. Already, the daylight was fading fast, deepening into gloom. The seas were rougher than before, he thought. He had listened in on some weather forecasts, but nothing scary was predicted.

He had now been aboard the *Sea Spectre* for almost twenty-four hours, and he thought it was a hell of a boat. Monahan knew damned well that the *Prebble* was within fifteen miles of them, and helpless. He didn't know what he would do in Norman's place. This thing was just ghostly.

A couple of times, he had daydreamed his excuse to Bingham Clay. He tried out McCory's argument. *I didn't feel I had the authority to countermand a captain's orders, Admiral.*

The response to that was a gritty, *Bullshit!*

Finally, he had decided to use the truth and try to ride out the storm that followed. Probably, he would face a court-martial.

Why did you not follow your orders, Commander?

I didn't want to follow them. I wanted to get the goddamned terrorist. Sir.

Monahan was post-Vietnam. The closest he had ever come to battle was service aboard a backup frigate during the Grenada invasion.

He had the training; he needed the action.

Bullshit, again.

The son of a bitch killed a lot of my colleagues. I wanted to wrap his head in a plastic bag and slowly fill it with water.

All right. Let's go with that.

Monahan didn't know all of McCory's motives. There were probably several grains of truth behind his comment about his father. Then, too, McCory had had the SEAL training. Those people tended to be very good, very disciplined, and very loyal.

All right. Let's buy that, too.

Monahan was at the commander's desk, plotting on the Atlantic chart.

McCory came up behind him. "Figure it out?"

He pointed out his markings. "Extrapolating speeds from our two radar readings, I can't tell much about the military ships. They seem to have changed courses and speeds from time to time. They're kind of milling around."

"Like ourselves."

"And like Badr, if we're thinking right. Over here, we're showing the six commercial vessels we spotted this morning. They're not all on the same course or track. With only two readings, we have to assume they've maintained their same tracks. If they have, I've got an approximate speed on each of them. Here, this one is making twelve knots. This one, sixteen knots. This one, eleven knots, and so on. The dotted lines project their future positions should they maintain course and speed."

"One of the six is our bogey," McCory said.

"I'd bet a steak dinner on it."

"They serve steak in the brig?"

"With luck, somebody will sink us, just after we blow the fucker out of the water."

Twenty minutes later, the Tac-Three channel sounded off.

"Night Light, Safari Echo."

Monahan was seated in the radar position, and instinctively, he picked the microphone off its clip.

McCory, at the helm, looked over at him. "They might try to get a radio fix on our position. There are enough ships out there to triangulate us five times."

He sat quietly.

"Night Light, if you're monitoring, give me a click."

He looked at McCory, who shrugged.

Monahan clicked the transmit button twice.

"Night Light, my money's on the *Hormuz*. She's tracking north on seven-one, one-five."

Monahan clicked twice again.

Within fifteen seconds, CINCLANT was broadcasting on the command net.

"CINCLANT to all Safari elements. Both stealth boats are to be considered hostile. This is not a guessing game, and we will not take chances. By order of the president, through the Chief of Naval Operations, weapons systems are freed for Safari Charley, Safari Delta, and Safari Echo. Written confirmation to follow. Upon contact, Target One and Target Two are to be given one minute to capitulate. Failing that action, they may be fired upon."

"Who's Target One?" McCory asked.

"I believe we've been included," Monahan told him. "You want to put this son of a bitch in gear?"

"Careful how you talk about my girl."

McCory eased the throttles forward until the readout showed fifteen knots.

2110 hours, 36° 21' North, 71° 15' West

"All right, Omar. One sweep only."

Heusseini activated the radar, then quickly shut it down. "It is the *Hormuz*, Colonel Badr. Six hundred meters dead ahead."

"Very well," Badr said.

The night-vision screen was blurry, coated with salty water splashed against it by the heavy waves.

Several minutes passed before Badr made out the tall black shape rising from the sea. A few minutes later, he concluded from the silhouette that it was indeed the tanker.

"All of you may secure your stations. Amin, open the cargo doors and prepare to attach the lifting cables. Allah has done well for us."

1730 hours, 12Jan87, Fort Walton Beach

McCory and his son sat in back of the marina office in the late afternoon, drinking Budweiser, and looking out at the new main dock. Fifty yards offshore, a barge was unloading sections of the new floating docks. Over on the left edge of the marina, the floating crane had shut down for the day. The boats had all been moved out of the area, and the crane was pulling old, rotten pilings.

They were both in cut-off jeans and T-shirts, the shirts stained with the sweat of a hard day. McCory had some lines in his face, and his hair was mostly gray, but the damp shirt conformed to bulging muscles that hadn't lost their tone. Kevin was a lot leaner but just as hard.

"Lookin' good, Kev." McCory pointed at the dock with his beer can.

"We should have done it ten years ago, Devlin." About the middle of his second year in college, Kevin had dropped the "Pop," and started calling him Devlin. McCory didn't mind too much, but he kind of missed being "Pop."

"Yeah, but ten years ago, we couldn't afford it. You pay for what you get, then you take it and go home."

McCory had paid off the mortgage the year before, then floated a new loan to upgrade the marina. It had gotten so that new paint wouldn't cover the cavities in old wood. He had lost quite a few long-time renters to the newer and larger marinas. The shorefront lots on either side of him had become too expensive to acquire, but McCory had gotten permission to extend outward. The renovated marina would handle 250 slips, though he was still going to have to raise the slip rentals a little for most of his people. There would be some griping.

The first mosquitoes of evening moved in. McCory slapped his forearm a couple of times, then said, "Let's go in."

They got up and went inside the building, where Amy Clover was tending the counter. Swede Norlich was buying two cases of beer. Kevin picked up a couple of fresh cans of Budweiser from the display case, and they went back into the private office.

It wasn't much of a private office. A battered desk was shoved into one corner. There were three old, straight-backed chairs, a wooden swivel chair in front of the desk, and a stool in front of McCory's high drawing table. The walls were papered with drawings of ski boats and cruisers. Centered above the drafting table was a full rendering of the SeaGhost. Above the desk in a small, glass-fronted frame was the only Navy memorabilia McCory had kept: his Navy Cross.

"We need to replace Maintenance Building One, also," Kevin said.

"You want to take a cut in pay?"

Kevin grinned at him. "Only if you do."

"You could move back here."

Kevin lived in his own apartment. McCory knew he wanted the privacy because of the succession of women that went through it. Unlike his father, Kevin wasn't a one-woman man. Not yet. anyway.

"We'll do it next year," Kevin said.

"Sure we will, son. Provided we fill those new docks with people payin' good money."

"Are you talking about the Johnsons and the Wheelers and the Corcorans, for instance?"

McCory frowned. "Some of those people have been here twenty-five years and more, Kevin. They can't afford a big boost in their rents. And they can't afford to go elsewhere."

"Their Social Security checks have increased."

"Not as much as they should have."

"We're going to have a state of the art marina, with a

bunch of faded and damned near sinking Chris Craft museum pieces tied up in it, Devlin.''

"People have a right to their own lives. I don't give a shit what their boats look like.''

"They need to pay, just like anyone else,'' Kevin argued.

"Money ain't everything, Kev. It runs second place to principle.''

2115 hours, 36° 13' North, 71° 22' West

"There are some big boys between us and them, Kevin,'' Monahan said from the sonar console.

"How many?'' McCory was at the helm, keeping the speed steady at fifteen knots. The digital readout gave him a compass heading of seventy-six degrees, the intercept course upon which he and Monahan had decided.

Using Monahan's chart, they had identified the unknown ship on the seventy-one-degree, fifteen-minute track as the *Hormuz*, then projected her position with a dotted line. If Monahan was right, the tanker had been holding steady at around twelve knots.

Because of the overcast, the skies had darkened early. The seas were still choppy but hadn't worsened in the last few hours. McCory figured the naval ships were running without lights. He hadn't seen one.

"The tanker should be about sixteen miles away,'' Monahan said. "I've got readings for ships at eight-five hundred yards, nine-three hundred yards, and I think, at ten thousand yards. There are a few more of them out there, but I can't pinpoint them on passive sonar. Somebody is looking for us on sonar. We got pinged a couple times, but I don't think the return was strong enough to alert them.''

"Who's the closest?''

"It should be the *Prebble,* just north and east of us."

"And closer to the *Hormuz?*"

"Yes."

"Well, hell. I want to be the first one there, Jim."

"So do I."

McCory punched the throttles.

2119 hours, 36° 16' North, 71° 20' West

"Safari Echo, Deuce Two."

"Go, Deuce Two," Perkins said.

The CIC felt hypersensitive. The technicians manning the consoles leaned forward in their chairs in anticipation of something, anything.

Norman stood near the plot, watching the shifting symbols. Target Two, the *Hormuz* was eleven miles away. The group with *Knox* was seventeen miles north of the tanker. Safari Delta was coming up fast from the south, just over six miles out.

"Echo, Two has a Target One on infrared at Baker Two, five-nine, eight-one, bearing seven-six. We make the speed at six-two knots."

"Copy that, Deuce Two," Perkins said, turning to look at Norman.

One of the console operators keyed the data in, and a new, red symbol appeared on the plot.

"She's closing on us," Norman said.

"Yes, sir. And fast. Less than six minutes away. Do I alert the gun and missile stations?"

"Yes, Al. Do that."

While Perkins spoke into his microphone, Norman studied the plot. He looked up to the bulkhead where repeaters registered the *Prebble*'s speed and heading. They were making thirty knots on a heading of eight-four degrees. Both the destroyer and the stealth boat were aiming for the *Hormuz*. At her speed, the *Sea Spectre* would pass them and reach the tanker first.

Unless Norman released a couple of missiles.

On the command net, he heard one of the *Oliver H. Perry*'s ASW helicopters reporting a sonar contact.

On his last day in the Navy, Devlin McCory stood in front of Norman's desk, holding his baby boy in his arms, and grinning that big, Irish grin. "I'm sure as hell going to miss the Navy, Mr. Norman, but I'm proud to leave it in your hands."

"We are prepared to fire on your command, Captain," Perkins told him. He did not sound happy about it.

Barry Norman did not know Devlin McCory's kid, and it would not have mattered if he had. His orders were to blow either of the stealth boats out of the water.

His duty was to protect the United States of America, including its ships. If that was Badr out there, Mini-Harpoons could be flying at any second.

The blip showing on the plot could be Badr heading for his support ship, or it could be McCory and Monahan.

He reached out for Perkins's headset, and the commander handed it to him quickly.

"Give me Tac-Three."

"Aye aye sir," a technician told him.

"Night Light, if that's you, I want a barber shop set of clicks."

Dut, dut-dut-dut-dut-dut . . . dut-dut.

Norman returned the headset to Perkins, spun away from the plot, and headed for the hatchway. "Secure weapons, Commander. I'll be on the bridge."

As he entered the light trap, he heard one of the console operators reporting, "The *Perry*'s launched missiles."

Norman did not think he would get a battleship. And he would probably lose his destroyer, too.

2122 hours, 36° 12' North, 71° 15' West

The missile bay doors were open, and Badr, Kadar, Heusseini, and Rahman were in the bay, groping for the tanker's lifting cables.

Abdul Hakim leaned over the railing above, grinning down at them. "The news on the radio is glorious, Colonel," he yelled.

Badr nodded. He had been listening to the newscasts, also. The reports from Norfolk and Langley Air Base were gratifying. The fatality count was high. There would be fewer soldiers to harass Allah's believers.

"You know, of course, that American ships surround us?" Hakim yelled.

"I know that, Captain. It is not a concern."

"They are headed toward us."

That was new information. Though Heusseini had begged, Badr had not let him activate the radar in the last few minutes.

Badr was about to ask Hakim if his ancient radar had determined the speed of the ships, when he heard an explosion to the southwest.

Then, quickly, two more.

He spun around, peering into the darkness, but he could see nothing. Salt spray whipped over him.

Amin Kadar gripped the top edge of the missile bay door to steady himself against the surge of the sea. He stared out into the night. "They are coming, Colonel. We will die."

"If we die, Amin, it is Allah's will. But we will take many American devils with us." Badr released the cable he was holding.

"We will attack the ships now?"

"We will attack the ships. You will load missiles on the launcher."

"At once."

Rahman joined him eagerly as Badr and Heusseini headed back into the cabin.

Six minutes later, Ibrahim Badr turned away from the tanker and picked up speed toward the southwest.

"I may go active?" Heusseini asked.

"Yes. Choose your targets wisely, Omar."

2124 hours

"Son of a bitch!" Monahan had yelled. "Hard to starboard! Kill the engines!"

McCory wasn't good at taking orders, but he took those immediately, slamming the wheel over to the right, reaching out to stab the ignition defeat on each engine.

The *SeaGhost* heeled over, was battered upright by an oncoming wave, and began to lose speed. She bounced hard in the troughs.

White arrows streaked overhead. One, then two more.

McCory didn't see the impacts, but he felt the concussion of the explosions as they echoed through the sea and against the *SeaGhost*'s hull.

"They had us targeted on infrared," Monahan said. "Light 'em up, again."

"Where in hell did they come from?" McCory asked as he started the engines.

"Safari Delta."

"Your boss means business."

"He usually does. But I'd bet that Andrews is pressing him on this, citing technicalities. Andrews tends to be a regulations man."

"It's still lethal." McCory spun the helm back and picked up speed. "You want to risk the speed again?"

"Hell, I don't . . ."

The command net channel sounded off. "Safari Echo

to all units. Echo has two incoming missiles. Delta, you've got two headed your way."

"That's him!" McCory yelled.

"Full bore," Monahan shouted back.

McCory shoved the throttles in. "Open the cargo doors."

"Shit, Kevin," Monahan said, "you've fired one of these before. I haven't."

McCory rose from his seat, and Monahan slid behind the helm. McCory dropped into the center chair, activated the armaments panel, and saw four green LED's. He punched the pad for the doors, then raised the launcher. He felt an urge to go aft and check on them, but suppressed it.

Through the windshield, he saw two missiles cross the horizon ahead of them, headed south.

The command net was overrun with excited, but orderly, reports. Ships dodging missiles, mounting missile defenses.

"Maybe Safari Delta will forget about us?" McCory said.

"Don't count on it."

The *SeaGhost* took the choppy seas easily. By the time she had reached fifty knots again, the up-and-down rhythm had steadied.

McCory's screen was on night-vision video, but no ships or boats were visible. He tried infrared. Nothing. Well, no. A small red dot. Probably an aircraft.

Thumbing the keypad, he switched the radar to active and selected the thirty-mile scan. The screen immediately lit, and the scan displayed fourteen solid targets within the thirty-mile diameter. Three tiny, fast-moving blips would be missiles. Where was the fourth? "MITS," "PRBL," and "PERR," were still identified, remembered by the computer.

McCory picked out the *Hormuz*. The other stealth boat was not shown.

On the radio, one of the ships in Safari Charley reported a missile hit on the fantail.

Another reported a new active radar.

"I'm going to eliminate Badr's support ship," McCory said.

Monahan hesitated. "Hell, why not? I don't think any of the others will do it."

Activating the radar-targeting link, McCory manipulated the orange target blossom until it was centered on the tanker's blip, then keyed the target lock.

"LOCK-ON" appeared on the screen.

He pressed the launch keypad.

The computer launched immediately.

WHOOSH.

"Goddamn," Monahan said as the solid booster ignited and kicked the missile off the rail. The white flare burned McCory's night vision.

Safari Echo and Safari Charley ships reported the last three hostile missiles destroyed.

"New launch! New launch! From Target One. I think."

As his vision returned, McCory checked the screen. He blinked and checked it again.

Two moving dots.

"I've got incoming," he said. The adrenaline was pumping through him, but he felt like he was settling in. Another night exercise. He was onstage, and the butterflies had flitted away.

"Go passive," Monahan ordered, turning hard to the right and reducing speed. He counted aloud to ten, then turned left again.

The missiles passed overhead.

"Bet they were Harpoons," Monahan said, "targeting on our active radar. What's our range to target?"

"I read it as five miles."

"Badr's close by, judging by the launch."

"He doesn't know we're around, though," McCory said.

"Probably not."

The Safari command net reported four more missile launches and gave Baker Two grid coordinates for the launch point.

"That doesn't help us a damned bit," McCory complained.

A sudden explosion brightened the darkness. A yellow-white globe appeared on the northeastern horizon.

"Hot damn!" McCory said. "That's got to be the tanker."

"Was."

The reports coming over the command net confirmed their strike.

"Maybe that will spook Badr," McCory said.

It may have. Either that, or Badr was running from his last launch point. The Tac-Three channel came alive. "Night Light, Echo."

Monahan grabbed his microphone. "Go."

"My choppers have got him on IR at three-six, one-one, seven-one, one-four. He's heading home at six-zero knots."

McCory switched the armaments panel to infrared targeting.

"The ships will never catch him," Monahan said. "There's no coverage to the east."

"What about the choppers?"

"If they get close, Badr will just shut down. He can outlast their fuel."

"Let's have some more turns, Jim."

Monahan shoved the throttles all the way in. "Plot it."

"Plotting," McCory said, pulling the chart from the top of the instrument panel. He found the coordinates Norman had given them, estimated Badr's speed and their own position, then said, "Take it to eight-four degrees."

"Turning now."

Switching the monitor to the infrared, McCory scanned it for any sign of the other stealth boat. There was a heat source to the right edge of the screen, but he thought it was likely created by a ship in Safari Delta. Another red spot was high and probably an aircraft.

"CINCLANT, Safari Echo." Command net.

"Echo, CINCLANT."

"CINCLANT, I'm prepared to provide positive ID on both *Sea Spectre*s. My helicopters have both of them targeted. Request that firing on the western boat cease."

After a momentary hesitation, a new voice came on the air. "Echo, your request is approved. All Safari elements, cease fire on the western boat."

"That's my boss," Monahan said.

A minute later, McCory heard another new voice on Tac-Three. "Night Light, this is Deuce One. I was told to contact you on this channel."

Monahan pressed his transmit button. "Go, Deuce."

"I'm closing on Target One." The pilot provided the coordinates.

McCory plotted them. "Three and a half miles away, Jim."

"We won't catch him, if we're both making the same speed, Kevin."

"How do we slow him down?"

Monahan went back to his microphone. "Deuce, Night Light. Can you drop a torpedo on him?"

"Affirmative, Night Light. Checking with Echo." After a pause, the pilot reported, "Dropping a Mark-46."

McCory hoped no one would shoot at him and activated the radar. He found the chopper ahead of them on the first sweep, but the stealth boat wasn't visible. The ships of the Safari task forces were falling behind.

"He's taking her hard starboard, evading the fish," Deuce reported.

Monahan eased his wheel to the right. If Badr maintained a southerly heading for a while, they would close quickly.

The seconds ticked away.

"Two miles," McCory reported.

"The fish exploded, fuel depleted," Deuce reported. "He's too fast for them."

"Try the infrared," Monahan said. "By now, Badr knows he's got another stealth boat after him."

McCory switched over.

And the center of the screen held an orange glow. A hot red spot to the upper left was the chopper.

"Got him. I'm launching. Watch your eyes."

McCory brought up the infrared targeting circle, centered it, then launched all three of his remaining missiles, one after the other.

He shut his eyes until they were all away.

"Coming your way, Deuce," Monahan said on the Tac-Three channel. "Better back off."

"Wilco."

Ticking.

Ticking.

"Hey, Night Light! He's launched two."

McCory could see the three white dots that were his own missiles. They were curving down toward the sea far ahead.

But two growing black dots with white halos were headed his way.

"Shut her down, Jim. They'll be infrared-targeting."

Monahan pulled the throttles back and turned to port.

"Night Light, Deuce. I've lost both of you."

All five missiles missed their targets. The two from Badr's boat shrieked past on their right.

Monahan returned to his course and ran the throttles up.

"Night Light, Deuce. Two bits this sucker's headed for home again."

"You think east, Deuce?" Monahan asked.

"Damn betcha."

"Good as any direction," Monahan told the helicopter pilot

"He's got to hold it under fifteen knots to avoid wake and a heat signature," McCory said.

"We'll close fast. What then?"

"I'm not going to have time to load a missile."

"You're a spendthrift with missiles, you know that, Kevin?"

"Lack of practice. Under your right thumb? On the wheel?"

"I've got it."

"That's your cannon. I'll activate it."

McCory leaned over and pressed the two pads on the helm panel that enabled the gun. He switched both Monahan's and his own screen to night-vision video. A targeting circle with distance elevation markings appeared in the center of the screen.

"Under your left thumb is a rocker switch, Jim. It increases or decreases the target range, raising or lowering the cannon aim."

"Is it accurate?"

"Damned if I know. I've never tried it. I'll bet you a million bucks it's skittish as hell at this speed and in these seas."

"You got a million bucks?"

"No. So I don't mind losing it."

"Heads up!" Deuce One shouted.

Less than a mile away, one, then another missile blossomed. The black circles encased in a white border—exhaust flare surrounding the nose cone from McCory's view—grew rapidly. They never exceeded thirty feet off the sea.

Monahan threw the helm over so quickly that the *SeaGhost* almost went over. The starboard side rose to a fifty-degree angle, throwing McCory out of his seat.

The boat banged back down, took a wave over the bow that drenched the windshield, then popped back up. McCory came to rest on the deck against the banquette.

Monahan hung onto the wheel, then reached forward to kill the engines.

The *SeaGhost* had not come to rest when the first missile plowed into the sea off the port side and detonated. The erupting charge of water heaved the boat clear of the sea, canting her over to the right. When she slapped into the surface again, the impact threw Monahan against the wheel, then into the starboard window.

The second missile went somewhere else.

The *SeaGhost* came to rest, wallowing in the troughs.

Monahan sagged and slipped to the deck.

Shaking his head to clear it—his ears were ringing from the concussion—McCory struggled to his feet and crossed the deck.

Monahan was out cold. He pulled him out from under the helm, slipped into the seat, and started the engines.

He had a vague idea of where the other boat was.

"Night Light, Deuce Two. You all right?"

He didn't answer. Shoved the throttles in.

The boat skittered up the front of a swell, canted over the top of the wave, picked up speed.

Rolled the wheel back to the left, then straightened it.

Wondered if the *SeaGhost*'s skin had ruptured anywhere.

Hang on Devlin. You and me, we'll get this son of a bitch.

At forty knots, the fuzzy image appeared on the screen. Two seconds later, he could tell it was the other *SeaGhost*.

She was stern on to him. She was tinted green by the enhancement of the night vision. Two hundred yards.

He retarded the throttles.

Badr must have seen him in his rearview screen. The stealth boat leaped ahead as Badr ran up power.

McCory rammed the throttles forward again. The *SeaGhost* lurched, slid into a wave, came up on plane. She danced on the wave tops.

McCory pressed the firing stud with his right thumb. With his left thumb, he slowly brought up the arc of the gun.

The thunder of the cannon was deafening within the fiberglass boat. Ahead he saw shells ripping into the sea, creating miniature white fountains, advancing on the other boat, but erratically, due to the rocking of the *SeaGhost*.

Too short.

Thumb the rocker switch.

Too far to the left.

He brought the wheel slowly right.

Dance.

Dance.

Into the transom. That's one.

A second shell slammed home.

A brilliant silver-white mushroom.

16

On the fifteenth of July, Ricky Daimler took the call on the ship to shore and talked to his dad for a few minutes, then said, "Mac, Dad wants to talk to you."

McCory went back and took the chair at the desk. He picked up the phone. "Yes, Counselor?"

"It figures that you'd be going off fishing while I'm doing the work."

"Actual work? You can report progress?"

"Number one. The Navy's bringing court-martial charges against Commander Roosevelt Rosse. They think they can prove he slipped Devlin's drawings to Malgard."

"Good on number one. But do you really think that was your work?"

"My suggestion, buddy. Supported by Norman and Monahan, of course. And by the way, both of them are up for decorations. I think Monahan's embarrassed by it all. How did you swing him your way?"

"Irish ancestry. Did you have a number two?"

"Number two, the Navy's bringing fraud and conspiracy charges against Malgard, and I'm pretty certain the D.A. down your way is going to get an indictment against him for attempted murder."

"Attempted?"

"Against you. Even though Chambers was on Malgard's payroll at the time of Devlin's death, they don't have enough evidence to swing a jury."

"Shit."

"We do what we can, Mac. Here's the best part. I just got back from a meeting with the AMDI board of directors and its five attorneys, four of whom could use a good firing. The company is shy of cash, but they'll settle by naming Devlin as the designer of the *SeaGhost* and giving you thirty percent of the company's shares. That's enough to get you the presidency."

"I don't want to be the president. You be the president."

"I don't have an interest."

"I'll give you five percent of the shares."

"My interest is rising."

"Better, you work it so I get to be chairman, with no real duties, and you get to be vice chairman of the board. We'll hire a president. And fire the extra lawyers."

"For five percent?"

"Done."

"Now," Daimler said. "About my fee."

"I sent you a hundred bucks."

"That's right. Okay, we're straight, except for my boat."

"I'll give you *Starshine*. She's worth a couple hundred thou. You come out ahead."

"It doesn't go as fast as my *Scarab* did."

"You're getting older. Slow down."

"Aw, hell. All right."

"And there's only fifty grand owing on it."

"Jesus!"

"You're still ahead of the game," McCory said, and hung up.

In the panel ahead of him, there were a lot of gaping

holes where the Navy had retrieved their special radios and black boxes. He would have to rearrange what was left.

In the shipyards at Norfolk, they had also relieved the *SeaGhost* of its armament and ordnance, though they had left him the radar, sonar, and navigation computer. McCory had already sketched out the changes he would make to the interior.

He spun around in his chair and looked forward. Ricky was at the helm, driving hell-bent for the approximate location of the Bahamas.

Ginger was at the banquette table, leaning against the outer bulkhead, her nice knees pulled up on the bench seat. She was wearing cutoffs and a Miami Dolphins' T-shirt. When she saw him looking at her, she gave him the finger.

But she smiled, too. She was coming around. He didn't think her anger at being left behind was heartfelt.

Behind the platinum aura of her hair, the blue sea stretched into infinity, serene.

Wish you could be here, Devlin.

It's all right, son. It's all right, now.

They survived Armageddon
to sail the oceans
of a ravaged nightmare world

OMEGA SUB   76049-5/$2.95 US/$3.50 Can
On top secret maneuvers beneath the polar ice cap, the awesome nuclear submarine U.S.S. *Liberator* surfaces to find the Earth in flames. Civilization is no more—once-great cities have been reduced to smoky piles of radioactive ash. As their last mission, the brave men of the *Liberator* must seek out survivors in the war-blackened land.

OMEGA SUB #2: COMMAND DECISION
                    76206-4/$2.95 US/$3.50 Can

OMEGA SUB #3: CITY OF FEAR
                    76050-9/$2.95 US/$3.50 Can

OMEGA SUB #4: BLOOD TIDE
                    76321-4/$3.50 US/$4.25 Can